A

MISSION POINT PRESS

Published by Mission Point Press
2554 Chandler Rd.
Traverse City, MI 49696
(231) 421-9513
www.MissionPointPress.com

ISBN: 978-1-950659-82-1
Library of Congress Control Number:
2020919889

Printed in the United States of America

A School for the Great Game

A Steampunk Raj Novel

J.R. SEEGER

Mission Point Press

AT THE DAWN OF THE 20TH CENTURY, THE BRITISH EMPIRE CON-
*trolled India, and the British Navy ruled the seas.
Colonies and Commonwealth nations around the
globe swore allegiance to the British Crown. In those
years, a modern world of steam, electricity, and airships was taking shape alongside the horses and oxen
of the previous century. The British Viceroy living in
Calcutta governed the entire Indian subcontinent and
extended the influence of the Crown into the Arabian
Sea through a small number of British political agents
and military officers and a multitude of British Indian
civil servants and soldiers.*

*There were challenges to the British Raj. Agents
from the Russian Empire were extending the Tsar's
control into Central Asia almost to the borders of British India. The German Kaiser was building political
and military relationships with the new Ottoman
government known as the "Young Turks" in Istanbul.
Not yet adversaries, these two competitors could at a
moment's notice turn into enemies. Meanwhile, restive
tribal warlords and a nascent Indian independence
movement threatened the internal security of the Raj.
And on the periphery of India, ancient and mysterious
knowledge still thrived and held sway over the peoples
living in the remote mountains.*

*To protect British India, the government in Cal-
cutta turned to a well-trained, loyal Indian Army and
a shadow corps of agents of empire. This story is a tale
of the shadow corps.*

5

PROLOGUE:
A Knife Fight with a Sufi

Mazar-e-Sharif — Early January 1911

FRANCIS BANKROFT STAYED IN THE SHADOWS OF THE EXTERIOR WALL ON THE north side of the "Qalai-e-Jangi" — the house of war. He was dressed as a Sufi traveler — complete with a set of bells and ribbons attached to his walking stick and a long earring in his right ear. Weeks of beard growth and matted hair along with the ragged, striped cloak, thread-worn trousers and over-shirt completed his disguise. He had squatted at this north wall each day for more than a month, begging in a mix of Persian, Uzbek and Turkic languages and performing Sufi poetry and an occasional dance. The locals rarely offered much in the way of payment, barely enough for Francis to buy a bit of bread and yogurt each day. His weight was no disguise. A look at his ribs and his hips during a trip to the men's hammam bath three days ago told him that there was no fat left on his body. He was hungry, tired and impatient, but he continued to wait as the sunset turned to darkness in the late January sky.

"A poem, Sufi?" The Afghan Army officer looked down at Bankroft squatting against the wall.

Bankroft responded in Pashtu, "Of course, Agha. Of course." He then started a poem from the local and most famous Sufi poet, Jalaluddin Mohammed Rumi Balkhi.

Earth receives the seed and guards it,
Trustfully it dies.
Then what teeming lives rewards it,
For self sacrifice.

The Afghan officer completed the poem.

With green leaf and clustering blossom clad,
Or golden fruit,
See it from earth's cheerless bosom,
Ever sunward shoot.

After completing the poem, the officer said, "Well selected, Sufi. Here is a small gift for you." The coins and a scrap of cloth dropped into the brass bowl in front of Bankroft.

"A green leaf is the gift of a Sufi, Agha."

The officer waved a menacing arm at Bankroft. "Move on, Sufi, before you end up in the grave." Bankroft bowed so that his head touched the sand in front of the soldier's boots. "Yes, master. I am your slave." He picked up the brass bowl and shuffled along the dirt road toward the shrine city, the Sufi bells tinkling as his moved his walking stick.

An hour later, Bankroft climbed the back wall of the small bungalow that he had rented under the alias of Hussein Shirazi, pilgrim and carpet seller, and dropped into the garden. His partner, bodyguard, and fellow spy Mirza Khan approached him with sword drawn.

"Brother, have no fear from a witless Sufi," Bankroft whispered in English.

"Bankroft Sahib, you are late." Mirza Khan shook his head. "You look pitiful!"

"As I should, but the deed is done. We pack and leave tonight." Bankroft walked into the house, shedding the Sufi garments outside the door and entering the bedroom where his Indian partner, officially Indian Army Intelligence Bureau Pundit First Class Mirza Khan of Gilgit, had laid out his travelling kit and a bucket of lukewarm water to wash. He did so with sufficient vigor that the floor was covered in water by the time he finished. He toweled off with the cotton laid near the bucket and walked barefoot over to his clothes. Bankroft started by pulling on his single piece, cotton undergarment and then lacing a leather envelope around his waist. He opened the envelope and put the document dropped by the Afghan officer inside.

He knew that the information justified the discomfort of living this double life. As he walked through the streets of Mazar-e-Sharif, Bankroft had scanned the words written on the cloth. The message outlined discussions between his Russian counterpart, Colonel Alexander Naglieff, and an Afghan Army General named Mohammed Stanekzai. Stanekzai was based in Qalai-e-Jangi, that same fortress Bankroft had shadowed for the past month. Colonel Naglieff, the commander of a Cossack flying squadron on the Russian borders with Persia and Afghanistan was a resourceful agent for the Tsar. He was famous in Mazar-e-Sharif for his superior Persian and Pashtu language skills, often inserting famous quotes from Hafez or Khushal Khan Kattak when he spoke to the various regional leaders.

The report said Naglieff had established a clandestine relationship with a number of Afghan Army officers, some of whom he had trained already in Bukhara. His goal was to use these officers to work with the Pathans of Kunduz and the

Konar River valley. They would be his surrogates, attack the border garrison at Chitral and, if lucky, convince the tribals to join them in a move to overthrow King Habibullah Khan in Kabul. In time, they might even capture Peshawar and reclaim the ancient winter home of the Afghan kings.

While Habibullah Khan in Kabul might hold the Russians in contempt, some of his Army officers — especially those Pathans exiled to the North and surrounded by hostile Tajiks, Uzbeks, and Hazara Shias — were amenable to both the Russian's offer and Russian gold. The Afghan army officer had chosen Bankroft's gold instead, and provided the details of Naglieff's activities.

Bankroft's source also speculated that Naglieff's true purpose was to start a war between the Raj and the Afghans. The source was certain that none of his peers involved in the plot understood the power of the British Empire. He knew the British Army would win any war. Instead, he was convinced that Naglieff's goal was to use the Afghans to generate a never-ending conflict between the British Empire and the Pathans of the Northwest Frontier. That type of simmering tension would weaken both Afghan and British resources, potentially letting the Russians take as much of Afghanistan as they chose. Bankroft's source report ended with a quote from former Afghan King, Abdur Rahman Khan: "My last words to you, my son and successor, are: 'Never trust the Russians.'"

After he wrapped the leather envelope around his waist, Bankroft pulled on a thin vest filled with a number of different tools of his espionage trade. Then pants and shirt, followed by a paired shoulder holster. Under each arm was a new Colt double-action revolver chambered in .38 caliber. Lighter yet more powerful than the current British issue Webley and, just as important, a weapon not used in the British forces of India.

Bankroft was pulling on his left boot when Mirza Khan came through the door.

"Sahib…" Mirza Khan slipped on the wet floor and fell face first. Bankroft saw a Persian dagger was buried deep in his friend's back. The three killers followed through the door — barefoot, each clad in dark brown shalwar kamiz and carrying vicious Khyber knives nearly as long as cavalry swords. They were prepared for a night of quiet killing. The first one slipped on the wet floor and slid off-balance toward Bankroft. Bankroft turned to avoid the man and used what had to appear to the killer's partners as a simple, one-fingered touch to the back of the neck. The man fell dead without a sound. Bankroft's training made him a dangerous foe in hand-to-hand combat. Even when his adversary had a knife.

Bankroft picked up the Khyber knife where it had fallen from the dead man's hands. He spun and launched the knife, which found its mark just below the sternum of one of the attackers. The razor-sharp blade passed completely through the man, who was dead before he hit the floor.

Most men would have given up the night's mission at this point, but the third assassin only saw the most recent events as a gain for him. He no longer had to share the bounty when he completed the task. He did recognize that this would no longer be a simple stabbing in a sleeping man's bedroom. He would have to fight for his pay, but he was confident that in the end he would be the victor and the ferengi would be the victim. Then he would collect the Russian gold.

Bankroft looked the man in the eyes and then gently waved his left hand across his chest as if to greet his killer. The assassin smiled through blackened teeth and a foot-long beard. He never saw the small knife launched from Bankroft's right hand that buried itself in his forehead. Bankroft walked over to the killer and spoke to him as the dead man's eyes glazed over. "I know it was your karma to come here tonight, but you should have tried to avoid your fate." He pulled the knife from the forehead, wiped it off on the assassin's clothes and slid it back into the sheath that was embroidered into the shirt sleeve on his left forearm.

Bankroft knelt at the feet of his bodyguard and touched his chest. "Mirza Khan, I am sorry that you were killed tonight in such a cowardly way. I know you would have preferred to fight them face to face but instead you came to warn me. I can only say to you that you were avenged. I shall sing your praises to your family in Gilgit. Now, I apologize, but I must leave you here if I am to survive this night." Before he turned to leave, Bankroft spread cinnamon powder over his friend's body.

Bankroft stripped the first assassin of his clothes and traded them for his own — keeping only the leather envelope, the interior vest and the two Colts in their holsters. He added a carnelian ring and bracelet to the dead man's left hand. Anyone who had watched this house over the past weeks would have seen the ring on his finger and the silver bracelet on his arm. If anyone in the market had paid attention to Bankroft, known in alias as Hussein Shirazi, they would recognize the ring as well. To finish the identity switch, Bankroft dropped the heavy, marble-topped bed table on the head of the dead assassin to damage the face. It wouldn't fool the Russian, but it might just keep his minions guessing for a few hours while he rode away. He walked downstairs and gathered a small shoulder bag of food and water, his Mauser hunting rifle and a dark brown shawl that served as a Pashtun's coat and blanket. He pulled on the woolen hat known as a pakol that he took from the one of the assassins and left through the open door.

Bankroft departed over the wall and toward the stables where he kept their horses. By the time he reached the stables in the next block, his bungalow was blazing from the fire he set using the kerosene lamps in the house. With luck, it would burn until dawn. It was late and he knew the stable boy would be sleeping in the loft above the horses, so he had to take care, but there was no time to wait for daybreak. He had a long ride. His two horses would serve him well on the road back to Chitral and the Raj.

A Ride on an Airship

February 1911

ELIZABETH BANKROFT STOOD AT THE ROUND PORTHOLE, GAZING OUT WITH wonder as the solid Earth drifted away from her view. Buildings diminished into small models of reality; trees merged into a rough carpet of a thousand random green hues; farm fields showed a pattern of green and brown lines bordered by serpentine terraces. Elizabeth was 16 years old and this was her first airship ride. As the scene unfolded below, Elizabeth realized that she was literally staring in open-mouthed amazement. She pursed her lips, gained control of her features and looked furtively around to be sure no one had seen her with her jaws hanging apart.

The airship climbed from Rawalpindi, leaving the wide streets of the military garrison and housing area known as the cantonment, where mulberry trees were just beginning to leaf and the mauve flowers of the jacarandas promised an early Spring. Elizabeth felt a gentle sway as the airship began to fight the winds coming down from the foothills of the great mountains of the Himalayas. Inside the huge craft, she did not feel as if she was travelling up into the sky. Instead, it was as if she were standing still and the ground was gently pulling away from her.

She looked down one of the portholes on the starboard side of *HMFS Resolve*, her hands gripping the leather-covered rail that ran along the windows of the passenger cabin. It seemed as if the world she knew so well was turning into a miniature world viewed from one thousand feet above. Elizabeth was not one to be overcome by flights of fancy. She thought of herself as a modern woman and an amateur naturalist. The emotions of the moment were restrained by her pride in the science of the airship and the Empire that created it. Dressed in her formal travelling clothes of a sky-blue blazer over a long-sleeved, high-necked cotton blouse, a long wool skirt and riding boots, Elizabeth felt exceptionally modern and blessed to see the wonders of the British Empire from this god-like perch of airship travel.

Before Christmas, she read in the Khyber Mail and the Illustrated London Times reports of airships in India. His Majesty's Flying Ship (HMFS) *Resolve* and HMFS *Sabre* were lozenge-shaped, silver fabric airships the length of a football pitch. Based on the recent designs of the German engineer, Ferdinand von Zeppelin, the lighter-than-air craft used hydrogen cylinders inside the craft to create lift. Propulsion came from four external propellers turned by two lightweight steam engines from a design by Mr. William Henson. The large wooden propellers carved the air like propellers on steamships carved the water. Drawings that accompanied the articles showed a small bridge and command cabin, a passenger cabin with a dozen leather chairs used as "observing stations" and then a power cabin which held the fuel and engines that turned the propellers. Still, the papers had not prepared Elizabeth for the luxury inside of cabin nor the beauty of the distant vistas out the portholes.

Elizabeth felt well-travelled as a sixteen-year-old who spent half of her life in the cantonments of India and the other half with her grandparents in the London borough of Chelsea. She regularly travelled back and forth by rail and steamship on the luxury liners of the White Star Line. India was a life of adventure for Elizabeth, while Chelsea was mostly drudgery. In England, she suffered under tutors who worked her through lessons in mathematics, science, and literature. England was home, of course, at least everyone she knew said so. But Elizabeth found it cold, damp, and unfriendly even when she arrived in April each year allowing her to avoid the heat of the Indian summer.

Elizabeth adored her mother's parents. Her grandfather was a retired brigadier who served first in the Scot's Guards and then, on assignment, with the Bombay Engineers. Her grandmother was an artist who had watercolours on display in India and in Edinburgh. She was a senior member of the Royal Horticultural Society and a volunteer at the Chelsea Physic Garden. They exemplified to Elizabeth what a rich life she could have, and they tried very hard to let her enjoy the city of London. Elizabeth came to England with her India-based, Scottish-born tutor, Mrs. Edwards. They walked from her grandparents' home to the newly opened Victoria and Albert and Natural History Museums and to the nearby Chelsea Physic Garden. They took the train to the Royal Botanical Gardens in Kew. Each of these trips was part of her education and Mrs. Edwards seemed to know everything and everyone in what she called the Natural Philosophy community in London. Mrs. Edwards worked hard to expose Elizabeth to the scientists and she encouraged, some would say demanded, that Elizabeth read the publications of the female adventurers of the age.

She had a well-worn copy of the writings of Gertrude Bell, including her translation of Persian poetry and her accounts of travels in the Holy Land. She also had the three books published by two Scottish sisters named Agnes and Margaret Smith who travelled to Greece, the Holy Land and even to St. Catherine's monastery in the Sinai where they uncovered ancient Christian manuscripts. These were women to be admired and respected! Mrs. Edwards was especially proud of these two intrepid Scots, and she underscored to Elizabeth that the only limitations for women in this new century were limitations that they placed on themselves.

On those rare occasions in London when her grandmother hosted tea parties with girls her own age, Elizabeth was disappointed. She noted with some annoyance that most of her peers' education focused on reading romantic novels, writing poetry, and taking music lessons. If they were allowed outside — briefly of course because the sun would ruin the complexion — the young ladies enjoy garden parties and light sports like badminton and croquet. Elizabeth found she had nothing to say to these young girls and they made it clear to her that they thought she was some oddity from the colonies: not sophisticated; not worthy of their attention; and most definitely not a girl who would become the wife of a successful English gentleman. They were cruel, and the cutting comments hurt Elizabeth. In their point of view, living in India guaranteed Elizabeth's only future was to marry some Army officer and die in childbirth in the wilderness of the Raj. On more than one occasion, Elizabeth barely restrained herself from taking a butter knife to them in ways she learned years before from her Indian nanny.

Elizabeth suppressed her anger only because she felt that she was preparing for living in the new 20th century, while these young English ladies were preparing to live in the past century. Her grandmother warned her that just because she was right about her peers did not mean that she could let these girls know that they were wrong. "Elizabeth, we are determined to prepare you for a special place in the Empire. Your parents and we have worked hard to make your schooling special, but you have to learn to live in this world of London. Someday it may make the difference between a boring normal life and one that you deserve."

Guided by both her mother and Mrs. Edwards, Elizabeth was convinced that while an Army career was out of the question, she could still serve the Empire. Perhaps she would be a famous scientist or an explorer who would discover a lost city in the Himalayas. To make that happen, Elizabeth knew that she needed to attend a British University, ideally Cambridge or Oxford. Her grandparents and Mrs. Edwards recommended Edinburgh University, but Elizabeth just assumed that was because they were Scots.

As Elizabeth approached her 16th birthday, she worked hard at deciding what she would do with her life. Regardless of her location, Elizabeth was filled with wonder at the marvels of the scientists, explorers, and soldiers who made the British Empire the finest in history. When she returned each year to India, her luggage contained some example of the modern instruments of the natural philosopher — one year a sextant, then a barometer, a telescope, and most recently a microscope. And, each year, Elizabeth filled a journal with her observations and drawings of the plant and animal life of the Raj. When her family and servants weren't looking, Elizabeth even drew sketches of the servants and soldiers in the cantonment.

She wasn't sure what she might do, but Elizabeth was certain what she would not do. She would not marry a soldier and be a good wife. Of course, no one who cared for Elizabeth ever said that she should, but the criticisms from her London peers cut deep wounds that did not heal.

During the Christmas holidays, Francis and Mary Bankroft told Elizabeth the time had come for a formal education. In an explosion of emotion that surprised even Elizabeth, she refused. In England, "formal education" for young women meant a "finishing school" where she understood young women were prepared for marriage. She stood up from the dining room table and placed her hands on her hips. She had never been a recalcitrant child, but this was time to put her foot down. And that was what she did with a stamp of her slippered foot.

"Mother and Father, I will not be finished in some school so I can become a good wife. I want to be a scientist. I have read the writings of women adventurers and scientists. I want to be someone like that."

Francis and Mary Bankroft smiled at their daughter's forceful argument. This only made Elizabeth more determined to refuse their decision. Her parents were treating her like...a child. She was no longer a child and intended to insist on participating in the decision. Francis said, "My dear Elizabeth, I promise you that the school we have chosen is not designed to *finish* you in the way you think. Your mother and I are certain that it is just the place for you to advance your education. It is a college that will prepare you for your future. If you choose to go to university after college, then you may. If you choose a profession after the college, then you may do that as well."

Mary Bankroft could see her daughter was not persuaded. She decided that it would be useful to redirect the discussion. She used her most calming voice and said, "Dear, just as your brother went to Addison College before going to Quetta for his military training, you need to go to an appropriate college to ensure you get a well-rounded education before you decide what you want to do with your life. We are sending you to our alma mater, The Viceroy's College. I think you will find it just right for your interests."

Elizabeth didn't quite know how to respond. Her mother's voice was so calming and soothing that all of the arguments in her head suddenly seemed foolish. Plus, the fact that they were sending her to their alma mater suggested this was a very modern school. After all, it must accept both men and women. That was something that she had not thought possible in India. The offer of a trip on an airship had finally turned the trick. After all, none of the girls in London would ever ride on an airship for any reason. Elizabeth was certain that this was how a woman of the 20th century should travel.

The airship's nose pointed gently skyward, leveled out and then turned to the northeast. In short order, they left the Punjabi plain and began to climb above mountain forests, first of shesham and, eventually, pines of the snow-capped Murree Hills, the foothills of the Himalayas. Her mother's voice pulled Elizabeth back to the present as she stared at the forests and steep hillsides from the starboard side of the airship. Mary Bankroft stood next to her daughter and explained the geography. Mary always shared her daughter's interests in botany and geology and she pointed out key features in the countryside as the airship flew northeast. From the airship's cruising altitude, it was easy to point out geologic features that would be invisible to anyone on the ground.

Elizabeth relaxed and listened to her mother's lecture. The ride on the airship proved that she was well on the way to becoming a 20th century woman. She just didn't know what a 20th century woman might do after college in a remote part of India. It seemed unlikely this school would help her gain entrance to one of England or Scotland's universities, and India had no university available. Where would this airship ride lead? Elizabeth could not venture a guess.

Two hours later, Mary Bankroft turned to her daughter and said, "Elizabeth, we are nearing our destination, you will need to sit down." Elizabeth could see the propellers that seemed as tall as a house, turning in the air in time with the rumble of the steam engine through the floor below. She heard a young boy on the port side of the airship gasp as the engines reversed pitch and slowed. The destination was on the port side.

Mary Bankroft said, "Go ahead, take a look."

Elizabeth stood and walked to the port hole next to the one where the young boy was sitting with his father, a stern-looking fellow with a full beard and dressed in a formal black suit associated with the Raj government. Through the porthole she could see a walled garrison appearing and then disappearing through the mountain mists. It looked to have dozens of bungalows made of dark wood, three buildings that looked exactly like barracks that she knew from Rawalpindi and Peshawar, and a building in the center that reminded Elizabeth of the headquarters building in Rawalpindi cantonment. The barracks looked as if they were perched on the side of a hard-rock mountain face. The entire architecture of the compound was a mix of Victorian bric-a-brac, Mughal arches, and an internal courtyard. Inside the compound were two sports pitches, a cinder track, a circular area of dirt, and a set of stables. There did not appear to be any road up to the college. In fact, it seemed to perch on the side of the mountain like some raptor's nest.

"This is the college?"

"Yes, dear. Now you can see why we took an airship. There are no formal roads to this part of the Empire. You can get to the college by horse, but it takes days to travel from Murree and more than a week of hard riding from Rawalpindi. Students, teachers, and visitors always go up to the college by airship. It is a wonderful and painless way to travel, don't you think?"

Just as Elizabeth was about to respond, the young boy at the railing said, "My name is Michael O'Connell. I am going to go to school here and become an agent for the Empire." His comments generated a stern look from his father, who then offered a more friendly nod to Mary as he noticed the embroidery on the Kashmiri shawl around her shoulders. He offered his hand to Mary and said, "James O'Connell. Class of '02. We are coming from Simla. It has been a long way for a fifteen-year-old to travel."

Mary took the hand and said, "Mary Bankroft. Class of '90. I noticed your tie earlier and assumed you were delivering your son to school. My daughter Elizabeth starts this term."

"Mrs. Bankroft, it is not as if I wouldn't recognize you. Is your husband at the parade ground waiting to meet you?"

Elizabeth noticed her mother blushed slightly. What made this man say what he did about her mother? She knew so little about the college and about her parents' time there. She could only guess why a man nearly a dozen years her junior would recognize her mother.

"Yes, Francis is on the ground. We will be returning by horse after a day in the galleries."

"I'm afraid Michael's mother passed some years ago. Fever. It's just me and the boy now and soon just myself. I will be assigned to a field station soon enough once I get Michael settled. I believe they are sending me to our station in Aden. It is the language, you see. Once an Arabist, always an Arabist. Perhaps I could share tea with you this afternoon before we depart?"

"I certainly hope so. Let me see what is waiting for us on the ground."

Elizabeth was tired of these grown-up pleasantries, so she said, "Mother, where are we precisely?"

"As I said before dear, we are at your new school. It is called The Viceroy's College. It is a school for some of the most gifted children of the Raj. Your father and I are very proud you will attend this school."

"No, what I meant was where precisely are we? I do not recognize the terrain."

"The Viceroy's College is near a small village called Natiaghali. It is north and west of Murree in the foothills of the great mountain range."

"This gentleman said he knew of you and father. What did he mean? And where is father?"

Mary decided to avoid the first question and answer the second. "Father is waiting for us on the ground, dear. He had work with one of his cavalry troops and went on ahead earlier this week."

During the ride and because of her mother's lecture, Elizabeth barely noticed the other passengers: nine young men and women each travelling with a parent. Mothers with daughters, fathers with sons — three other girls and six boys including Michael O'Connell. Elizabeth guessed they were between the ages of 14 and 16. Convinced she was the oldest girl, Elizabeth wondered how each of them had been chosen for this school in such a remote place. She knew many of the boys in the cantonment in Rawalpindi and Peshawar were sent off to Eton, Harrow or Rugby in England. Those who hadn't met that social, academic or financial standard were sent to the best college in India, Addison in Lahore. Her brother Conrad had attended Addison and then went to Quetta Staff College to become an officer in the Indian Army. He was an ensign in the Baluch Rifles and would return for Christmas.

The loudspeaker in the cabin sounded three bells. The amplification in the cabin was through a brass horn not unlike the gramophone horn in the family library at home. The voice that came out next was far less clear than any of the singers she heard coming from the celluloid tubes on the gramophone. "Ladies and Gentlemen, this is your captain speaking. Please take your seats. We are about to dock at Fort Burnes. In the next few minutes, you may feel a gentle sway in the cabin. This is normal for an airship at well dock. Please do not leave your seats until you are instructed to do so by

Ensign Jameson. You will be on the ground shortly. Thank you."

"Ft. Burnes?" Elizabeth had heard of Alexander Burnes and had read his works on Afghanistan as well as the books outlining his tragic death in that country. But, she had never heard of a military cantonment named after him — at least not in India.

Mary Bankroft nodded and said, "Dear, we are on a military airship. It is only natural that the airship docks at a military cantonment."

Over the next few minutes, the ship did begin to sway first back and forth and then side to side. It reminded Elizabeth of her voyages by steamship from Karachi to Greenwich when the liner docked at the various ports on the way. She looked out her porthole and saw heavy lines, they were called hawsers she recalled, reaching to the ground and being taken up by uniformed men at least 100 feet below. They hooked the lines into cylinders that looked like a giant version of her grandfather's fishing reel. The ground crew began to reel in the lines using small steam engines. Slowly, they descended as the lines were taken up in the reels. Much sooner than she expected, Elizabeth felt a gentle bump as the ship docked against a raised platform 30 feet above the ground.

Ensign Jameson opened the door to the bridge and walked into the passenger cabin. Elizabeth was impressed with this young ensign, resplendent in his white cap, a navy blue RNFC blazer, white roll-neck sweater, sky-blue trousers and black boots. He appeared only a year or two older than she, but already serving the Crown; this was what young men could expect and young women could hope but not expect. She intended to change that — perhaps she would be the first female aviator as well as a scientist. Why not? After all, it was the 20th Century.

He said, "Ladies and Gentlemen, we have docked at Ft. Burnes. God save the King! Please follow me to the aft passenger door to disembark from the *Resolve*. Also, please take care to mind the gap between the door and the dock. Ladies, I will be there to assist you."

Mary Bankroft rolled her eyes as she stood and took Elizabeth's hand. "Do mind the gap, dear. But do not accept any help from the good ensign," she whispered. "Our boots are no more or less sound than his and I suspect we have both ridden far more challenging horses than this airship."

Elizabeth smiled. She was her mother's daughter to be sure.

Elizabeth was very proud of her mother. In Elizabeth's view, her mother was the perfect example of a modern woman. Mary Bankroft was in her early 40s though she looked ten years younger dressed in a modern-cut shalwar kamiz made of brilliant cream wool with a similarly coloured, long scarf called a dupatta. The scarf had three vertical stripes along the border coloured red, saffron, and a brilliant white that stood out from more cream-coloured wool. Fitted inside the pajama pants known as the shalwar, were brown suede ankle-high boots. These were not consistent with the shalwar kamiz in style, but certainly more practical than the leather slippers that most women wore with such an outfit. Elizabeth had seen her mother in these clothes, but never with this dupatta. She normally wore a simple white-on-white dupatta with a jacquard pattern covering her stylish cut of ample chestnut hair. Elizabeth had a similar travelling outfit with a green dupatta, though her mother had encouraged her to wear her "English" clothes today: a white blouse, navy skirt and blazer. She noticed the other three girls were also in English dress, though the blouses and the skirts seemed more restricted and their button shoes, while stylish, looked to have dangerously high heels.

Before they headed to the door, Elizabeth noticed all the mothers were wearing scarves like her mother's scarf and all of the men were wearing ties with the same stripes running diagonally across the tie. Elizabeth thought, "Some sort of club?" She knew British regiments, universities and clubs had ties made that allowed alumni to identify each other at a distance. Perhaps this was a new club that she would hear about on the ground. As Elizabeth reached the door and stepped onto the docking platform, she decided to ask that question later.

Elizabeth climbed down the stairs from the platform to the parade ground where the *HMFS Resolve* was docked. As she looked back at the enormous craft that seemed to fill her entire view, she noticed a lower deck that had been obscured in the Rawalpindi terminal. Crewmen from the lower windows waved to the departing passengers. Unlike the formal uniforms on the upper deck, these fellows were wearing leather jackets and leather helmets. Their portholes had no glass and Elizabeth could just make out gun barrels protruding from inside. It was a gunship after all! The newspaper articles had described the airships as part of the defense of the Indian frontier and even said the hostile tribes on the border referred to the airships as the "talons of the Raj." Now she knew why, though she still thought it odd she was travelling on an armed airship to a remote school. She supposed the airship was always armed in flight — especially on the frontier.

The thought did not last long as she looked out over the parade ground. A mix of military uniforms and formally suited men gathered near the deck. Beyond them, a full complement of Frontier Force lancers were on parade, resplendent in khaki and red astride twenty perfectly matched black chargers. All present and correct as her father said when Elizabeth and her brother Conrad arrived at breakfast each morning. Standing at attention beyond them were twenty men and women each dressed in white shalwar kamiz, brown wool coats, and caracul hats. Elizabeth puzzled over the scene as her father greeted her mother and her at the embarkation platform. Even her father looked strange in the uniform of the Frontier Force with khaki and a turban in that regiment's colours.

"Father, you haven't been reassigned again, have you?"

"Beth, my dear, is that the first thing out of your mouth after a month away from me?"

Mary said, "Francis, it is a bit of a shock seeing you in this uniform. You do look splendid of course, though rather thin."

"Thank you, my love. Young Beth, I have been on temporary assignment here and the commander wanted me to wear the local uniform."

"You mean the colonel is here as well?"

Bankroft and his wife shared a quick glance. Mary took the lead. "Elizabeth, you know we don't talk about our colonel in public. Your father was talking about the post commander here, Colonel…"

"Colonel William Stephenson, at your service, ladies." Stephenson was greeting each of the families and had arrived just in time to end what might have been an embarrassing conversation. Stephenson had the look of an old Raj hand. Wrinkled skin the colour of maple wood from too many years under the Indian sun and a white mustache and whiskers more common in Indian regiments than in British Army regiments of the 20th century. He was tall, thin, and glorious in his Frontier Force uniform, turban, and riding boots. Elizabeth was struck dumb at this giant warrior of the realm.

Mary smiled. "Colonel, you have done something no man has done before, you have silenced my daughter with a simple greeting. We need to learn a lesson from you. Thank you for greeting us with your surprise parade."

"Mrs. Bankroft, when Francis told me you were coming and the fact that you were both illustrious alumni of this school, I simply couldn't help myself. A little pomp is always good for everyone, especially the troops. At least, that is what Sergeant Major Bailey tells me."

A discrete cough from behind the colonel revealed the

presence of an equally resplendent man, the size and shape of an oak stump. Sergeant Major Bailey had a full mustache and mutton chops and, instead of a sword, he carried a large, knobbed stick nearly as long as most police lathis Elizabeth had seen in the cantonment. "Sir, we will need to load the mountain troops immediately. The captain of the *Resolve* says the winds are favorable only for another hour."

"Righto, Sergeant Major! Make it so, if you please. I will join you presently."

Bailey did a formal right turn, walked four paces along the dock and slammed his staff on the wood with a sharp report. "All right, boys. Quick March and load the airship!" He didn't seem to strain at all, but his voice carried across the entire parade ground. Elizabeth noticed a movement from behind the lancers. Twenty Pathans in battle khaki, helmets and mountain boots came on the run to the docks and then started marching up the steps to the airship.

"Ladies, we need to get out of the way of the scouts who are heading up country." As Elizabeth walked down the separate gangway, she took one last look at these men called scouts. All bearded, dark hair and skin and the look of the pirates she knew from her readings of Mr. Stevenson's book. She also noticed that even though they were armed and carried light packs, they made almost no noise as they moved past and onto the airship. Their uniforms were clean, but worn at the knees and elbows. They smelled of nothing but gun oil and leather.

The colonel turned to Francis Bankroft. "Francis, they will do the job now that you have found the key."

"Thank you, sir. I am sure Captain Dodd's men will be more than enough and the *Resolve* will be a fine addition to the operation."

"Francis, Bailey and I and the headquarters staff have to go now, so we will bid you farewell and thanks. Until the next time."

Elizabeth's father came to attention and rendered a formal salute. "God speed, sir."

The colonel returned the same and joined five others carrying bags and map cases as they climbed aboard the airship. Elizabeth noticed that all of the men were now looking out the windows of the lower deck as the airship engines began to turn.

Ensign Jameson leaned out from a lower deck window in the bow of the airship. He had a megaphone and shouted down to the ground crew. "Port side, Starboard side, clear! Dock clear! All clear! Ground crew release hawsers!"

The crew worked carefully to release the hawsers from their reels as the crew on the dock pulled away the gangway. "All clear?" The ground crew master chief saluted to the ensign. "Stand by."

The roar of the steam engines surprised Elizabeth. With a sudden jolt, *HMFS Resolve* took to the sky and turned away from the loading dock. They quickly gained altitude and the hawsers seemed to withdraw into the ship on their own. In what seemed like a blink of the eye, the airship became just a small balloon, then a dot, and then nothing at all. Elizabeth was amazed at this wonder of the age.

Elizabeth walked hand-in-hand with her parents toward the group of white-clad men and women standing in front of a large stone building on the far side of the parade ground. It was in the design that Elizabeth had seen in Rawalpindi and Lahore — a mix of arches and towers that her mother called Raj Victorian after the former Queen. She recently learned that the design was made famous by John Lockwood Kipling, the father of the writer Rudyard Kipling. Family ties were always part of the history of the Raj, and the Kiplings, father and son, were no exception. Mrs. Edwards had focused one

of her more interesting classes on teaching the architecture
of British India using the family Holmes Stereoscope and
a series of slides of government and commercial buildings
across India. The stereoscope made the images seem almost
real. This stone building had not been one of the slides, but
Elizabeth recognized the design almost immediately. Definitely a Kipling building.

A senior gentleman in the front of the civilian parade
spoke. "Ladies and gentlemen, as alumni of our school, you
know that the time has come to say goodbye to your children.
We promise to take excellent care of them and prepare them
for the life that they will lead in service to King and Country.
Please say your farewells and then move to the dining hall to
take tea with the faculty in the galleries."

Francis turned to his daughter. "All right, my little darling.
It is time for your mother and I to say goodbye. We will see
you at the end of term in December — in time for a Christmas holiday. This is the first of two years at the school, but I
believe it is the hardest."

Mary smiled and said, "It was hard for you only because
you are terrible at trigonometry and map making..."

"Thank you, old thing. I don't need reminding."

Elizabeth missed the joke. She sounded worried as she
said, "Father, will the school really be hard?"

"Dear, it will be hard because work in service of the Crown
is hard. But, as we say in the regiment, train hard, fight easy."

Mary Bankroft shook her head and said, "My dear, you
need to remember you are talking to our daughter, not one of
your sepoys. Train hard, fight easy isn't exactly how I would
frame the school."

Elizabeth thought to herself, "I've been polite and open
minded, but what is going on?"

She was frustrated that she still didn't understand why she

was attending this college and why in the world it was so remote to be almost like a prison. It was hardly a college she had expected and certainly not her image of a where you received a 20th century education. Elizabeth knew she had only a few seconds left before she had to leave her parents and join her classmates. If she was going to succeed, and Elizabeth was determined that she would succeed no matter what, she needed to know something, anything about the college. She said, "While you are having this conversation, you haven't told me anything about why I am here. What is this school? Why am I here?"

Francis Bankroft bent down and whispered in her ear. "My lovely Elizabeth, it is a school for the greatest game of all. The Viceroy's College produces the intelligence officers for British India. It is what your mother and I do for our King and you may join us once you graduate from the college."

Elizabeth's mouth dropped open and she gasped. She knew it was a less-than-attractive trait, but she couldn't help it. She whispered back to her father and Mary Bankroft who was now slightly bent over to hear the conversation. "It is a school for the spies of the Empire? You are both…spies?"

Mary Bankroft replied. "We prefer not to use that term, dear."

Francis Bankroft smiled at Mary. He took Elizabeth's hand and said, "Got it in one, dear. That's where you are. You are to attend His Majesty's Indian College for espionage."

A tall wizened man with skin the colour of burnished oak walked up to Elizabeth. "Young madam, it is time to join your classmates."

As this man looked her in the eyes, Elizabeth felt calm. She knew that she was starting a new life and it was time to take that first step. She squared her shoulders, drew in a strong breath and began to follow this teacher. Elizabeth looked over her shoulder and said, "Mother and Father, I will see you at the end of term."

"Of course, dear. Be careful and study hard." Francis waved to his daughter and then turned to Mary. "Do you remember that moment?"

"How could I forget? At the time, I didn't realize what was happening, but it seemed so wrong that I was unable to say farewell to my parents."

"Elizabeth is strong-willed. She will be a handful even for Guru Naismith."

"I do believe you are right, Francis. I do believe you are right."

And so, in the first week in February in 1911, Elizabeth started her career in service to the British Empire.

The Viceroy's College

ELIZABETH FOLLOWED THE MAN IN THE WHITE WOOL SHALWAR KAMIZ AND karakul hat until they reached a small courtyard where the rest of her class already stood along a yellow line. They were not exactly in formation in the way that Elizabeth had seen her father's soldiers in formation, but nearly so. She joined the line and faced forward as one of the ten new students at the school.

The old man said, "Ladies and gentlemen, I am Guru Naismith. I am the master of this college and I want to welcome you personally to our center of learning." Elizabeth thought his voice had the sound of caramel sweets. Soothing. It was hard to imagine feeling anything but at home with Guru Naismith. All of her concerns about the school and her parents seemed to evaporate. "You have been selected to join the ranks of many honourable men and women in the British Empire. Our job is to provide you with the skills to succeed in your future responsibilities. The Viceroy's College has been here in the mountains for twenty years and we are proud to have been part of the success of His Majesty's Empire. Our graduates have continued on with their studies in many universities throughout the Empire, but with a single task in mind — service to the Crown. I hope you will agree that this is a most important task."

The teenagers nodded in unison. Naismith smiled. The mix of altitude and his voice were calming them. They would no longer worry about the departure of their parents. It was as it should be.

"Now, you will each be assigned your own guru who will serve as your guide for these first few months. Please follow the guru's instructions and make sure you understand what you are being asked to do before you do anything here at the college. We expect our students to think and sometimes to express disagreement. Please meet your guru and go to your quarters. Dinner will be served in the main hall promptly at sundown. There will be three strikes on the bell to let you know you need to come to the parade ground and then to dinner." Naismith motioned to his left and slightly behind the students.

They turned to face a massive bronze tubular bell suspended from a carved wooden frame with three pillars. At the top of the pillars were three carved demon faces. Elizabeth had seen the faces before on a ceremonial dagger that her father kept in a bowl of sand. He had told her it was a Tibetan spirit knife and it was used to keep misfortune in check. The three faces on the knife were the same three on the triangular frame. In dark carved wood in these mountains, the faces were terrifying. Elizabeth could almost imagine they were alive and staring at her. She shook her head. As a natural philosopher, Elizabeth knew there were no such things as spirits.

Elizabeth heard a soft voice with a Welsh accent in her ear.

"Elizabeth, it is time to go to quarters." Elizabeth tried not to appear as startled as she was. She could have sworn there was no one behind her and yet here was a woman in a white wool shalwar kamiz with a white wool shawl wrapped around her head and shoulders. The dupatta had the same three stripes as the shawl her mother had worn today.

"Elizabeth, my name is Guru Marian and I am your guide for the time you are in college. Please follow me." Marian turned and walked silently up the path from the courtyard. She started up a series of twisting stairs between stone buildings that somehow Elizabeth had not noticed from the airship. Elizabeth guessed that Marian was probably her mother's age and from her accent she clearly was from Wales. Unlike her mother's amber hair, cut in a stylish bob, Marian's was a raven black which she kept in a long braid down the middle of her back. The braid shifted slightly back and forth as she climbed the stairs. Elizabeth strained to follow her. She thought she was quite fit, but somehow the thin air did not seem to fill her lungs.

Marian turned back to watch her new charge. She started to walk backwards so that she could talk to Elizabeth face to face. Elizabeth puzzled over how this woman could know every step along the stairs even though she was walking backwards. "Elizabeth, I know from your mother that you are quite an amateur naturalist. You must know why you are having trouble breathing."

Elizabeth worked hard to get enough air into her lungs to say anything. Eventually, she gasped, "We…are…at…some…altitude higher than Murree."

"Yes, Elizabeth. We are at 9000 feet. What does that mean regarding the atmospheric pressure?"

Elizabeth had not expected to be quizzed as she walked uphill to her new room. In fact, she hadn't expected to be challenged at all as she climbed the stairs. Still, she did not want to appear foolish. If the atmospheric pressure at 1 mile was half that of sea level, then another 4000 feet later would be…. She said, "It…means…there is approximately…30 percent of the atmospheric pressure at sea level."

"That is very good, Elizabeth. Now, we need to move along even if you only have 30 percent of your atmosphere." Guru Marian smiled and continued to walk backwards up the stairs. Elizabeth suddenly noticed Guru Marian appeared to be not walking but actually gliding slightly above the stairs — almost flying.

"Guru Marian, are you flying?"

"Elizabeth, you know that can't be so. We haven't suspended the laws of physics here at The Viceroy's College."

Elizabeth looked again. "But, I can see your feet are not touching the ground."

"Elizabeth, we are going to teach you that sometimes what you see and what is really happening are two very different things. Now, come along." They finished the climb and Elizabeth and Marian walked along a line of doors on the barracks. Each door had a Sanskrit letter painted in red. Elizabeth's door had the letter pronounced "Kha."

Marian gestured to the door, "First termers live in the high barracks. All of your books, your clothes and your boots will be red. Second termers live in the middle barracks below. They are dressed in saffron. Midway through your second year, you become seniors. Seniors live in the barracks around the parade ground. They dress in white."

Marian opened the door and guided Elizabeth in. Even though there were no windows, the room was bright as if lighted by gas lamps similar to her father's study in Rawalpindi. Elizabeth looked up to see a round hole in the ceiling covered with what appeared to be a web of glass.

Marian nodded. "Ah, you noticed the solar lamp! Excellent. We use the sun during the day. The light from the sun is stored in a chemical battery and provides light at night. A design Guru Naismith invented years ago. It saves on lamp oil which would have to be carried by wagon from Murree." Marian pointed back to the door and said, "The switch for the battery light is next to the door."

The room was spartan. Polished wooden floors and plank panels on the walls. There was a bed, a small desk and chair, a bookshelf and a dresser. There was a smaller room off the side which Elizabeth assumed was the water closet. Marian paused and then said, "This is your room Elizabeth. You will be expected to keep it clean. I will inspect the room every day for the first three weeks and then once a week for the rest of the term. You will make your bed every day. The dhobis will provide clean sheets once a week. As washermen, they will also collect your dirty clothes and the towels from the hamper there in the corner. You will put them outside your door every Monday. As you can see, your desk is opposite the bed and your clothes dresser is at the back of the room. Your bookcase is already full of books that you will be expected to read by the end of term." Elizabeth was struck by how small the room was and how many books were in the glass-covered bookcase. "What languages do you speak?"

"I speak French and some Urdu and some Persian."

"Elizabeth, we are precise here. On a scale of one to four with four being a native speaker and one a person who can order food but nothing more, what languages to do you speak?"

Elizabeth paused to be certain that she was not exaggerating. "I speak French at a three level and both Urdu and Persian at a two level."

"Very good. After the first three weeks here at College, we focus great attention on language skills. We have four houses for language: Persian, Arabic, Turkish and Russian. I believe you are currently set to be in Russia House, but that will be dependent upon your demonstrated skills over the next three weeks. Do not worry. There are no 'good houses' or 'bad houses.' There are only language houses." Marian pointed to the corner of the room. "Now, you see that the staff have brought up your portmanteau. Please change into your school uniform and place your civilian clothes in the portmanteau. We will put it in storage and you will see your English clothes again at the end of term. I will expect to see you at dinner. Please settle in."

"Yes, Guru Marian."

"One last thing, Elizabeth. Always lock your door. It is a habit you must maintain for the time you are here and, when you graduate, for the rest of your life. You must be certain that you will not be attacked in your own home." With that warning, Guru Marian was gone.

Elizabeth walked over to the closed door. There was a slide bolt which she fastened. She also noticed two wooden wedges next to the door. Elizabeth had seen these sorts of wedges in her parents' suitcases and noticed that they always applied the wedges to the doors in any hotel that they stayed in when travelling. Perhaps this school was where they picked up that habit. Elizabeth decided it was a good place to start. She placed one wedge in the top of the door and a second in the bottom.

Once the door was secured, Elizabeth walked around the room to see if there was anything that she had missed in her first glance. The bed was a simple Indian charpoy — a rope bed. On top of the charpoy was a cotton-batten mattress and on top of the mattress was a quilt in a coverlet and a single pillow. Elizabeth studied how the bed was set up so that she could copy it precisely in advance of her mentor's inspection. This part of the school would be easy. Her father and mother had been inspecting her room for as long as she could remember.

She turned to the desk. It was a wooden writing desk with pens, an ink well, pencils, a small knife to sharpen the pencils and writing paper. There were also a series of bound notebooks stacked in the upper right corner of the desk. Each was empty. Finally, she turned to the bookcase. On the top shelf, were a mix of books on mathematics, geometry, trigonometry and map making. The second shelf held histories, poetry and philosophy texts addressing the various parts of the Empire. One of the books on this shelf she did not recognize. It was called *Arthashastra*. Elizabeth was curious, but she assumed there would be time enough to sort these questions out. There were books in Russian that seemed to be part of the language course. There were also books in French. In total, there were forty books.

Elizabeth liked to read, but these books seemed much harder and much more "adult" than anything Mrs. Edwards had ever offered. Elizabeth understood now her father's comments about how hard this term would be. This was by no means a "finishing" school.

Perhaps she would learn more about the school over time. One thing was for certain, Elizabeth recognized this college would be a challenge and she always loved challenges. But what would be the biggest challenge? For the first time in her life, Elizabeth was surrounded by strangers. No allies to be seen. Based on the books on her bookshelf, it was clear she would be tested on subjects that she did not know. What other troubles were ahead? Elizabeth decided that she could not change her course at this point. She was in a college which, as near as she could see, was on the edge of the earth. One of Mrs. Edwards' favourite quotes from Seutonius was *Alea iacta est* or "the die has been cast." Well, Elizabeth was certain that her current situation was not as dramatic as Caesar crossing the Rubicon, but there was absolutely no going back. At this point, for her own honour and for the honour of her family, she would do whatever it took to survive this strange college.

As a first step in this new commitment, Elizabeth turned to the clothes dresser. She opened the first drawer and there were eight sets of folded, one-piece underwear in undyed cotton. Next to each set were two pairs of cotton socks. Elizabeth found to her amusement that the socks had toes in them. The next drawer had eight sets of shalwar kamiz dyed a dark red that looked much like the red in the tribal carpets on the floor of her father's study. In the bottom drawer were eight folded woolen dupattas in white with a broad red stripe. In front of the dresser were two pairs of leather sandals, dyed red, two pairs of red canvas shoes with hard rubber soles, and two pairs of black, highly shined knee-high riding boots.

"It will be easy to choose what to wear," Elizabeth said to no one in particular as she put on the red uniform. Just as she finished putting on her new uniform, she heard the striking of the bell. She put on the canvas slippers and headed out the door. As she left, she saw the rest of her class leaving as well. The other girls and boys seemed far less comfortable than her in their new uniforms. The girls seemed to have decided that the sandals were the correct answer to the evening call and the boys were wearing the riding boots. Elizabeth had to laugh at this mix and match as they headed down to the parade ground. They looked like a waterfall of red as they moved down the stairs.

"Do not run, first termers! We need you to live through the next three weeks!" On the sides of the stairwell, nine mentors stood watch. The tenth mentor — Elizabeth's Guru Marian — stood at the bottom of the steps to guide them to their proper place on the parade ground. Four students in white and six students in saffron shalwar kamiz were already in place. Marian carefully filed the red first termers into the last row on the parade ground. They were all facing the flagpole and looking to the east toward the Pamirs and Kashmir. Behind the flagpole facing west was the squadron of Frontier Force Lancers, now on foot at what Elizabeth knew from both her father and her brother as a position called parade rest.

Guru Naismith and a major from the Frontier Force stood

facing the three rows of students. Naismith spoke in his gentle voice. "Guru Lawrence."

"All present and correct, Guru Ji."

"Guru Macintosh."

"All present and correct, Guru Ji."

"Guru Marian."

Marian spoke from the right side of her section. "All present and correct, Guru Ji."

Naismith did a formal left turn and faced the major, who had just completed a formal right turn. He saluted. "Major, the school is assembled."

"Thank you, Major Naismith." The major completed another right turn as Naismith completed another left turn. They were now facing the flagpole and the Frontier Force squadron. The major spoke in a formal parade-ground voice. "Colour sergeant, retrieve the colours if you please."

Elizabeth watched as best she could from behind a very tall young man dressed in saffron as the colour sergeant and two troopers walked out of formation and marched to the flagpole. When they reached the flagpole, the colour sergeant turned to the squadron.

"Squadron. Attention!" The troops snapped to attention as one.

Naismith turned to look back at the students. "College. Attention!" The students in the first two rows immediately snapped to attention. Elizabeth's row was less skilled and instead of a single movement, it seemed to be a cascade of action from Guru Marian to the end of the row. Elizabeth could see which students were from military families and which were from civil servants. In a military family, you learned about formal ceremonies before you could walk on your own.

"Squadron, present arms!" Another set of movements in unison as the troopers brought their rifles to present arms and the squadron guidon bearer lowered the guidon. The Frontier

Force officer and Guru Naismith rendered hand salutes as the British colours were recovered and folded properly. The ceremony ended quickly, once the colours were recovered and the colour sergeant and his team returned to their position. The two majors exchanged salutes, shook hands, and walked in opposite directions. The gurus followed Naismith and the students followed the gurus with the ten students in red at the end of the column.

The dining hall for the school was large enough for at least 100 guests. On a small platform at one end was the table where Naismith and his three senior mentors ate. Directly below, was the staff table with 40 mentors and instructors sitting together facing three parallel rows of tables and chairs — students stood at table until instructed to sit. The dining hall staff stood at attention until all were seated. The walls in the hall were without decoration except for dozens of lamps hanging from forged iron hooks. In addition, twenty chandeliers hung from the ceiling. The room was bright and, once dinner started, exceptionally noisy.

During dinner, the young girl sitting next to Elizabeth said, "My name is Martha."

"Elizabeth."

"I just heard from one of the second-term boys about the Reckoning. What is the Reckoning?"

Elizabeth frowned. It didn't sound very encouraging. She said, "I don't know."

"Well, the second-term student said they were making bets on how many of us would survive this Reckoning."

Elizabeth did her best to sound calm. She was anything but calm. She said, "I'm sure they are just trying to frighten us. Boys will do that."

ᵀᵇᵉ Reckoning

DURING THE FIRST DAYS AT THE COLLEGE, ELIZABETH WAS CERTAIN THAT THE instructors were determined to either kill her or make her quit. Early morning exercises before dawn were followed by a quick march through mountain trails. The students never knew how long the march would be. Sometimes it was a simple short jaunt into the surrounding forest and sometimes an hour-long march that ended with a desperate run to the parade ground. The instructors barely broke a sweat while the students struggled with each step. While the shalwar kamiz was loose enough to survive any exercise, Elizabeth's sweat made her kamiz around her armpits and the legs of the shalwar rub arms and legs raw. After each morning program, they were marched into the dining hall where they were given a bowl of porridge mixed with stewed apricots and a cup of unsweetened tea. They were expected to eat their porridge standing up and eat it they did. After the second day, it was clear that they would not see much food later in the day.

Following breakfast, they were given time to take a cold bath and change clothes for a day of classroom work. Classes focused exclusively on mathematics and geography. Thankfully for Elizabeth, these were easy repeats of subjects she had long mastered with Mrs. Edwards. She could see that several of her classmates were struggling with the material and, in the case of the younger students, struggling just to stay awake. At lunch, they were allowed to sit and have a bowl of yogurt and raisins and a glass of water. Students were not allowed to speak. Speaking at the lunch table meant the end of the meal for the violator and for whoever the violated had addressed. It took only one day of punishment to ensure silence in the dining hall.

After lunch, they changed back into their exercise uniforms, barely dry from early morning efforts, and conducted another set of exercises and another quick march. This exercise routine was followed by a horseback ride or a land navigation exercise in the forests surrounding the school. Each day ended with the parade and dinner in the great hall with the second term and senior students. Once again, Elizabeth and her peers were singled out. They had to eat standing up and in silence under the watchful eyes of both instructors and more-senior students. After dinner, each first termer was issued a writing assignment to be provided to their mentor at morning exercises. The writing assignments focused on describing the events of the day. They were graded on the ability to accurately describe what they saw and what happened. An assignment would receive a poor grade if it included errors in the description or, worse still, if it focused exclusively on what the student felt or thought as opposed to what they actually observed.

By the end of the second week, two of Elizabeth's classmates, one young boy and a girl Elizabeth's age named Nancy, had walked into Guru Naismith's office and asked to be sent home. There was no argument and no recrimination. Down the mountain on horseback they went. By the next formation, any sign of their presence had disappeared from the college. Their rooms were cleared and the parade formation was shortened by two spots. By that time in the Reckoning, Elizabeth was too tired to ponder what had happened though she was shaken by how quickly both the instructors and the students seemed to forget about Nancy. Worse still, Elizabeth was troubled that she didn't seem to care. Her only concern was to make sure whatever happened to her colleagues did not happen to her. She was focused on survival.

Elizabeth had never faced such severe evaluation nor high risk of failure. Mrs. Edwards might have been a task master with her assignments, but she never pushed Elizabeth beyond her level of comfort. During this training, Elizabeth felt continual stress and fear that she might not make the grade. It didn't matter whether it was in the formal aspects of classroom and written product or in the outdoor activities of running, marching, riding or navigation in the Himalayan forests.

Elizabeth was working at her desk on her nightly assignment. She was quietly sobbing. She was ashamed that she hadn't asked any of her instructors about Nancy. She was concerned that some weakness that Nancy demonstrated might be part of her own daily routine. Earlier in that day, Elizabeth had been the last to finish the morning march. She had twisted her ankle during one of the navigation exercises and the long morning march had been one torturous step after another. She knew from Mrs. Edwards' teaching that she needed to rest and elevate the ankle. In an effort to do so, she was working on the nightly writing assignment with one foot on the floor and her injured foot, wrapped in a wet towel, on the desk. This pose made many other parts of her sore body ache even more.

She wasn't entirely certain why she was crying. It wasn't from sadness. In part, it was simple exhaustion. In part, it was fear of failure. How could she face her parents if she did not survive this training? After all, they had survived and graduated. Elizabeth asked herself why had she abandoned her friend Nancy without a second thought. She had no answers. She was just too tired mentally and physically to do anything but cry. Even in that, Elizabeth was embarrassed to be sobbing like some little girl. Suddenly, Elizabeth heard Guru Marian's voice say, "Have you reached a point where you want to quit our school?"

Elizabeth looked up from her desk. She was certain that she had locked and chocked her door. Yet, here was Guru Marian standing behind her. Elizabeth carefully placed her injured foot on the floor and straightened her back. She took a deep breath. Without turning to look at her guru, Elizabeth said in the most polite tone she could muster, "The only way I am leaving this school is if you throw me down the mountain. I will not quit."

With that, she stood up and turned to face her instructor and realized there was no one in her room. Had she imagined Marian's voice? In Elizabeth's frazzled brain and body, there was only one explanation. She imagined Marian. Or, perhaps, there really were things such as ghosts. Anything seemed possible. She returned to her assignment and her sore ankle.

At the end of the third week, Guru Marian appeared to Elizabeth a second time as she was working on her evening assignment in her quarters. Elizabeth had survived the bruises and scrapes of the program and felt stronger than ever. Marian asked if she was ready for school to begin. This time Elizabeth stood up and walked toward Marian. She could now be certain that her mentor was in the room. Her question puzzled Elizabeth completely. "Begin? I thought we had already begun the term?" Elizabeth was more than a little frustrated. She had survived the first three weeks simply because she was determined not to let her parents down. Now, Guru Marian was asking her whether she was ready to start school? If the last three weeks hadn't been school, what in the world was it?

Before Elizabeth could express these feelings, Marian said, "Elizabeth, you already know we call this time the Reckoning. It is simply a means of determining if students really want to be here and if they are ready to be here. You all arrive for many reasons. Most students arrive simply because their parents want them to follow a family tradition. Some expect this to be no different than some college in England that is used to prepare them for university. Of course, we can't know for sure what our students think or feel when they arrive. So we have the Reckoning. Two from your class have already decided to leave. We want to be sure that when we start training the art of espionage, we have students who will stay the course. The Reckoning usually eliminates those who were not ready. They may come back next year or they may not. We can only wish them well in whatever they choose to do next, but we know they are not ready to begin our program. Some of your classmates are still not entirely certain that they want to stay. It is understandable."

"And you are certain I want to stay?"

Elizabeth wanted to sound very adult but she feared the question came out as a bleat. She was, in fact, almost in tears again. She took a deep breath and straightened her back and shoulders. Long ago, Mrs. Edwards had taught her that an adult faced challenges standing up straight. This certainly was a time for a straight back.

"Elizabeth, when you said to me last week that we would have to throw you out to get you to leave, we knew you would stay the course. I suspect you didn't know it at the time, but you were very tired, very hungry and frustrated with us and with yourself. You still said the right thing and at that point, we were convinced you would survive the Reckoning. I just wanted you to know the hard work was worth it. You will see soon enough."

Elizabeth was angry. The three weeks were just designed to make her suffer? Just to see if she had the will to continue? Why not just ask her? She bowed her head for a moment, struggling to put her thoughts into words.

Guru Marian broke through those thoughts in a voice that seemed to Elizabeth to have originated in her own mind. Marian said, "Yes, we need to see if you have the will to survive. You need to see for yourself how hard you can work even when you are tired, sore and hungry. The trade demands resilience. We must know if you have this before we send you out in the world. Otherwise, you might not survive. Now, finish your assignment and sleep well. Tomorrow is another day and you will find it more to your liking."

Before Elizabeth could reply, she looked up and realized that Guru Marian was not there. The door was locked and the two chocks were still in place. Did she imagine Guru Marian coming to her? Was it a dream? Elizabeth decided to return to her assignment and then go to sleep. That night, for the first time since she arrived, Elizabeth slept without dreams.

Guru Mason stood before Michael O'Connell. The young man looked bedraggled. He was covered in small scratches and bruises caused by the Reckoning. O'Connell was definitely not the most agile student Mason had ever instructed. Still, he seemed determined. At least as determined as a fifteen-year-old boy could be. There was something about the child that made Mason uncomfortable. On the one hand, he was an awkward boy. On the other, Mason could see that the boy was hiding some dark secrets deep in his mind. What sort of dark secrets could a fifteen-year-old have?

"Michael, are you ready to start school tomorrow?"

O'Connell had been waiting and hoping each night to hear that question. His father had prepared him in advance to expect the Reckoning. He had also taught his son some of the basics of mesmerism years ago so that he could survive the bullying that he had faced living in the Navy lines in Bombay. During those hard years, when he realized that his mother had died because of some sort of English prejudice, Michael had nurtured an anger for the English that sometimes consumed him. His father spent many evenings preparing him for The Viceroy's College to be sure that he would not become so angry that he would be eliminated during the Reckoning. During one of those sessions, he taught his son how to conceal his anger so that even the most careful instructor would not see how he felt. Also, it would allow him to conceal his father's shared anger and commitment for revenge against the British. So now, the instructor wanted to know if he was ready to start school.

Michael O'Connell focused his thoughts so that he would express to this instructor both how excited he was and also how compliant he was to college instructions. "Yes, Guru Ji. I am very happy to start school tomorrow."

What Michael O'Connell didn't realize was that Guru Mason was not actually in the room. He was projecting himself deep inside Michael's brain. The deeper he entered the student's brain, the more he saw that was disturbing.

First a Daydream and Then Classes

March 1911

STARTING THE NEXT DAY, THE SCHOOL BECAME MORE LIKE A SCHOOL AND less like a complex torture ritual. After a standard morning set of exercises and breakfast, the eight remaining students were taken into a hall inside the main Anglo-Indian structure where they were seated in a semi-circle around a small podium. None of them had seen the inside of the building, much less the assembly hall. The walls of the hall were covered with paintings of men and women who were considered most honoured alumni of The Viceroy's College. Elizabeth was stunned to see a single portrait of her parents in this "hall of fame." She could not guess what her parents did to deserve such an honour. What was most interesting was the portrait was not one of a younger Francis and Mary Bankroft. It was a portrait of her parents as she knew them now. Questions upon questions filled Elizabeth's mind.

The eight students waited quietly with their mentors: One mentor behind the chair of each student. Elizabeth was at one end of the semi-circle next to the other two girls in the class and five young men including the young man named Michael, who she met on the airship. He caught her eye and smiled. Elizabeth did her best not to blush, but she knew herself well and expected a red blush was climbing up from her collar.

The large wall clock in the rear of the hall sounded the hour with nine paired bell tones like a ship's bell. At the end of the ninth pair of tones, Guru Naismith walked into the room dressed in a black silk shirt and pants and a white, wool knee-length coat known in the Punjab as a kurta. His perfectly groomed, short grey beard matched his nearly shaved, short grey hair. He was wearing black slippers that looked more like something to be worn in an exercise room than a bedroom. The only bit of ornamentation in this uniform of black and white was a black leather band on his left wrist that held a large watch. Elizabeth had seen her father wear a watch like that in the past, but only when he was about to depart "on a tasking" as he liked to call his missions. He had explained that wearing a watch on his wrist rather than in a pocket in his waistcoat made work far easier. Elizabeth could see how useful this might be and wondered if her mother had one as well.

Naismith took a moment to look each of the students in the eye. He then said, "Welcome ladies and gentlemen to The Viceroy's College. In the past three weeks, I know you have wondered what you did to be punished so brutally during the Reckoning. Our commitment to the Crown and, honestly, our commitment to your parents, is such that we have to be sure you are resilient. We are about to introduce you to a life that will require you to work on your own in very dangerous circumstances. Before we teach you how to do this work and to survive these circumstances, we want to be sure you have the mental and physical ability necessary to succeed. The Reckoning may not be a perfect mechanism to make that determination." He paused to look at the eight students. Naismith continued, "But, it has proven to be a useful tool for us to sort out those who are ready and those who are not. Often, students who fail the Reckoning the first time are very successful when they later return."

Elizabeth noticed how the light from the solar lamp in the ceiling was hitting the watch crystal on Guru Naismith's wrist. It sparkled as he spoke. His voice seemed to be more gentle than she had remembered. Perhaps it was just that she was tired. Elizabeth realized that despite herself, she was starting to daydream. Naismith paused and observed the students as he stepped in front of the podium. He used his most powerful mesmerism voice and said, "I am going to tell you a story and like all good stories, it starts with once upon a time. Here, we say that in Persian. We say: *Yek-e-bud, yek-e-nabud, pesh az khoda, hitch kas nabud. Once there was a man, once there wasn't a man, before there was God, there was no one.* Repeat after me...." The students began to repeat the saying over and over while Naismith watched their auras change colours to the deep violet that suggested they were entering a trance state. He noticed that his eldest female student, Elizabeth Bankroft, and his youngest male student, Michael O'Connell, were the last to go into the trance. He wasn't entirely surprised. Elizabeth's mother, Mary, had been a student with strong telepathic powers as had Michael's father, James. It was entirely possible that the two new students had faced mesmerism in the past. He walked closer to Michael and repeated the phrase until he saw the young O'Connell's aura change colours. He saw into Michael's mind that there was anger there from years of being called a half breed. Naismith understood those taunts and that anger. It was anger that he had owned in the past. He focused more carefully at Michael and continued the chant.

Michael O'Connell knew what was happening. His father had taught him the basics of mesmerism years ago. He also taught him how to protect himself from the powers of a master of mesmerism. To make this defense, Michael felt himself withdrawing into the small, locked room his father had taught him to imagine inside his head. It was his memory castle. He still heard the voice of Guru Naismith and knew that he would need to comply with Naismith's demands, and that he would have to remember that task when Naismith released him from the hold of his mesmerism. He quietly closed the locked door in his memory castle and allowed the rest of his consciousness to slip away. Naismith was surprised to see a novice use such a technique and he was dismayed the boy thought he could hide that ability from a master guru. Still, there would be plenty of time to consider what Michael O'Connell knew and didn't know.

Once O'Connell's aura changed to purple, Naismith walked over to Elizabeth and focused his voice and attention on this strong personality. He worked slowly to ensure she felt no fear and no challenge from his voice. Eventually, she slipped away and her aura also turned deep violet. Naismith looked up at his assistants who were observing their charges. One by one they nodded. The children were ready for instruction.

Naismith started to speak in a gentle, almost parental voice. He said, "You have been chosen to become intelligence officers for the Crown. There are many skills that you will be tasked to accomplish before you finish your time here. But before you receive any training in our skills, there are four standards that you must remember forever. All other training will be merely techniques of our trade. These are the principles of our trade. Nod your heads if you are ready to accept the standards."

Naismith watched as each of the students nodded. The initiation of the students was always a powerful moment in Naismith's year. He accepted this as his responsibility to develop honourable men and women in what could easily become a dishonourable profession. Previous leaders of the school realized through bad experience that even the most ethical of intelligence officers could reach a point where their honour was challenged. When that moment occurred, it would be important that the officers have a rock to anchor their honour. So, previous instructors chose to embed hypnotic suggestions to reinforce their good nature.

Now he began the instruction in his most soothing, parental voice. He said, "Repeat after me. Standard one: I must always tell the truth to my colleagues. It may be good news or bad, but it needs to be the truth and nothing but the truth." The students repeated the standard. Naismith continued, "Standard two: I will never abandon my colleagues. These include my native colleagues who serve as my guides and my scouts. My life depends on their lives." They repeated the second standard. "Standard three: Mission success means I must return alive. It is not brave to sacrifice my life in reckless effort." They repeated the third standard. Naismith concluded, "This is the final standard: You must never reveal the existence of our school or the names of your fellow students. These must remain secret to the outside world. Forever."

After the students repeated the final standard, Naismith checked their violet aura. They were all steady. Of course, Michael O'Connell was working as hard as possible to make him believe that he was in a deep hypnotic trance. Naismith was puzzled why the young man would choose this time to hide in a memory castle. Still, the rest of the students were clearly under his control and the hypnotic suggestions would remain embedded unless removed by him. Naismith knew that he would never do so.

Now, he began slowly to take them out of their trance state. Two minutes later, with a snap of his fingers, they awoke with no memory that they had been anything but paying attention to his lecture. To reinforce this, he continued a discussion by starting a speech that he had given every class since he was taken from the field and put in charge of the College in 1900. "The Viceroy's College is a result of the disaster of the Indian Mutiny in 1857. When the Mutiny was finally suppressed and the British government took over from the East India Company, seniors in Whitehall in London and in the Viceroy's office in Calcutta understood that they had failed the Crown. They were surprised by an uprising that could have been avoided. They needed to *know* threats to the government and to the people before they became catastrophes. To accomplish this mission, they decided to create a secret service attached to the Military Intelligence Bureau of the Government of India and a second service attached to the police force. These two services took some years to take form because government bureaucracies are slow moving creatures. We all work to serve the Crown, but government departments work as much to preserve their power as they do to serve the Crown. Years after the Mutiny and even after another war with the Afghans, finally the secret services were created when Viceroy, the most honourable Marquess of Landsdowne served as the head of government here in India."

Naismith paused to observe the students. He continued, "Our service would be made up of a select number of men…" — here he looked at Elizabeth and her two classmates Elizabeth knew only by the first names Martha and Susan — "and women who would be trained to conduct more than simple reconnaissance operations. Before the creation of the college, intelligence was conducted by British Army officers, usually brave cavalry officers, who were sent some distance afield to "go spy the land." Some Britons and some brave Indians served the crown as individual agents as they explored the far reaches of the Empire.

But, as we faced a growing threat from soldiers of the Tsar and internal threats from local insurgencies that are the nature of Empire, the Crown needed more than just a man, a map, and binoculars. The government in the United Kingdom has had a secret service since the days of Elizabeth the First. There are men and women stationed around the world who report on friend and foe alike. Since 1890, the Government of India has the same. The Persians like to say that if you see a leaf moving in the forest and lift it, you will find a British spy underneath that leaf. We are not that good nor are we that big, but we are a very elite group. You are about to join that elite group of important men and women."

This mention of 1890 caught Elizabeth's attention. If the service was established in that year and since her mother told Michael's father that she was in the class of 1890, it meant that her mother and father were graduates from the first class of The Viceroy's College. That would explain their portraits here in the Great Hall. But then, who taught Guru Naismith? Was he in the same class? That didn't seem possible since he was easily ten years older than her parents. If not, what guru taught her guru? And where did he learn his skills? This puzzled Elizabeth in the same way her understanding of the geology of England and the ancient sea creatures of Lyme Regis made her wonder about what came before them. Elizabeth decided to make this her own special mission.

Elizabeth's loss of concentration came to Naismith's attention. However, he came to the wrong conclusion. Every time Naismith gave this speech, he wondered how many of these young people, children really, understood the life they were about to begin. Would they care at first about their tradition? Probably not. They would see their new life as one of adventure, something that would appeal to any bright, well-educated child. But it was also going to mean times of loneliness, and very high risk. Naismith thought of the men who were early members of the Intelligence Bureau who did not return from missions. Sometimes, their sacrifices were not known. No one knew where they died or why. Other tragedies, like the deaths of Captains Stoddart and Connolly, became well known to the general public as their torture under the Emir of Bukhara became the source of graphic newspaper articles. Naismith spent half of his adult life living like a hunted animal in the various emirates of Central Asia, living under cover as a travelling mystic. He was successful because he never forgot to balance success against risk. He reported on Russian operations in the region, he reported on clan, tribe and ethnic conflicts on the borders of British India and deep in Afghanistan. He received quiet praise from the seniors in Calcutta and, even once, from Queen Victoria herself, passed to him via the Viceroy. Now, he trained men and women to take up this challenge. These eight were the next set to be trained.

North of Kandahar, Afghanistan — August 20-22, 1880

"Lieutenant, I need to know precisely the nature of the Afghan forces surrounding our people in Kandahar. Your commander said you have the ability to conduct scout missions in ways that no other can accomplish. Is that so?" General Frederick Roberts looked up from his campaign desk. The young officer he captured in his icy gaze didn't quite seem the model of the sort of hero he needed for this mission. The lieutenant was thin and only five and a half feet tall. Probably not more than 10 stone, he looked as if a stiff wind could blow him off a saddle. He had a wisp of a black beard that was not trimmed and grew in bits and pieces over his face. His black hair was long and unkempt. He was in an unremarkable khaki uniform that was worn in ways that suggested he lived rough and rode hard.

Definitely not the spit-and-polish image most of the Indian Army cavalry presented to a general officer. This lieutenant was more reminiscent of Roberts' combat experience in the Indian Mutiny. This young lieutenant looked very much like a member of the irregular cavalry of Skinner's Horse. Good fighters to be sure. Those men saved the day in Delhi, but they were hardly soldiers. The general was not impressed and he wondered what officer cadre in what woe-begotten regiment of his Kabul field force would have generated such an officer. Still, Roberts' chief of intelligence had described Naismith as both brilliant and resilient. Well, Roberts thought, this mission will certainly test both skills. So far, Naismith's face remained impassive, so Roberts decided to be clear about his intentions.

"Lieutenant, we are about two weeks march from relieving the Kandahar garrison. We might push a bit and get there in ten days. But that will only happen if we know how to avoid the Afghan troops between here and there and push directly to our objective. We have our cavalry screen in front of us letting us know what to expect each day, but our trapped forces in Kandahar cannot afford any delays. I need to know the correct route for each mile between here and there. THE CORRECT ROUTE. Am I being clear?" The lieutenant remained unresponsive. Hardly a good sign, but Roberts was used to lieutenants who were overwhelmed by their first one-on-one with a general officer.

After nearly a minute of silence, Naismith said, "Sir, I will need ten native couriers to travel with me. They will return each day to report to your staff the next day's route of march. I will need men from a regiment that you can trust because their mission will be the most critical. I will advance each day to determine the next leg of the route. I have already been forward twice and I think you are correct that we can make this march in ten days. Of course, after that will be the fighting."

Naismith's voice was clear and calm with a slight accent that Roberts could not identify. It was definitely not from any of the counties of England. Roberts wondered if, like

Skinner, this lieutenant was the product of a British officer and a native princess. If so, that might explain his less — than-sterling image.

"Sir, if that is all, I will be on my way immediately. With your permission." Naismith stood at attention and offered a very formal, very correct salute. Roberts replied in kind and dismissed the officer.

Later, in the tent, Roberts asked his chief of intelligence about this puzzling young man who had a mission that could bring success or spell disaster for the Relief Force. Lieutenant Colonel Manchester shook his head as he started to explain why he chose Naismith for the job.

"Sir, I'm sure you were dismayed at the lieutenant's appearance. He is a bit of an eccentric when it comes to day-to-day discipline, but he is well and truly a wizard when it comes to reconnaissance. You probably noticed he is Anglo-Indian. Father was an officer with the Assam Rifles, mother was one of the princesses of a local raja. The story is that Naismith was raised by local mystics in those foothills of the great range. I don't know if I believe it or not, but he is one of the few men I know who can truly disappear into the native community and reappear with the necessary intelligence. Accurate and on time. He is nominally assigned to the Fifth Gurkha Rifles, but I have pulled him for special duty from the time we left Peshawar. He speaks Bengali, Punjabi, Persian and Pashtu and for all I know ancient Greek and Sanskrit. When he isn't spying for us, he sits in his tent reading. He had to leave his library in Kabul when we issued orders that every cavalryman had to keep to one horse. He was most displeased about his books. He didn't seem to care that he had to live for a month with one uniform."

Roberts nodded and said, "I noticed he wasn't properly dressed."

"Sir, when you called for him, he had just returned from a

ten-day scout. He hadn't slept or eaten when he went to your tent."

"A man with a backbone."

"Indeed, sir. A backbone and more than a few secrets."

While the two officers were debating Naismith's capabilities, Lieutenant Burgess Makepeace Naismith was already riding at a full gallop with ten members of the Bengal Cavalry behind him. By dawn on the 21st of August, he was already twenty-five miles behind Afghan lines having bypassed a screen of Ghilzai riders who were tracking the British approach. He stopped at dawn in an eroded dry water channel long enough to eat two of the dried dates he carried in a small pouch hanging from the saddle and for a swallow of water. He turned to two of the cavalrymen. In perfect Bengali, he said, "You will stay here. Stay unseen and wait for our message tonight. As soon as you receive it, take the message to Colonel Manchester. We will be trusting our lives to you. Your honour is at stake. Do not fail."

The two men had been captured by the dark gaze of the lieutenant who rode like he was born on a horse and who had a reputation as the bravest Englishman in the Gurkha Regiment. Somehow, with his gentle voice he seemed to ask rather than order. Very different from their other English officers. They were determined to perform their task or die trying. They promised they would not fail. With the promise in hand, Naismith and the eight remaining riders took off to the South. It was unlikely that the Afghan villagers would be awake for at least another hour. The men would ride hard and scout the nearby villages and fields and then rest in the heat of the day. If they were seen, they would be identified as nine men on Raj mounts: lone scouts far from friendly forces and a certain target for Afghan cavalry.

As they rode, Naismith understood it would be a long few days, but he was confident he could accomplish the mission. This confidence was based on the fact that well before he was called to meet with General Roberts, he had scouted all the way to the outskirts of Kandahar. He knew the route already and knew what they would face along the way. All he needed to do at this point was to confirm that there were no changes. After that, he would send reports back to the general. He couldn't expect his men to ride the way he rode or to melt into the community the way he could, but they would be reliable couriers and that was all he needed.

Later that morning, the riders settled into another remote wash known locally as a nullah or gulley. They set up their security watch under what little shade was available under a 100-degree sun. Once they were settled, Naismith recovered a small canvas bag from behind his saddle. He pulled from this bag what looked to be a pile of rags, which he put on in place of his uniform. He broke a six foot limb from a tree and tied a series of ribbons and bells to one end. Before he left, he walked over to where the horses were picketed. He grabbed dirt churned up by the horses as they settled for the day and covered his face and hands. Then he grabbed some horse dung and rubbed it on his clothes. Just enough dung to keep locals away from a wandering Sufi. As his riders settled into their hot, restless sleep, Naismith headed toward a village that he knew was only three miles away. A barefoot Sufi would be just the sort of "invisible" traveler who could observe and then prepare a report for the next leg of the Kandahar Relief Force. His men never heard him leave and the villagers never saw him arrive.

Naismith heard much and said little as he wandered the streets of Tir Andaz. He heard from Pashtuns on the streets that they had decided to lift the siege of Kandahar. Their leader, Ayub Khan, intended to move to a new location to face the arriving Indian Army force. The Afghans were headed to the Arghandab valley and preparing for their battle. As Naismith passed from tea shop to coppersmith to the vegetable market, he periodically stopped to listen to the stories of the Pashtuns who were bored with the siege of Kandahar and convinced there would be little to loot even if they finally did defeat the British. Naismith was not surprised. The resistance to the British in the south was motivated by calls from clerics and tribal chiefs for "jihad" or Holy War against the infidels. None of the young men who joined the fight knew much of the Koran or even how it made sense to fight the British who controlled land on the other side of the Safed Koh range. What they did understand was the prestige of the title of mujahedin, holy warriors, and, more importantly, the personal benefits of plunder or *ghanima'at* as they called it in Pashtu.

Most of Ayub Khan's men were young farmers who joined his force based on the promise of gold and English weapons when they defeated the infidels. Now a quick fight had turned into a long siege with little promise of either gold or weapons. Worse still, the siege offered the risk of being killed by a well-placed rifle round from a trained Indian Army sniper. Everyone wanted to kill for jihad, but no one wanted to die for jihad. Mostly, the young men were bored. They intended to move on to a more lucrative traditional trade of raiding villages and attacking caravans headed to Kabul. Those fighters who were members of Ayub Khan's tribe would stay with him in the Arghandab and fight the British, but even those who stayed were reluctant warriors.

By the time the sun had gone down, the barefooted Sufi was on his way out of the village with everything he needed for a report back to the general. This was no longer a ten-day reconnaissance. It was an intelligence report of significance. As he left the village, two of the young fighters decided to have a bit of sport with this dirty Sufi. While most villagers in the north of Afghanistan and certainly all villages in northern

India respected the mystics from all religions, Kandahar was a different story. Islam in Kandahar was of a literalist variety and mystics were considered troublesome heretics. Sufis were famous for making sport of the poorly educated mullahs. In other locations, that might be considered amusing. In Kandahar, it was considered treason. Those young men who answered the call of jihad were more fundamentalist than most. Naismith could see in their eyes that they had already decided their sport tonight would include cutting the head off a Sufi. Their biggest mistake was they did not draw their swords before approaching within arms-length of this small, dirty man leaning against a wooden staff.

As the first tough reached out to grab the rags wrapped around Naismith's shoulders, Naismith raised his left hand as if to beg for forgiveness. He even asked for mercy as a last attempt to avoid a conflict. No mercy was likely from this young man and Naismith's hand gently reached the base of the black beard of the Pashtun. As soon as his palm was near the lips of his attacker, Naismith blew a red powder into the eyes of his attacker. Red chili powder from a specific plant that grew only in Bengal filled the man's eyes, nostrils and open mouth. He was blinded and the deep burning sensation caused him to put his hands up to his cheeks. Disabled for a moment, the attacker cried out that his face was on fire. The more he rubbed his eyes, the worse the burning sensation.

The second attacker had not seen what Naismith had accomplished with the red powder and for a moment he stood to watch his colleague coughing, crying and beating his face with his hands as if trying to put out a fire that was rising from his beard. He decided the Sufi was the blame, and raced up behind the slight man. Just as the man was about to grab him from behind, Naismith dropped to one knee. He used the blade edge of his right hand to strike the man's knee. The ugly crunch meant the knee was smashed. As he fell, Naismith reached up and grabbed his assailant's right hand.

He stretched the arm out straight and then drove his fist into the man's armpit. Naismith knew that one of the major nerve centers for the body was buried deep in the armpit. The right strike at the right moment could disable a man. More power could kill. This man was dying as he crumpled to the ground.

Naismith had time enough now to handle his first attacker. The chili powder had disabled the man, but not convinced him to stop his attack on this travelling heretic. He reached to draw his tulwar blade from its scabbard. Before it could clear the scabbard, Naismith had unwrapped a ribbon sword from around his waist. He suspected the flexible blade was something that the Pashtun could not imagine. It was not well known in Afghanistan, though common enough in Southern India. A thin ribbon of steel unraveled like a rope, but with edges as sharp as any tulwar. Swinging the ribbon up and across his body, Naismith's weapon ended the fight with a deep cut to the Pashtun's midsection.

Naismith turned to each of the dying men and reached into another of the pockets disguised by the exterior rags. He dropped a pellet of opium on each of their lips which dissolved immediately. They would not suffer their last minutes on earth and the barefoot Sufi continued to walk into the darkness and toward his men. It wasn't the first time Naismith had been forced to kill on this job, but he did not pretend that it would not affect him — body and soul.

He would not report the incident to any of his superiors. After all, what was the point? They were all soldiers and killing was an expected portion of their job. Naismith had started his career as a young Indian Army lieutenant and had seen more than his share of close-in fighting, Indian Army bayonet facing Afghan tulwars. The difference in his current trade was that there were no comrades to the left or to the right and no pretense that there was honour in death. Later, he would spend time in meditation focusing on his actions and purging the negative spirit that always came from surviving an attack.

Naismith ended his moment of reminiscence and looked at his new students. He decided to forgo his normal lecture on the Intelligence Bureau and its missions. That could always come another day. He could see from their flickering auras that these students were bored with history. They wanted to *do* something. He jumped forward in his prepared speech to explain the course. After that, he would have the mentors take these students on a vigorous run through the mountains and let them ponder their future on their own tonight. He said, "So, here you are. What are you going to study this term? First and foremost, you will study mathematics, especially advanced maths that will help you draw maps of unmapped reaches of the Empire. You will also study natural philosophy including animal and human physiology, botany, chemistry and astronomy. These skills will make you a valuable reporter for the Crown as you observe new and different worlds. You will learn a language. Not just as a student learns a language but as a native speaker learns a language. At the end of the first term, you will have some skills to sound like a native speaker. At the end of your second term, you will be a native speaker in your new language. You will dream in that language. You will find that sometimes you prefer to think in the new language. Finally, this term, you will learn ways to protect yourself. That will include skills in hand-to-hand combat, fighting with weapons, and using modern and primitive firearms."

Michael O'Connell decided the time had come for him to ask the question that had been on his mind for the last hour. He used his most deferential voice, "Guru Ji, at what point do we learn how to be intelligence officers? The skills you have described do not seem to me to be how a spy might work his trade."

There were a few gasps from O'Connell's classmates. It was, after all, a very blunt question, no matter how polite the voice. Naismith was interested in O'Connell's tone as well as his question. He had watched as the boy's aura changed from a calm green to yellow and almost to orange. This boy would have to be watched carefully. He might be young, but he was deep. Naismith's own instructors from the mountains of Tibet might even call him an "old soul." There was an edge there. Not common in a fifteen-year-old. Naismith thought it interesting, but also troubling. He had a history with young men who thought they knew more than they did. It just hadn't happened at the college before this.

Naismith responded, "Master O'Connell, just as you would not build the walls of a house before you built its foundation, we focus on fundamentals and foundational work in the first term so that when we add what are, admittedly, complex…" Naismith looked up at his instructor cadre and smiled, "complex skills. One thing at a time. What we call 'tradecraft' will be imparted over time at the end of this term, but mostly during the second term when you trade your red uniforms for saffron and eventually to white."

O'Connell was clearly not pleased with the answer, his aura switched to almost crimson. Naismith thought, "This one is impatient. What does he already know about the school and why does he want to jump ahead? I need to keep a close eye on his development." What he said out loud was, "Students, we are done talking today. I want you to follow your instructors out the classroom and into the parade ground. After we do some stretching exercises, we will go for a good long run so that you are not bored listening to an old, shaven-headed guru." He clapped his hands, creating a loud bark in the hall, and walked out of the classroom, followed by eight of his instructors and then his first-term students.

The next day, the first bell rang just as the sun was climbing over the Himalayas. This was the bell for the first-term students. They were expected to be dressed and on the parade ground before the second bell, which rang thirty minutes later. In the next half hour before the third bell rang, one of their individual mentors would lead them through a set of yoga stretching exercises and slow martial arts movements which Elizabeth learned were called *tai chi*. After this half hour, the first-term students were marched to the dining room for a morning meal of apricot porridge, sweet tea and flat bread. As they marched off the parade ground, they could see the arrival of the saffron and white robed second-term students taking their place for morning physical training.

After breakfast, they were marched back to their individual rooms up the stairs at the top of the campus. Elizabeth noted that by the time they were marching toward their rooms, the parade ground was mixed with saffron and white robed students conducting exercises that looked as much like ballet routines as they did a martial-art program. Careful examination as the days passed made it clear to Elizabeth that the "dance" routines were advanced martial-arts training exercises. Each saffron-robed student partnered with a white-robed student, leaping, dipping and dodging as they tried to strike each other with an open palm. And, as the term continued and their physical training became more obviously martial in structure, the saffron-robed and white-robed students added long staffs, pikes, and swords to their routine. Elizabeth was jealous of the mix of dance and weaponry.

From that first day and, as the weeks progressed, Elizabeth

and her classmates learned intelligence officers had to understand complex mathematics to support their mission. Trigonometry and logarithmic scales would allow them to observe a distant location and determine within a hundred feet the distance to the objective. Basic physics and chemistry were used to understand the nature of materials and how they can be modified by heat, by electricity, or by chemical additives. They studied botany and plant physiology and learned to make accurate drawings of plants. They learned that plants in Asia were already being used for medicines in England and they might find new plants that create new medicines to help the Crown. The routine was much the same for six days each week. One hour of mathematics followed one of physics, followed by one of chemistry in the morning and finally an hour in their language house. Elizabeth shared Russia house with two students — Michael O'Connell and Jason Mackenzie. Elizabeth learned quickly that O'Connell was the youngest of the three and the most effusive in his joy of being in the course. Guru Standish solved O'Connell's determination to talk happily and continuously by forcing him to only converse in Russian. If he broke into English, Standish would make him stand on his head in the corner of the room while counting from one to 100 in Russian. Soon, O'Connell was less loquacious but an expert in arithmetic conducted in Russian. This time in language was the first opportunity to be with young men other than her brother. Elizabeth found herself attracted to both boys. Michael for his openness and laughter and Jason for his seriousness and intellectual interests. They made a good team and Guru Standish regularly complimented them on their willingness to take their language study seriously and to hold real conversations about art, science, and politics in Russian.

Elizabeth had not spent time with young men before. She was puzzled by the way they acted and equally puzzled by her own emotions when she saw them. They were attractive to be sure, but they were also funny and serious and kind. They were nothing like the young men she met the previous summer while in England. Those young men in England tried so hard to be adults that they demonstrated that they were boys. Michael and Jason made no effort to pretend to be men. Because of that, they seemed more mature than the young men of England. Each evening, Elizabeth had to focus hard on her schoolwork as her attention wandered as she thought of life after The Viceroy's College. Would she find a husband at the school or would she leave these young men behind when school was finished? She knew her parents met at the college. But, was that the norm or was it unusual? Did she even want to share her life with a young man? Elizabeth had to use the meditation skills she was learning to keep focused on work and not some future life.

A brief lunch of bread, fruit and tea split the workday in half. After lunch were technical drawing classes (focused on map-making and accurate depictions of everything from flowers to buildings), then two more hours in a language house. As the days progressed, Elizabeth spent more and more time with Michael and Jason. They grew close as they pushed each other in their language training and argued over who was better at mathematics or drawing or even botany. In those arguments, both of her classmates acknowledged that Elizabeth's skills in technical drawing and her understanding of all the disciplines of natural philosophy were far better than their own. This was the first time in Elizabeth's life that she had received praise from her peers, and especially praise from young men. She wasn't quite sure why she liked it, but Elizabeth was very pleased when she received it from her compatriots.

Each day ended with another hour of exercises and competitions in a circular sand pit known to the cadre and the students as The Circle of Decision. It was in the Circle of Decision that students learned basic hand-to-hand combat. First-term students learned basic holds, blocks and throws. Again, as the first-term students worked in the one half of the Circle, Elizabeth observed the saffron and the white robed students in full scale competitions with Guru Naismith as the referee.

Personal feelings were not appropriate in the Circle of Decision. Each first-term classmate at some time during the weeks of training would be paired with another classmate to practice holds, blocks and throws. Anyone who appeared to take the instruction less than seriously was required to run the Circle — sometimes on foot, sometimes on all fours in what the Guru called a bear walk, and sometimes backwards and on all fours in what was called the crab walk. Guru Maloney was the master in the Circle of Decision and Elizabeth spent more than her share in the first weeks running around the circle because she could not understand Maloney's English accent. It sounded like a fusion of his Irish-Indian heritage. Asking for him to repeat an instruction resulted in yet another lap around the Circle. Elizabeth realized that, if nothing else, she was becoming more fit than when she arrived at school.

Finally, she began to learn the techniques required for survival in the rough and tumble of the Circle of Decision. She discovered that the tricks taught by the martial arts gurus allowed her to defeat boys who were heavier and far stronger. Elizabeth was determined to succeed and her determination showed as she mastered the intricacies of holds and throws. Along with learning the basic skills, she realized that she needed to anticipate the actions of her adversary. Over time, Elizabeth found that if she concentrated, she could know in advance what her adversary intended to do.

She was not one to be carried away by what Mrs. Edwards would call "folly," but Elizabeth felt as if she was reading the minds of her counterparts so that she could act with certainty when she needed to block a blow or counter a throw. By summer, she became the leader in her class. Even Jason Mackenzie, a good 20 pounds heavier and six inches taller, had no luck throwing Elizabeth, while she was able to use leverage and her increasing skill to throw every member of her class. To win, she had to either throw an adversary on his or her back or force them outside the circle. Sometimes, she had to deceive her opponent to succeed and it was in those bouts that she made few friends.

In the early fall of her first term, Elizabeth was enjoying the martial arts practice in the cool, damp air. It reminded all who had lived in Northern India that winter had already arrived in the great mountains. The end of monsoon always meant the start of autumn. At this altitude, autumn would quickly change to winter snow. That morning, Elizabeth was paired with Michael O'Connell at the end of the martial arts training. Over the previous weeks inside the Circle, she had formed a soft spot for Michael as she watched her slight partner from Russia House regularly tossed to the ground by the other students. He always landed poorly and generally ended up with some small injury. Nothing broken, but more than a few strains, cuts and bruises that he took with him to class. Of course, everyone sustained these small injuries, but, unlike Jason, who wore his injuries like medals of honour, Michael remained glum for days until the injury faded. When finally paired against him, Elizabeth decided to be less aggressive. She allowed Michael to try out some of his moves on her. Of course, she could not bring herself to allow him to win, but at least gave him an opportunity to try his moves. Eventually, she used a simple arm-lock technique matched with a simple hip throw to force him out of the Circle. He did not suffer any bodily injuries, but as he left the Circle, Michael suffered derision from his male colleagues. He fumed as he heard the cheers for Elizabeth.

Later in his room, Michael focused his evening meditation on why he had lost to a girl who was lighter and smaller than he was. He was furious with himself because he had lost focus during the fight. He had strong feelings for this young woman with the auburn hair and grey eyes. He had expected to win not because he was stronger than Elizabeth but because he was smarter and better at disguising his moves. Or, that was what he thought. In fact, she had accepted his fakes as the bluffs that they were and instead made him look the fool as she forced him out of the Circle. Now he told himself she had just been playing with him so that she could finish the fight with a flare that had become her style in the Circle of Decision. The jeers from his five other classmates reinforced the feeling that he had been played the fool. He vowed to himself that he would never make that mistake again.

Evening meditation was supposed to be used for two purposes: first, to consider what the student learned that day and, second, to calm emotions. In that way, positive experiences were reinforced and negative experiences understood. Instead of reducing his anger through meditation, Michael allowed the anger to grow and focus. For years, he believed there was no one he could trust in the world except his father. It was his father and Michael against the world. Everything he saw at the school and in the world at large reinforced that belief, and it was underscored by the day's events in the Circle of Decision.

At the end of his meditation, the one lesson he did realize was he had to suppress his anger and disguise his opinions of his classmates, his gurus, The Viceroy's College and even the British Raj. He knew enough about mesmerism and advanced mental skills from his father's instruction to realize he was surrounded by what normal adults would call "mind readers." Of course, they couldn't *read* minds but they would read and interpret body language. He had to be careful or his secrets would leak out from his actions.

As he was about to end his meditation, he was stunned by the voice of his father. Not coming from his room but coming from inside his head. In the past, his father had used what he called his very own "trickery" to pass messages to his son when they were trapped in some terribly boring government event. Michael was as used to his father's mental voice as his father's real voice. In the past, they were close to each other and he could look at his father's face as they "talked" without speaking. Here, his father was nowhere to be seen, but distance had no effect on the clarity of the message.

"Michael, can you hear me?"

Michael concentrated. He closed his eyes and remained in his full lotus pose that he used during his meditation cycles. He said, "Father, I can hear you."

"Excellent. You are doing so well in class. I am proud of you."

"Father, a girl defeated me in the Circle of Decision today."

"Michael, you learned an important lesson today, so that defeat was useful. Was it not?"

"Yes, indeed it was useful."

"Now, you need to focus on a different point. I need you to make maximum progress in this term. It will be your last term. After this year, you will be coming to work with me. By the end of the term, you must have all the skills you need to begin working directly with me. Any further skills, I will teach you myself. Are you ready?"

"I am ready, Father."

"Know that I am watching over you as much as I can. I am working on something right now that will ensure our personal success. I will let you know when I have completed that task. We will be together soon."

"I love you, Father."

"And I love you, my son. It the two of us against the world, but the good news is the world doesn't know this yet."

"I agree."

"Keep safe, son. Keep the memory castle in your mind. You are going to need it. I have to go now. Farewell."

"Safe travels, Father."

After her meditation cycle in her room, Elizabeth was visited by Guru Marian. This time the visit was real and preceded by a knock on her door and a request by Marian to enter. She was surprised because it was the first time that Marian had visited after dinner and during "study hours" when students were restricted to their quarters. Elizabeth couldn't imagine why her guru would visit. She was doing very well in her mathematics and science classes, her language skills were improving every day and she was the current winner of every bout in the Circle of Decision. She was especially surprised with Guru Marian's comments.

"Elizabeth, I watched you in the Circle of Decision today. Why did you choose to make the bout with Master O'Connell last longer than needed?"

Elizabeth had not noticed her Guru near the Circle nor did she realize that anyone had noticed her actions. Without doubt, her peers had been cheering enthusiastically in support of Michael O'Connell, so she thought she had disguised her intent. Still, she knew that lying to a guru was considered improper at best and a violation of the school code, so she said, "I feel sorry for Michael. He is the weakest of our class and is always hurt after a bout. Also, he is a nice boy and is trying very hard to succeed."

"Elizabeth, do you think that making it easier for him makes him better?"

Elizabeth had not thought about that. She never had a plan. She just decided to avoid harming Michael in the same way that she might have avoided harming a stray cat or dog. "Guru Marian, I had not considered the point."

"The Circle of Decision is not just a lesson on how to protect yourself. It is also a lesson on how to accept your own limitations. So far, you haven't been forced to face your limitations. But, I promise you will. When that happens, you won't learn any more if we make it easy for you and allow you to avoid that moment. Do you think Master O'Connell really thought he had a chance in your bout?"

"I don't know."

"I do know. He knew as soon as you both faced off that he had no chance. You did not deceive him. And, you did not deceive us. You did deceive your colleagues, but only for that brief moment when they started to cheer Master O'Connell on. By defeating him in the end, you did nothing for him. In fact, you may have done more harm than good. We shall see."

Elizabeth blushed and lowered her eyes. She had not considered any of this. She said, "I am sorry, Guru Marian. I had not thought of the consequences of my actions."

Marian smiled. Her charge was learning. This was a good moment, so she switched to her soothing mesmerism "voice" to both reinforce the teaching moment and to make it "feel" positive for Elizabeth. She said, "Today, you have learned about your own limitations, Elizabeth. You have feelings for Master O'Connell and that is not a bad thing. But, you did not control those feelings. They should be expressed in a more appropriate time and place. That place and time is not at this college. You have to learn that expressions of those sorts of feelings, especially at the wrong time, may do more harm than good. Now I want you to spend some time tonight meditating on your own actions. Not as good or bad, but as events where you learn something new about yourself."

"Yes, Guru Marian." Elizabeth had responded in the dreamy voice demonstrating she was under the mental control of Marian. When she returned to her studies, Elizabeth would think her choice to review her actions was not a directive from her guru but her own decision. She would not even remember that this was a directive.

Marian switched to her normal teaching voice so that Elizabeth would return to full consciousness and said, "You need to also remember that sometime in the future, a person who you think might be a friend will disappoint you. That person may be using you just long enough to get something or accomplish something. It is not easy in our trade to identify friend from foe. I am not saying that Michael is that person, but you need to consider how you keep your distance until you can put a person in your circle of trust. Until then, you should always defeat them as quickly as possible in the future."

Elizabeth had come out of the dream state and heard only Guru Marian's observation as something to consider in the future. "Thank you, Guru Marian."

"Return to your studies, Elizabeth. Tomorrow is another day."

When Elizabeth looked up to say farewell to her guru, she was puzzled that Marian was nowhere to be seen. She had not heard the door open or close. How did her guru come and go in such silence? In a moment of amusement, she said aloud to no one, "Obviously, she simply walked through the wall." As she said that, she walked to the door and locked it. Elizabeth wondered if that was possible.

Sundays at The Viceroy's College were reserved for personal

time. Students were expected to attend a silent sunrise vigil on the parade ground. The gurus pointed out that the college student body and cadre included Hindus, Sikhs, Muslims, Christians, and Jews. There was no room for houses of worship for all of them. The Sunday meditation was designed to allow each student to quietly practice his or her own belief. After the meditation, the students ate a late breakfast together. At the end of the dining hall, cold lunch and hot dinner meals were set aside in brass tiffin pails: three enameled tins stacked with a single handle. Tiffins were common among the working classes of India, but several students from the upper classes of British India had never seen one in real life. Enormously practical, they allowed the students to choose when (or even if) they intended to eat a meal. The students were encouraged to spend the rest of their Sunday in whatever way they chose, but entirely on their own. There were horses to ride, trails to hike, and, of course, books to read.

Sunday was Elizabeth's favourite, the single day of the week she could have to herself. She took her tiffin, her food, her binoculars, her sketchbook, and hand lens into the remote mountain trails north and east of the college. There were plenty of wonders in the mountains that she intended to find, observe and catalogue. She observed nature in ways that she hoped were consistent with her natural philosopher heroes like Darwin, Humboldt or Banks. She filled her notebooks with observations as the seasons changed. Even during the heaviest of monsoon downpours, Elizabeth would walk trails to see how plants responded to the seasonal rains.

By fall, Elizabeth was observing the birds heading south and the small animals in the forest building their winter hideaways under trees and bushes. She wandered far into the ridge lines that surrounded the college. The trees on the ridge bent by wind and weather offered an almost magical environment of drooping limbs over mossy rocks. At one point, Elizabeth slipped on one of the rocks and caught herself as she came down on all fours. In front of her was the most delicate of flowers, a mix of mauve and white.

Elizabeth knew this was an orchid, but not one she had ever seen in a book or a drawing. Orchids were hardy creatures, but this one seemed to be clinging to the rocks overlooking a southern exposure at an altitude of 9000 feet. It obviously survived the winter because the southern exposure provided the light and warmth for most of the year. Elizabeth was excited. Might this be a discovery that needed to be reported to the world? She wondered if during second term she would be able to bring a glass plate camera to the school. She doubted it and redoubled her efforts to accurately capture this orchid and then describe where it was so that she could find it again. It was in this natural environment that Elizabeth kept her balance between the requirements of classes, the Circle of Decision and her own emotions about school, family and boys. The discovery of the orchid clinging to a rock on the edge of a cliff seemed to capture the essence of her current life.

As the term approached its end, Elizabeth thrived in classes that blended hard science with art and culture. Her favourites included trigonometry, map-making and botanical illustration. She still found Russian difficult, but studied hard and stayed in Russia House for the entire term. Guru Marian encouraged her to expand her journals of her Sunday hikes and she looked forward to showing them to her mother. Sketches of mountain scenery were interspersed with observations of the plants, animals, and climate in the areas around Fort Burnes, as well as notes to remind her of a difficult map-making technique or a clever Russian phrase. Marian asked Elizabeth for a formal report on the orchid she had found, and told her that she would be forwarding this report to the Botanical Survey of India and the botanists at the Royal Botanical Gardens at Kew.

Elizabeth was as proud of this discovery as she was in

excelling in all physical aspects, including horsemanship, archery, and firearms. For the first time in her life, Elizabeth was allowed, actually encouraged, to compete with both boys and girls. Her classmates from Russia House found this amusing even when they were occasionally defeated "by a girl." Elizabeth's friendship with both Michael O'Connell and Jason Mackenzie generated a degree of rivalry between the two boys which meant that when one was defeated by Elizabeth, the other would do his best to remind their classmates of Elizabeth's success. Elizabeth was puzzled by what she saw as a bit of childishness, but her only real experience with young men was with her brother, so she reserved comment until she could ask her mother what it all meant.

In the last days of the term, Elizabeth expected to begin receiving training to be an intelligence officer. But, right to the end, her schooling included her favourite subjects of natural philosophy and some training on how to throw men into the dirt. Guru Marian reiterated that intelligence officer skills started and finished with good observation, detailed reporting and a willingness to go to places no one wanted to visit. She promised that when Elizabeth returned for her second term, she would receive training that was more focused on "the Trade."

For now, science, mathematics, drawing, and the Circle of Decision would have to be enough. A puzzled Elizabeth accepted the advice from her guru, but still had more than a few questions.

Perhaps she could find out the answers from her parents.

A PAIR OF INTERLUDES
Interlude #1: A Second Ride on an Airship

01 December 1911 — Rawalpindi

AT THE END OF THE FIRST TERM, ELIZABETH RETURNED TO RAWALPINDI CANtonment via *HMFS Resolve*. This was the first time in her life she had travelled alone and the opportunity to enjoy the trip was complicated by the fact that the airship was filled with the remainder of her class under the watchful and strict eyes of a Viceroy's College graduate. Elizabeth could see their chaperone was less than pleased with his mission. All of his classmates had already returned home with onward assignments across the Empire. As last place in his class, Peter Carolton had one mission before he began his career and that was to deliver these "children" to their parents. He suffered the tasking with no sense of humour as he sat in the front and scowled all the way to Rawalpindi. The eight survivors of the Reckoning had dwindled to only six students who completed the first term. The two missing students were injured and sent home to recuperate. They would return as first term students in time to start classes at the same point that they left.

Elizabeth had expected her colleagues from Russia House to sit with her on the way home. Instead, Jason sat with two other boys who had been part of Arab House and Michael sat alone in the passenger deck, making no effort to talk to anyone. Elizabeth had observed a change in Michael in the last month of class. Less frivolous, less engaging and certainly less fun to be around. During evening meditation, she explored her own behaviour to see if she had done something to create the rift. She could find no explanation. On the ride home, she sat next to her remaining female classmate, Martha. There had been little time to "just chat" over the previous weeks and suddenly she was sitting with a classmate who was, for all intents, a stranger. Elizabeth had never been good at engaging girls her own age, but she was determined to do her best.

Both girls tried to build common threads of conversation. There were some successes like their mutual confusion about boys in general and specifically boys in their class. Martha was in Persia House with one of the remaining boys named Frederick. She revealed she had a crush on Nathaniel, one of the boys in Turkish House, and hoped over the holidays to see him in a more convivial setting. Elizabeth wasn't entirely certain what a convivial setting might look like in her house, but she understood Martha's interests. She would certainly like to see Jason over the holidays. Unfortunately, he had told her that his family was travelling for the holidays to enjoy the beaches on the Arabian Sea. His father was one of the consular officers responsible for Goa and, across the Arabian Sea, Zanzibar. They would not return until just before the start of the next term.

Everyone travelled in English clothes. Once again, Elizabeth was wearing her long, navy-blue skirt and white blouse with a navy-blue blazer and cream-coloured scarf marked with a red stripe at the bottom. The boys were in khaki trousers and white shirts with a sky-blue silk tie with a first-term red stripe. She thought they looked quite dashing in their English clothes. No longer boys, now young men. After ten months living in a shalwar kamiz, Elizabeth found her formal woman's clothes itchy and very annoying. Of course, over those ten months, Elizabeth's body had transformed from a spindly young girl to an athletic young woman. She would have to ask her mother if it would be possible to have new clothes, and especially new shalwar kamiz, made before she returned in February.

The arrival of the airship in Rawalpindi was cause for less ceremony than the arrival had been at Fort Burnes. The same instructions were given by the executive officer of the airship but this time no one warned of the gap at the dock and certainly no one offered to help the students disembark. The senior graduate led the six students off the docking platform and down to the meeting hall where parents reunited with their children, seeing them for the first time in 10 months. Greetings shouted and hugs given were the standard. In the mix-up of greetings, Elizabeth lost track of her two classmates from Russia House and her travelling companion, Martha. She was surprised to find only her father waiting for her this time, dressed in civilian clothes and with only his carefully trimmed military style mustache instead of the full beard that she expected.

Francis Bankroft had never been one to express emotions in public and most especially inside the cantonment. He said, "Elizabeth, welcome home and congratulations on completing the first term at The Viceroy's College." Elizabeth noted that her father looked healthier than she remembered him when she last saw him at Ft. Burnes.

She also understood the formality of the reception even

though she would have preferred to run into his arms. Trying her best to sound like an adult, Elizabeth said, "Father, you look well and most handsome in your suit. I have to admit, I prefer seeing you in uniform, but I suppose different missions require different clothes."

"Too right, dear. For now, I am a simple government staff officer assigned to Rawalpindi."

"And, not a…"

"Hush dear. Let's save that sort of discussion for when we get home. We have a carriage waiting."

"Father, where is Mother?"

"Your mother is away on a work assignment, dear. She will be home for Christmas, but for the next few days, you will have to be entertained by my good self."

Based on a telepathic message from his father late in the term, Michael O'Connell knew his father was not going to meet him. As the families departed by carriage or motorcar, he was left alone on one of the polished oak benches, waiting for contact from his father's new colleagues. There were two men in uniform at the door who might be able to help, so he stood up and headed toward them. He was nearly there when he heard his father's voice.

"Michael, turn left toward the baggage office."

Michael couldn't see where his father was; the voice was only in his head. When he approached the baggage office, the voice said, "There is a small office to your right. Enter the office. There are two men waiting for you there. They will take you to me. I am sorry to miss picking you up, my son. I will explain when I see you. Very soon."

Michael obeyed the directions and entered the small office. There were two men dressed in formal European clothes. Fit men with very short haircuts and highly shined riding boots. Michael was immediately relieved. Clearly his father had sent two military colleagues to meet him.

The taller of the men did a slight bow and said in accented English, "Master Michael, I presume. We are here to take you to your father. He was unable to attend. He is, as you know, on special assignment."

When Michael turned 12 years old, his father had revealed that he was in Indian Military Intelligence. He was aware that his father's travels were in support of the secret service and he never asked questions, though he wanted to know more. Now that he was starting down the same path, he understood the wisdom of knowing only as much as you needed to and nothing more. Michael straightened his shoulders. He was carrying a small leather Gladstone bag in his left hand which made it harder to assume the military posture he would have preferred, but he did his best. He said, "Gentlemen, I am ready. Please lead on."

His departure from the airship terminal would soon become more of an adventure than he had expected.

The taller of the two smiled and said, "Excellent. Follow me."

With military precision, the men did an about-face, headed out a side door and immediately loaded into a polished black motorcar with a canvas top and side curtains. Inside the cabin of the motorcar, Michael sat amazed at the red leather seats and the polished wood coach work. The vehicle looked more like some naval torpedo boat than a motorcar. One of his two guides was driving in the front seat of the motorcar while the taller man was in the back seat with Michael. He noticed the young man's interest in the car and said, "Master O'Connell, my name is Captain Wiess. And this," he touched the vehicle lovingly, "this is the only automobile of its type in all of South Asia. It is called the Benz Prince Heinrich. It is very fast."

Michael was unable to disguise his fascination. "It is a marvel."

As soon as the doors closed, the driver headed out of the military cantonment and joined the main Grand Trunk Highway that ran across India from New Delhi to Peshawar. As they entered the highway, the driver began dodging camel caravans, oxcarts and an occasional military vehicle lumbering along at almost the same speed as the oxcarts. The driver accelerated past some the vehicles and forced others aside using a hand cranked siren that warned all in the vicinity that a person of importance wanted the right of way.

"It is a testament to German engineering. We had it shipped out specifically for our missions here in India and Afghanistan. We have been testing it for weeks. It has withstood the tests of mountain roads and the winter cold. We are confident that it will withstand Indian heat as well."

As they hit a small pothole in the Grand Trunk highway on the way out of Rawalpindi, Michael said, "But, perhaps, not the rocks on Indian roads."

"For now, we have been careful to keep the vehicle like new. I suspect you are correct. As we use the vehicle, we will see damage. An automobile is designed to be used. It can always be repaired."

Michael watched as they left the outskirts of Rawalpindi and entered the rolling countryside of small farmsteads and brick kilns. The smoke from the kilns and the dung fires in the houses made the sky a grey-brown colour. The driver switched on three large electric lamps that were mounted in the front of the vehicle. Michael remained glued to the window as he watched the countryside flash by at what he calculated must be at least thirty, perhaps forty miles an hour. He asked his guide, "How fast are we going?"

"The Benz has a top speed of eighty-five miles an hour, but of course that would be on German roads. Here, we travel at a moderate pace." He leaned forward and asked, "Albert, what speed are we travelling?"

The second man said, "Graf, we are travelling at forty miles an hour. I did not think any faster was prudent."

"*Genau.*" He turned back to Michael and said, "Forty miles per hour."

Michael could not think of anything to say. It was an amazing speed.

They drove west for an hour to the outskirts of the ancient ruins of the Gandharan city of Taxila. The car stopped next to a two-seat monoplane. His guide said, "Master O'Connell, I wish you a pleasant journey. We intend to follow you in the Benz, but we will take some time on these roads. I hope to see you soon." He opened a small turtle-backed trunk strapped to the rear of the motorcar and pulled out a leather flying suit like the ones Michael had seen in the airship. Also in the trunk was a long leather overcoat and a leather flying helmet. All of the items fit Michael perfectly.

In his head, he heard his father's voice, "Michael, the aero plane will bring you to me. Please do not worry."

Michael wasn't worried. He was thrilled. He was headed on a secret mission all his own.

He expected a brief ride to meet with his father somewhere in India, perhaps even as far south as the port of Karachi. Instead, the aero plane headed west toward the setting sun, flying over rugged terrain he had read about in Mr. Kipling's books, but had never seen. He was glad to be wearing the leather flying suit and helmet as he looked out over the terrain from the front seat of a craft that seemed as fragile as a butterfly. The wind whistled through the wires that controlled the wing surfaces. Michael had read about the Wright brothers aero planes while living in Simla years ago. He had even seen a small biplane fly when his grandparents took him to Germany for his twelfth birthday in 1908. Of course, that airplane was little more than a powered glider. Now he was riding in a true flying machine. It was wonderful.

They landed in a farmer's field just over three hours later as the sun was starting to settle in the southwest. The pilot slapped him on his back as they climbed out of the craft. He said, "Das ist gut, ja?"

As Michael puzzled over the pilot's language and slowly recovered the feeling in his legs after sitting in the wicker seat of the aircraft, he was approached by a bearded man dressed in a heavy sheepskin coat with an equally heavy karakul wool hat. Standing nearby were four dangerous-looking men wearing the same coats and hats. They were in front of six saddled horses. Even with layers of clothes and a heavy beard, Michael recognized his father immediately. He ran forward and wrapped his arms around James O'Connell's chest. "Father, I knew you would be waiting."

"I promised, Michael. And, I live up to my promises. By the way, welcome to Afghanistan!"

"Afghanistan? But Father, I thought you were in Aden."

"Another assignment, son. Now, we are working in Afghanistan."

"We?"

"Of course. I have been following your training and I decided you didn't need to spend another year in that dreadful school when you already had the skills needed for our trade. I wanted to be your tutor myself, and so, I arranged your mysterious travels."

"It was wonderful, father. It was cold, but it was wonderful. How did you get the Germans to take me on this trip?"

"We are now working with the Germans, my boy. They were willing to help bring you here so we could work together. I am sure you will find this work far more interesting than anything that the gurus could have taught you next term."

Michael heard the enthusiasm in his father's voice and saw

the light in his eyes. Michael was certain that his father was absolutely correct.

December 1911, Christmas Holidays — Bankroft home, Rawalpindi military cantonment

The first few days in their bungalow in the cantonment was a special time for Elizabeth. She had spent time with both of her parents over the years, but rarely alone with her father. Like many fathers of the era, Francis demonstrated his love for his daughter, but seemed outwardly more distant from her than from his son. Still, Elizabeth knew that when her parents envisioned one child carrying on the family tradition, she had been chosen instead of Conrad. While the school and "the trade" were still confusing, one thing was certain for Elizabeth. Her parents had decided she was the one to follow in their footsteps. With pride in her voice, Elizabeth told her father all that she had learned and how she had been the best in the Circle of Decision.

Francis Bankroft was not surprised by his daughter's successes. But, he listened with a heavy heart as he realized his young daughter was becoming both a woman and a member of the Secret Service. He knew the challenges ahead and knew precisely the dangers that Elizabeth would face. They were the challenges and dangers that her mother was facing even now.

He asked her about the academics and quizzed her on her language skills. Elizabeth learned for the first time that her father spoke Russian in addition to Persian and Pashtu. He commented that her Russian was far better than his. After some prodding, he agreed to teach her some rude colloquialisms that he expected her language instructors would not ever reveal. Elizabeth was greatly amused by the barracks talk that her father knew and, most especially, by the songs he sang at the table. After sharing many smiles and much laughter, they agreed to use Russian at the dinner table so Elizabeth would not lose ground in her language skills before she returned for her second term.

"And what of the other students, dear? Did you make any friends at College?"

"Father, it was hard to find friends there. Two other girls survived the Reckoning, Martha who studied in Persia House and Susan in Turkish house. Susan just disappeared one day about mid-term. I thought we were friends. We ate together and studied geography together. She was in Turkish House so I couldn't practice languages with her, but we were close. Suddenly, poof. She was gone."

"Sometimes the gurus see something that you don't see. It is a hard school."

"Did you lose friends in school, Father?"

"Yes, dear. My class started with fifteen and we graduated five." Bankroft smiled and said, "Of course, you know one of my classmates."

"That would be Mother?"

"Yes, that would be your Mother. You haven't said anything about the boys in your class."

Elizabeth blushed. She had not expected her father to ask this question. She wanted to raise it first with her mother. Elizabeth was still not entirely sure how she felt about the boys in her class or about boys in general. Some days, she felt a strange sort of glow when spending time with her Russia House classmates. Other days, the boys seemed to focus exclusively on showing off, which seemed to her the worst possible trait. She was certain that her mother could explain. Still, she knew her father could be a relentless interrogator of either Elizabeth or her brother Conrad. There was no good way to avoid his eyes when he started asking questions. In a flash, Elizabeth suddenly realized that the gurus at the college also had that way about them.

Her father's gaze was not exactly withering but capturing. She could only compare it to something she saw years ago when she watched a tiger hunting a deer. After a vacation to see the Red Fort of Lahore when Elizabeth was ten, the family visited a game preserve along the canals south of the city. They spent the night in a treehouse designed specifically for hunters, though neither Francis nor Mary Bankroft were hunters. Now Elizabeth knew that they were not hunters of animals but hunters of men. Francis wanted to watch the jungle from the safety of the treehouse. He told his children that the jungle had its own rules and so long as they did not violate those rules, they would be safe. He said it was important to learn to live by the rules of the jungle. One never knew when it might be useful. At the time, Elizabeth did not understand. Now, she realized that her father's comment was based on real experience.

At dusk, just after they saw a flight of bats fill the sky and a hawk on the wing capture a bat in his talons. Francis pointed into the jungle. "Watch now. This is the way a tiger hunts. The tiger and the deer are part of one circle of life, but until now, the deer did not know it."

At that point, Elizabeth noticed the tiger's gaze seemed to prevent the deer from running away. The deer appeared to lose all independence of thought or movement, as if the tiger already owned the deer well before the kill. Every one of the gurus seemed to have this same skill, and as she recalled the tiger and the deer, now she realized her father did as well. She had to answer. Actually, when her father looked at her this way, she wanted to answer.

Elizabeth said, "Most of the boys are too interested in their own world to notice me. Only two of the boys seemed interested in me. Both are with me in Russia House. One is

Michael O'Connell and the other is Jason Mackenzie. They don't seem like the other boys. They are nice."

"I met Mackenzie's father when we were waiting for you. He is assigned to Bombay and responsible for the Arabian Sea. O'Connell's father is currently in Aden, I believe. He is one of the best Arabists in the Service. I wonder why his son is in Russia House?"

"He was supposed to be in Arab House, but after the Reckoning they moved him to Russia House. There are three of us there, two in Persia House, and one in Turkish House. This term, after they pulled Michael, they did not fill any students in Arab House. I suppose one or more of the students we lost in the Reckoning were supposed to be in Arab House. They are talking about adding a German House next term." Elizabeth was trying her best to avoid any further discussion of Michael O'Connell. She hoped her father wouldn't notice the subtle change in topic.

Francis Bankroft was well aware of his daughter's effort to avoid further discussion about a potential boyfriend. He could use his guru taught skills to get her to say more, but he decided not to press. It was not time to reveal his refined skills to a daughter who was just at the beginning of her training. After all, young men and women often formed attachments at the college as he and Mary well understood. To allow Elizabeth to believe she had avoided further discussion of Michael O'Connell, Francis said, "German House. That is very interesting. You know there is a growing concern over what the Kaiser is doing to expand his Empire and build a formidable navy. It is no threat to us here, but someday it could be. For now, the threat remains from the Tsar's forces rather than the Kaiser's. Still, the deans of the college are very wise to add a German House." This time, Francis did decide to use "the guru voice" so that his daughter felt no concern. "By the way, I didn't see James O'Connell at the reception area. I think your friend Michael was met by one of the senior officers from the Frontier Force. I'm sure James was just delayed."

Elizabeth decided to turn the tables on her father. She said, "Father, I noticed that you and mother have a portrait in the Hall of Honors at the school. Why didn't you tell me you were famous?" Her smile was between a smirk and a grin as she watched her father blush.

"Elizabeth, your mother and I were in the first class at the college. We have worked now for almost twenty years in service to the Crown. I suppose the college seniors decided as first class, we deserved a portrait."

Elizabeth could feel as well as see her Father's reluctance. She decided to let him off the hook at this point. She said, "Father, I think there is more to this story than you wish to say. I am more than willing to wait until you want to tell me."

Christmas Eve — December 1911

On the morning of Christmas Eve, Mary Bankroft returned to the Bankroft bungalow in the cantonment. She looked tired and thin. In the past, Elizabeth had not paid attention to her mother's "personal travel." Now she knew there was nothing personal about those journeys. Elizabeth had trouble imagining her mother working in the same trade as her father, but now after a year at college, it was clear to Elizabeth that her mother was, in her own right, a secret agent for the Crown.

At noon, Conrad arrived by train on holiday leave from his regiment which was currently assigned to guard the Bolan Pass from Afghan bandits. He also looked tired and thin, but Elizabeth suspected for far different reasons. Ensigns in the Indian Army were expected to lead patrols and to be the officers responsible for "pickets" or observation posts on key high ground in locations like the Bolan or Khyber Passes.

Long hours spent in the saddle or on foot patrol, as well as life and death responsibilities, were certain to tire anyone and Conrad was no exception. But Elizabeth wondered what responsibilities her mother had recently assumed that made her look as tired as her brother. The holiday reunion of the entire family — including the Christmas Eve church service followed by an exceptional Christmas Day dinner and Boxing Day exchange of gifts — kept Elizabeth from asking any hard questions for those three days.

She finally had time alone with her mother one day before the new year. Mary Bankroft and Elizabeth took tea on the patio of their small garden in the cantonment. Black and white magpies, known as bulbuls in India, were bouncing around on the grass while making their distinctive whistle. It was a gentle moment that both mother and daughter appreciated after months of hard work. Elizabeth asked, "Mother, where were you?"

"I took a small trip for the colonel. I took the train down to Karachi and then a steamship to Basra. I was in Mesopotamia for about four weeks."

"You look tired. Was it a hard trip?"

Mary Bankroft thought for a moment. Was it a hard trip? It was hard and dangerous and sad. The images of her time in Mesopotamia flashed through her mind as she tried to avoid showing her emotions to her daughter.

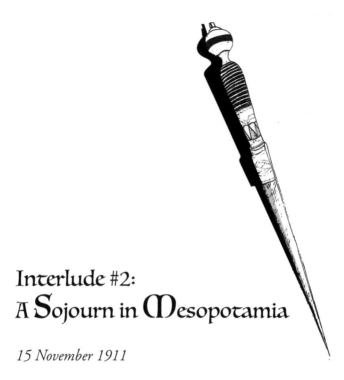

Interlude #2:
A Sojourn in Mesopotamia

15 November 1911

"MRS. BANKROFT, YOU CAN'T BE SERIOUS. A WOMAN JUST DOES NOT TRAVEL up-country on her own. *It is just not done.*"

Bartholomew Hastings, the British consul in Basra was a traditional member of the Indian Civil Service and an experienced Arabist. He believed his primary responsibilities were to keep British shipping interests safe and to explore building a relationship with the Ottoman governor of Mesopotamia. The Navy had made it clear they wanted oil from the region. While the consul didn't know why they wanted oil when the Royal Navy ships ran on coal, he certainly wasn't going to let some woman adventurer create havoc on his turf. He knew there was already enough of *that sort of thing* going on in Arabia with the female adventurer named Gertrude Bell. He had a comfortable relationship with the local Ottoman civil servants and a growing friendship with the Ottoman governor. He worried that any British visitor not under his personal control could create trouble that would disrupt that relationship.

Mary Bankroft looked around the office of the consul. Whitewashed walls with the obligatory portrait of the King and the Viceroy. A print of Egypt from the Royal Academy artist, David Roberts. Oak furniture which was very British, but much too heavy in design for the rest of the room. She was sitting in a straight-backed oak chair across the enormous desk from the consul. One look at him had warned her of trouble. He was dressed in a style that was ten years out of date with a stiff wing collar, bow tie, and heavy wool vest. Sleeve guards ensured his French cuffs and gold cuff links stayed at just the proper distance from his wrists. His five-button jacket was on a hanger behind him. Mary could sense that this man lamented the new century, the new King and the fact that the world moved faster than he could think.

Mary knew she could have used "the voice" which gurus at the Viceroy's College had long ago perfected to make unwitting individuals compliant. However, during all of her years working for the Indian Intelligence Bureau, she had never used it on a fellow Briton. In this case, Mary knew the Indian bureaucracy would soon render a compliant if not supportive colleague. She handed him an oilskin envelope with the formal waxed seal of the office of the government of British India and said, "Sir, before you dismiss my request, please open the dispatch that I have carried from the Viceroy."

Bartholomew Hastings took the envelope the way a person might receive a cobra handed to him tail first. His white mustache puffed up as he tried to act as if he regularly received a dispatch from the Viceroy. In fact, he rarely received any dispatches from any part of the Indian government much less from the Viceroy in Calcutta. He took it to his desk, sat down and used a silver letter opener to break the seal which he recognized as the personal seal of Lord Minto. He placed his pince-nez glasses on his nose and read the hand-written note on very fine writing paper:

My dear Bartholomew,
I am most pleased to send you regards from Calcutta.
I have heard many good things from both the Navy and my own people on the work you are doing in Mesopotamia.
It is always a pleasure to work with a man willing to accept
a challenging assignment.
It would please me greatly if you would assist Mrs. Mary Bankroft. She is travelling in your area of responsibility at my direction and on a special service mission.
Yours most respectfully,
Minto

Now the consul realized that this *woman,* Mrs. Mary Bankroft, wasn't a tourist or private adventurer. He was already familiar with the term "special service" from a dispatch he received earlier in the year from Calcutta. At that time, he had been tasked to support the travels of a man named James O'Connell who was based in the Royal Navy coaling station in Aden. He had provided the necessary transit papers and sent him on his way. He never heard from O'Connell again. These individuals on "special service" were generally disruptive, but there was no way to avoid helping them. The previous dispatch was from the Military Intelligence Bureau. This one was a personal request from the most important Briton east of the Suez. It was clear that he would do as requested, if for no other reason than it would allow him to respond to this personal note. One never knew if establishing such a dialogue might enhance a career in the Indian service. It certainly couldn't hurt.

Hastings looked up from his desk and said, "Mrs. Bankroft. I will be happy to help. How can I be of service?"

"Sir, I have to travel up the river, possibly as far as Baghdad. I will need appropriate letters of introduction, a letter of approval from the Ottoman governorate, and, if it is not too inconvenient, two of your consulate guard force to ensure I do not have any difficulties along the way." Mary Bankroft smiled her most engaging smile and tried, she hoped successfully, not to gloat at the way the consul had been transformed by the letter from the Viceroy.

"Mrs. Bankroft, I should be able to provide all of those resources in the next two days. I assume you have sufficient funds to travel by steamer?"

"Sir, I do have sufficient funds. Thank you for your assistance."

21 November 1911 — Aboard the MV Persepolis

Mary was sitting in her cabin on the steam ship as it slowly made its way up the Tigris toward the city of al-Kut. As she had expected, the consul had dragged his feet just enough to demonstrate who was in charge in Basra. If forced to admit it, Mary would have said that the extra few days in Basra were part of her plan. She was picking up the threads of James O'Connell's travel by reaching out to his known informants in the city. Gold sovereigns and a few interview tricks later, Mary believed she had as much information as they could provide. After years of working against Russians and Persians, where her mesmerism skills were challenged, it was honestly too easy to "enchant" the local shipping personnel and shopkeepers. Still, she made sure that they were also paid well for the information they gave up while under her spell. Her instructors at The Viceroy's College once warned her, "It may seem easy to confuse and even control the mind of a shopkeeper, but remember, once the spell is broken, if they don't get paid, you can expect a knife fight."

Her information from Basra pointed to O'Connell's departure from the city sometime in the middle of September. That would have been consistent with his role as a circuit traveller in southern Mesopotamia. As an Arabist, O'Connell's job was to obtain detailed reporting on the relationships among the city dwellers, the tribal nomads and the Ottoman government. The Ottoman government seemed to be weakened under the leadership of a new triumvirate of the "Young Turks," and the Government of India was concerned that Russian agent provocateurs were working to incite unrest in Mesopotamia. O'Connell would have known that their British colleague, Captain William Henry Shakespear, had just been dispatched to Kuwait to explore the nature of tribal unrest in Eastern Arabia.

Mary Bankroft was not entirely certain why a man serving in Aden had been dispatched to Basra. Surely, Mesopotamia was an entirely different challenge from the Yemen. Mesopotamia was riven with tension due to sectarian differences between Sunni and Shia villages and between the larger rural and urban populations. The marsh lands along the Tigris and the Euphrates even had a population that lived on houseboats more like Kashmir than anyplace else in the region. O'Connell was a well-respected Arabist, so perhaps the Intelligence Bureau wanted a fresh set of eyes. Having met with Consul Hastings, it was entirely possible that the Bureau was certain they needed a fresh set of eyes. Another possibility was that O'Connell had picked up some information in the port of Aden that needed to be tracked to sources in Mesopotamia.

Calcutta had not sent any explanation to Mary when they tasked her to travel. It was clear enough they were worried about James O'Connell, and they simply ordered Mary to find him. O'Connell's trip had been scheduled to be completed in early October, with his reports to be on the desk of the Intelligence Bureau in Calcutta later that month. When it did not arrive and, in early November when there had been no word from O'Connell, it was time to find out what happened. Given the hazards of their trade as well as the dangers of travel in any part of Arabia, Mary was not optimistic that she would find a positive answer to the question.

Mary was preparing to go ashore during the ship's brief scheduled stop to take on supplies, off-load cargo and board passengers in al-Kut. O'Connell's contact list included a shopkeeper near the city's docks. Perhaps he would know something. If he did, Mary would get him to talk. She opened her steamer trunk and pulled out all that she would need for two hours in the city. She started her preparations by donning the one-piece undergarment that was part of her issued equipment. The one-piece served as storage for such tools of the trade as a pair of throwing knives, a set of skeleton keys and shims that could be used to open locked doors, a small magnifying glass, and six small, sealed packages that carried phosphorus charges to start a fire or a series of powders that could either disable or kill a man depending on the dose.

Mary then chose a set of loose trousers that looked like those worn by every other tribal woman, except for the sturdy belt loops that allowed her to wear a leather belt. That belt carried a dagger on her right hip and a new Belgian Browning automatic pistol in a cross-draw holster on her left. Francis might swear by his Colts, but Mary found the Browning pistol smaller, lighter and, most important for concealment on a woman's body, flatter than the big revolvers her husband preferred. It was chambered in .32 caliber which Francis considered an anemic cartridge, but when Mary pointed out she was the better shot, he surrendered. She also knew, but did not tell her husband, that her past use of pistols had been at ranges of less than three feet.

Mary pulled a long, brightly coloured tribal dress from the trunk. It was modified with slits in the skirt so that she could access the knife and pistol without difficulty. She added a set of Persian slippers that looked like every other woman's scuffed shoes. They were not what they appeared to be. Like most of her clothing, they had been modified in India by the Bureau's quartermaster to serve under any conditions of running, riding or swimming. A leather satchel carrying gold sovereigns and a number of smaller Ottoman coins went across one shoulder. To complete her trousseau, she added a long black wig and a black cotton shoulder wrap known locally as an abaya. The wrap served as headscarf, veil and shawl. She checked herself in the small mirror in the cabin. Next to the mirror was a bag of well tarnished nomad jewelry which she added to her hands, feet and ears. The transformation was complete. She would travel the streets of Kut not as an Englishwoman but as a nomad wife looking for supplies. Mary knew little Arabic, but her Persian, coupled with a working knowledge of the Baluch language, would further enhance the image of the nomad traveler.

Earlier, she had told her two consulate guards that she would be staying in her cabin until they reached Baghdad. They were berthed in the next cabin. Mary watched carefully as the two guards headed to the "native" deck to play cards with the crew as the steamer ambled along the Tigris. With some degree of caution since a "native," man or woman, would not be allowed on the colonial deck, Mary Bankroft slipped out of her cabin and headed immediately down to the deck where the locals were waiting for the steamer to dock.

The arrival of the *MV Persepolis* in al-Kut caused great excitement. Cargo and local passengers left the ship, traders interested in selling local goods to the remaining passengers pushed up the gangway, and the expected chaos of Middle East trade occurred on the dock, on the "native" deck of the ship, and even over the side as locals pulled small boats against the side of the vessel. Mary Bankroft blended into the teeming mass of people, animals, and goods and reappeared as an individual only when she cleared the docks. She looked at one of the pieces of jewelry on her wrist which held a disguised wrist watch. She had one hour to meet with the source and less than an hour after that to arrive back at the ship before it departed for Baghdad and points north on the Tigris.

On board, she had memorized the street plan from the dock to a brass- and tin-smith shop where O'Connell's contact in al-Kut, Mohammed Sultani, worked. She arrived after a brisk, ten-minute walk. It was mid-day, but the sun barely penetrated the narrow street with shops on the ground floor and three levels of apartments above with laundry, bedding and carpets hanging from small balconies. The smells of cooking oil, spices, livestock, humans and sewage made her eyes water as she walked into a progressively narrower alley.

Sultani was sitting outside his shop on an overturned brass cooking pot, eyes closed, fanning himself with a filthy handkerchief. The arrival of a tribal woman surprised Sultani but he immediately transitioned into his most structured sales pitch that he used with tribals. They came often enough to his shop with very little money, but also very few demands. Sultani was convinced this would be an easy sale of one of his lowest quality brass or tin cooking pots. He always made a very tidy profit from the fools of the desert. Tribal women were his favourite customers.

Mary started in Baluch language but quickly shifted to Persian so that she might encourage Sultani into his shop where the real interrogation would begin. Once he heard the much more sophisticated Persian coming from behind the veil of this woman, Sultani smiled. She might be a tribal, but the language argued she was a rich tribal. So much the better. He agreed to enter the shop to show her all of his wares. Mary followed him into the shop and before he could turn, she applied pressure to the right side of his neck along specific nerve ganglia. He was paralyzed in an instant. She spoke in Persian and using a hypnotic voice made it clear that Sultani had one choice to make, answer her questions or die.

"What do you know of the British man O'Connell?"

Already living in what the instructors at The Viceroy's College called "the waking dream," Sultani replied calmly, "I saw him last month. He asked of the current situation in the area, how we are treated by the Ottomans, and I gave him my reports. He paid me."

"What else, Sultani?"

"He asked how he could meet the German engineers who are working with the Ottomans on the river. They say they are improving river traffic."

Mary did not expect that response. Germans? There were no requirements from the Bureau on Germans. "Did you help him meet the Germans?"

"I did."

"And…"

"He was carrying a suitcase and a long leather tube. We had to use horses to get him and the cargo to the Germans."

"And then…?"

"And then, he told me to leave. He said this in a way that I feared him. I left. My contacts said O'Connell and the Germans headed east into Persia. I know nothing else."

Even under this spell, individuals with exceptionally strong wills could hide information. But, their pulse would quicken as they struggled to lie. Mary would have felt that change through her fingers which were still on Sultani's neck. No changes noted, she felt he was telling everything she knew. There was no time to waste. Mary increased the pressure on Sultani's neck just enough that he collapsed as if he was a marionette whose strings had been cut. He would be unconscious for no more than ten minutes.

Mary took the first few minutes of that ten to search the

back of the shop for further clues. She found none. Before she left, she reached into her purse and placed five Ottoman silver coins into Sultani's right hand. After paying him for the "inconvenience" which he would never remember, Mary dashed out of the building and along the street.

Much later and once she returned to the ship, she realized that her haste caused the next bit of difficulty. Just before she turned the corner on her return to the dock area, she brushed against two dock workers. Mary did not know for sure if they were drunk from wine or intoxicated from hashish, but either way, they were not about to let a tribal woman touch them without her paying for it. The first one grabbed and tore her abaya as she passed, pulling her to a halt. The second mumbled some sort of insulting phrase in Arabic about her profession while his partner pulled Mary closer and started toward her. She could see both salacious and vicious intent in their eyes.

Years of training and experience allowed her mind to work quickly through what was known in her trade as the "ladder of consequences." Mary was first introduced to this topic during her second year at The Viceroy's College. An ancient looking guru stood in front of a class of very fit young men and women. He had already demonstrated what looked to the class like some sort of magic act. He had chosen the most fit of the class, a tall, lean-muscled, 17-year-old rugby player named Francis Bankroft who had already caught the attention of Mary. With no apparent effort, the guru tossed Francis across the sand training pit as if he was tossing a cricket ball.

"Students, there may come a time when you have to use the skills I am about to teach you. However, your job is never to stand and fight. Your job is to collect intelligence for the Raj. If you can run away, you must run. If you can talk your way out of a problem, you must do that. If you have to do harm, do just enough to get free and run away. But, if you must kill, do so quickly. This is known as the ladder of consequences. Your opponent will climb that ladder. It is up to you to decide what to do next. Now, we will practice." Over the next few weeks, they learned how to disable and, if need be, kill a man. The ancient guru led them through the ladder of consequences first with bare hands, then with a simple walking stick, and finally with a knife.

Mary did her best to avoid a conflict. She realized that these two men had already cut off her escape. This meant she would have to stand and fight. First, she engaged the two men in her most polite Persian offering apologies and even a small compensation for her mistake. Again, they made clear what sort of compensation they expected. It wasn't financial. They leered at what they saw as a tribal woman caught in their web. They had done this more than once. It was always a pleasure to take what they wanted and listen to the screams of their victim. Mary shook her head at their foolish decision. They were climbing to the top of the ladder of consequences. It was very dangerous at the top.

As the first man approached, Mary bent over as if to cower under the assault. In fact, she was reaching inside her dress to access her dagger. She held it low and hidden until he was right on top of her. With one hand, the attacker pulled her abaya and with his other hand he reached out to grab Mary's throat. As he leaned forward over what he took to be a cowering woman, she drove the dagger up under his rib cage and into his heart. Once she pulled the thin blade out, the wound sealed and little blood followed. The man was dead before he knew he had been stabbed. He dropped like a stone.

The second man could not understand what had happened to his partner, but he knew he could not let their prey escape. He charged, moving too quickly and without a plan. Using her now freed abaya to disguise her movements, Mary sidestepped her new attacker and used the back of her hand to strike just between his skull and neck. Just a tap in the right place and his spine dislodged from his brain. As her guru had said, many parts of the human skeleton are very resilient. Many parts are not. Much of the human skull is very fragile and it is easy to die from a head wound. He showed them where the skull was most vulnerable. The guru emphasized that it was easy enough to kill, but much harder to manage regret afterwards. Again, this one was dead before he hit the ground. Mary had little time to manufacture a credible scene in the alley that would explain the dead men. She did find a small blade on one man and placed it in the hand of the other. If anyone cared, it would look like a fight between two villains. That would satisfy the local Ottoman authorities who had better things to do than wonder over the life and the death of the dockside villains of al-Kut.

It was time to get back to the boat. Mary cleaned her dagger in the sand and returned it to its sheath and walked to the dockyards and onto the boat. She had to concentrate to keep from breaking into a run. A run would draw attention. A tribal woman would meander back to the ship. Mary used her skills to dampen the urge to race to the ship. The ship's crew did not take any notice of what seemed to be a tribal woman calmly coming on board. From their perspective, her passage would be paid by her husband or father who was certainly already on board. *Persepolis* did not charge by the head down in the native area. They charged by the family. By the time the ship departed al-Kut, Mary was in her cabin and changed out of the tribal disguise. She wrapped the clothes inside the abaya to be tossed overboard later.

From one of her bags, she pulled out a small Persian prayer rug and rolled it out on the floor of her cabin. Still in the single-piece undergarment, though now "unloaded" of all her tools, Mary sat on the rug and completed a series of yogic exercises to wash out the tension rushing through her bloodstream. She knew from experience these exercises would reduce the negative emotions that always followed a fatal confrontation. During the hour following the exercises, Mary pondered the information that she acquired and began to formulate a plan. Baghdad would be the next stop for the *MV Persepolis* and it would most certainly be the place where she would determine whether O'Connell had been kidnapped or whether he had joined forces with another European power.

"Mother? Are you there?" Elizabeth looked directly into her mother's eyes. One minute Mary had been talking, and the next she stopped as if pondering some complex mathematics equation. Elizabeth didn't know what had happened, but she seemed to feel tension and even fear coming from her mother.

"I'm sorry, dear. You asked if the trip was difficult. It was difficult and I was just thinking about what these difficulties mean to all of us."

"All?"

"Yes, dear. You need to know the reason I was travelling. I was searching for a lost officer in Mesopotamia. He is the father of your classmate, Michael O'Connell."

"Michael's father is lost?" Elizabeth's response came out of a choked mouth. Mary realized at that moment her daughter had feelings for young Master O'Connell.

"Yes, my dear. James is not at station and could not be found in Mesopotamia where he was last seen. I don't know if you will see Michael this term. If you do, please don't tell him what I have just said, but please be kind to him. His holiday will have been most unpleasant."

"Do you know what happened to him, mother? Did you

report to the colonel? Did you report it to the consul in Mesopotamia? Has the Army started a search?"

"Elizabeth, these are questions I could not answer even if I knew. You have to learn that sometimes, in the trade, we do not share secrets even with our loved ones."

Mary watched as her daughter transitioned from a pout to anger and eventually to determination. "Mother, we must find James O'Connell. We must."

"Indeed, Elizabeth. We must. But for now, we must enjoy our own family and our holiday. And, you must go back to school to learn the skills necessary to search for a lost one. I promise, this term will be far more interesting than the last."

Mary decided to apply a small bit of "the voice" to her daughter so that she could calm her down. She looked directly into the young woman's grey eyes, changed her tone slightly, calmed her voice and said, "This is what you must do so that you can join us in the Trade. And, Elizabeth, you must not talk to your brother about this. You must promise."

In the dreamy voice that revealed the success of the mesmerism, Elizabeth nodded and said, "Yes, mother. I promise."

Mary switched back to a normal voice and said, "Elizabeth, do finish your tea."

Elizabeth shook her head as if to clear it and said, "It's gone cold, mother. I will go to the kitchen and ask Mohammed to bring a fresh pot. Would you like some biscuits?"

"Thank you dear." As Elizabeth walked across the green yard toward the bungalow, Mary Bankroft realized this was probably the last time she would be able to use mental tricks on her daughter. After next term, Elizabeth would know what was happening and would have the skills to fight back.

Adventures on the Border

January 1912 — Afghanistan

THEY TRAVELED FOR WEEKS ON HORSEBACK, BYPASSING KABUL, HEADING north through the Sorubi Pass of the Kabul River. Once north of the capitol, they turned northeast into the Panjshir Valley. Along the way, James O'Connell introduced Michael to the wonders of Afghanistan. The winter winds were harsh, and several times they had to stop in local caravanserai to shelter from blizzards. Michael was captured by the high peaks, by the mines filled with lapis lazuli, carnelian, and turquoise, and by the sparkling clear rivers that ran too quickly to freeze. As they approached the mountain passes of the Hindu Kush, Michael was reminded of the foothills of the Himalayas he had visited while living with his father in Simla. He had always been a good rider. Still, travelling through the narrow passes of the Hindu Kush in the middle of winter was more than a challenge. It was life threatening.

They had been travelling for over a month when they finally approached a snow-covered pass leading from the Panjshir Valley to the plains of Northern Afghanistan. Michael did not want to sound like he was complaining, especially in front of his father's soldiers, but he was concerned about the snow, the ice, and the cold. He was a confident young man, but he had never been a risk taker. Now he was facing a risk far greater than anything he had seen before. He wasn't entirely certain why they were pressing forward at such a pace. And, he still didn't know why they were rushing headlong into the mountains. Michael realized over the past month that he could sometimes intrude on his father's thoughts without his father noticing. Those thoughts were all about a place north of the mountains called Mazar-e-Sharif, and about an Afghan general. Michael's abilities were limited and the information came in sudden bursts that had little to do with their travel. It was time to make some progress in understanding what was going on.

"Father, it is January. I know we never tried to force a mountain pass in India in the middle of winter. Why are we doing so now?" He tried not to make it sound like a bleat, but he was certain that his voice gave him away.

"Michael, we have an appointment in the north that we must keep by early March. If the passes are closed, then we shall wait. We have a house at this end of the pass that we shall use. I just want to see if there is any chance to enter the pass. If not, then so be it. If so, we have a house on the other side as well. First, we must see."

Michael realized at that point his father was telling only a portion of the truth. He decided it was his turn to do the same. "Father, I am ready to follow you anywhere."

James O'Connell looked at his son. He hoped that the boy meant what he said because they were heading toward treachery and violence. And the treachery and violence would be of James O'Connell's making.

20 January 1912 — Rawalpindi Cantonment

With the New Year's celebrations completed, on 15 January 1912, Conrad Bankroft had boarded a steam train south and returned to his regiment on the Bolan Pass. Before leaving Rawalpindi, he received a promotion with his parents looking on during the ceremony. Now, Lieutenant Bankroft would take on new duties that, to the relief of his parents, would rarely include serving as the only officer on the picket line defending the pass.

The rest of the Bankroft family also was called back to work long before they would have preferred. Elizabeth had planned to travel with her mother on the airship back to The Viceroy's College in time for the new term beginning in February, but that was not to be. Mary and Francis both apologized as they bid her farewell on the embarkation platform for the newest of the Royal Flying Corps airships, *HMFS Mace*. They were sending her back to school a full ten days before the term started, but there was nothing to be done about it.

Elizabeth accepted the decision as part of the process of growing up and joining the service to the Crown. She concealed her disappointment and presented her most straight-shouldered, adult pose as she said, "Mother. Father. I know why I must leave early and why you can't go with me. I am a young woman now and I can easily make this trip without any problems. Please be careful as you do your service. I will study hard and hope to join you on future adventures."

Francis Bankroft took his daughters hands and looked into her eyes. "Elizabeth, you need to study hard this term. It is when you are asked to learn the most. I know you will do your best. I love you very much."

Mary Bankroft thought for a moment her tough husband, survivor of so many hair-raising adventures, would break down and cry. Of course, that wouldn't be proper. Instead, he simply hugged his daughter, did a formal about-face, and walked off the platform leaving Elizabeth and Mary to say goodbye.

"Elizabeth, don't forget what I said about young Michael. I don't know if he will even be taking this term, but if he is, he will need someone he can talk to about his father. Please be that someone. Also, I know your father would want you to write to us. In the second term, you are allowed to send us small notes about your progress. The notes will be reviewed by the gurus, but you can let us know about your health and any scientific discoveries that you might have made."

Elizabeth blushed. Her mother had found out that she had discovered a new Himalayan orchid during her summer studies in the mountains. Elizabeth's drawings and her plant press were dispatched almost immediately to the Royal Botanical Gardens at Kew. The plant was confirmed to be a new sub-species of a terrestrial orchid. Plant hunters would arrive in the spring and the college had already instructed Elizabeth to take them to the location where she saw the orchids. They would take a sample back to Kew. Botany was a hobby of Elizabeth's and this was her first discovery. She was very proud of the orchid and knew that her grandmother and Mrs. Edwards would be most pleased. Elizabeth was captured by the emotions of the moment. She could only offer, "Of course, Mother. I will do my best…" Then the klaxon sounded and she and the other passengers had to board.

27 January 1912 — Rawalpindi Cantonment

One week after dispatching Elizabeth, Francis and Mary were in the Rawalpindi office of the regional commander of the Military Intelligence Bureau of the Indian Army. Lieutenant Colonel Gareth Winslow-Heath was another example of the survivors of years in the Raj: his face, hands and arms permanently tanned from the Indian sun, his commitment to tea drinking renowned, and his family life non-existent. Different from his peers, Winslow-Heath was avowed tea-to-tal. He was considered a less-than-jolly member of the officers' club in the Rawalpindi cantonment because he would not enjoy a "peg" of whisky at the end of the day. The Bankrofts' knew why Winslow-Heath was "less than jolly." During a holiday entertainment at the Bankroft house in 1904, Winslow-Heath waxed nostalgic as he watched Elizabeth and Conrad playing a more rigorous than usual game of croquet. He revealed that he lost his wife and child to cholera fifteen years earlier while serving in the Bombay Engineers.

After that tragedy, Indian Army seniors offered him compassionate retirement in England. He refused. Instead, he accepted an assignment to the senior staff college at Simla, where he stood out as one of the rare mid-level officers who appreciated the many cultures of India. The head of Indian Army Intelligence Bureau, Sir Charles MacGregor, recruited Winslow-Heath and within a few years, he had risen to become one of the Bureau's leaders. Winslow-Heath focused on threats to the frontier from Russia. The Director of Naval Intelligence, Rear Admiral Alexander Bethell, told MacGregor he was most pleased with Winslow-Heath's results. Now, he could focus more of his attention and resources on the same threats in the Indian Ocean and the Arabian Sea.

Winslow-Heath opened the meeting with the Bankrofts in the avuncular style he used with his collectors. He said, "Francis and Mary, thank you for coming today. I hope you had a good holiday and that you were able to spend some time with your children."

Francis responded, "Sir, we did have a good time for a bit. It is always difficult to say goodbye to children." Francis realized that he had made an error and Mary noticed her husband blushed just at his collar.

The colonel nodded and looked down at a photograph on his polished-oak desk. Neither of the Bankrofts had stood behind that desk, but they assumed that the frame held a picture of his wife and son. Winslow-Heath let the moment pass gracefully and asked, "How is your son doing with the Baluch Regiment?"

Mary responded this time, "Sir, Conrad is doing very well. You were there for his recent promotion. He has returned to the Bolan Pass and I expect we shall hear from him by post. In the meantime, over the holidays he said that he was enjoying his work, though managing pickets along the Bolan Pass is a challenge."

Winslow-Heath seemed to grow beyond his six-foot frame as he said, "Well do I remember my days on the Frontier. I can tell you that your son will be having far more fun chasing bandits than we have chasing ghosts here." Winslow-Heath nodded to a map table on the other side of the room. As he stood up, he waved the Bankrofts to join him. The map on the table included all of British India as well as the "areas of influence" of the Raj including Afghanistan, Persia, Mesopotamia and the Persian Gulf.

Based on the map, Francis realized this was an entirely different sort of briefing. In the past, his chief usually had maps that focused on a single pass or a single tribal area. Suddenly, the game board had shifted and they were looking at grand strategy of the Empire. This meant their assignment would be filled with different opportunities, but also greater challenges.

"Now, we are facing two different adversaries." Winslow-Heath put his left hand down on the portion of the map focusing on the Persian Gulf and Arabia. "On this side, we see a growing influence from the Kaiser. Since the imbroglio in Agadir last year, the Germans have been building heavy battleships and flexing their muscles across Europe. We must no longer consider Germany just a land-based power limited to continental Europe."

The Bankrofts nodded. The events had been in the papers last year. The French had forced the sultan of Morocco to sign a new treaty that obligated him to consult the French government on all foreign treaties. Germany initially accepted the new Franco-Moroccan relationship but when violence broke out in Morocco, the Germans sent a gunboat and then a new battle cruiser to the port of Agadir on Morocco's Atlantic

Coast. The British Navy saw this move as a potential threat to their control of the waters off North Africa. For weeks, British newspapers covered the crisis as the possible beginning of a land and sea war, with France and England on one side and Germany on the other. In November, negotiations calmed the crisis and France ceded a portion of its sub-Saharan African colonies to Germany. But for the British military planners, and most especially for the Royal Navy, the expansion of German seapower raised troubling questions about the Royal Navy's ability to control the seas.

The colonel continued, "Now, the Germans are working in Africa as well as building ties to the Ottomans. The Kaiser has made two visits to the sultan in Constantinople and once even to the Holy Land. He has offered to help build a railway from Berlin to Baghdad and, more importantly to our interests, he has obtained lucrative contracts to sell the Ottomans military equipment and to train their military. In short, the Germans are very close to building an alliance with the Ottomans and that means they are very close to the Suez. It was this concern that led us to send O'Connell to Mesopotamia. And when he disappeared, Mary, we dispatched you to find out what happened."

Mary nodded. She expected the colonel had read her full report outlining what she knew: that James O'Connell would not be returning to his post in Aden; and what she thought: that O'Connell had joined the Germans in their efforts in the region. What she did not expect was the next question.

"What do you two know about navigation?"

Francis spoke first, "Sir, my experience in navigation is on land where you work using map and compass. I suspect that is more or less the same for airships. I have seen, but don't honestly understand, how ships' officers navigate using a sextant, ship's clock and charts."

Mary began to explain how a sextant can be used to navigate by the stars, when Winslow-Heath waved his hand and said, "Mary, I suspect you know more about this than both of us together. However, I suspect you are not familiar with the newest Royal Navy methodology using an analytic engine."

Mary nodded. Like a prize student in some university class, she began by saying, "Sir, is that a modification of the difference engine Mr. Babbage designed last century? It was some sort of computational machine. If I remember correctly, Countess Lovelace had some involvement in designing the computations. I thought the machine was a design only. It seems to me I read that there was no way to power the complicated gears of the difference engine."

Winslow-Heath laughed and said, "Once again, Mary, you have demonstrated knowledge in an area that baffled me and, looking at your husband, completely confused him. In short, you got it in one. The analytic engine is about the size of a library table and can be powered by the electrical current running to a ship's bridge. Far smaller than the difference engine designed last century by Mr. Babbage, which was never a practical device. The analytic engine is a computing device which works out trigonometric functions far faster than any human. The Navy thinks that analytic engines will transform the accuracy of their navigation and, most especially, the accuracy of their gunfire."

Francis did not want to be completely left out of the conversation even if he did not understand the technology, so he said, "Sir, with our new battleships powered by oil and the addition of the analytic engine, we will have far greater success on the seas. It may even transform the capability of our airships."

"Indeed, Francis. So long as we can keep our analytic engines a secret. Unfortunately, the design of one of these computing devices is missing from *HMS Skirmisher,* a scout cruiser that was passing through the Arabian Sea. The *Skirmisher* has an analytic engine on board for testing at sea. They weren't planning on testing the engine until they were in Indian waters where they could experiment with the use of the engine for both navigation and naval gunnery. When they arrived on station in Indian waters, they opened the crate and found the device was there, but the detailed plans, drawings and instruction manuals had disappeared. Without those documents, the *Skirmisher's* commander, navigators and gun crew were unable to use the device. They had checked their inventories at the last port of call, Aden. The *Skirmisher* is on her way to Bombay, but I doubt any search of the ship or crew will uncover the material."

Mary nodded and said, "And O'Connell went to Mesopotamia just after the port visit?"

"Indeed, he did. A very handy trading tool if one wanted to change sides. Even better if one wanted to change sides and convince an adversary to support some Irish independence movement."

Francis huffed, "Against the Crown? Surely that is a fool's errand."

"Perhaps, but what would you say if a spy offered you the designs of a secret weapon in exchange for a promise of future support?"

Mary said, "We would more than likely say anything to a traitor to get what we needed from him."

"Just so, Mary, just so."

Winslow-Heath moved over to the center of the map and placed his right hand down on Afghanistan. "Francis, you of all people know Russians continue to play their games in Afghanistan. They are expanding their presence, both official and unofficial, in Herat, Mazar-e-Sharif, Konduz, and Kabul. They are playing a deep game in Afghanistan. I know there are some both in Calcutta and Whitehall who still think the Russians intend to invade Afghanistan and eventually India. I think their plan is more subtle. They simply want to encourage the Afghans to be more hostile. It is in the Afghan nature to be hostile to foreigners, so it doesn't take much persuasion.

"Why do they want to do this? Because, they want us distracted while they target the great oil reserves in Persia. After the loss of their entire Pacific fleet against the Japanese, the Russians are working double-time to build new warships. And those warships, like our newest fleet, are oil-fired, not coal-fired."

With that, the colonel looked up at his two intelligence officers and suddenly he said, "Time to take tea, don't you think?"

The Bankrofts nodded and the colonel used his parade ground voice to call his subaltern into the room. "Smythe. Tea if you please." A junior officer appeared at the door and nodded. He returned immediately with a full tea service, cups and saucers and a plate piled with pastries and dried fruits. Clearly this was the time of day when the colonel always called for tea.

"Good man, Smythe. You can leave us now. I will serve." The colonel gestured for the Bankrofts to return to their seats in front of his desk. As they sat down, Winslow-Heath handed Mary Bankroft a full cup of milky tea and a small plate. "Please serve yourself, Mary." He repeated the action with Francis and then walked behind his desk to recover a large ceramic mug for his own tea. After he returned to his seat and drank nearly half of the mug, he said, "Much better, eh?"

He didn't wait for an answer before returning to the reason for their meeting. "The Ottomans already control what oil reserves exist in Southern Mesopotamia. If they ally with the Germans, that oil will no longer be available for the Fleet. If the Russians somehow control the oil in Persia through influence with the Qajar Shah, where in the world do we get our oil? We need enough oil for our ships and, soon, for our airships as we transition them to petrol. The Americans will sell us all the oil we want and at a fair price too, but how in the world are we going to get that oil to India? No. Not acceptable. We have to think up our own ploy to deter the Germans and the Russians. Short of war of course, because the current government in Whitehall, bless them, believe we should love peace and avoid war. I wonder how many of our mandarins in Whitehall have ever faced a dedicated enemy on a battlefield. Precious few, I would guess."

This was the beginning of a standard diatribe the Bankrofts had heard many times from Winslow-Heath. It usually lasted at least five minutes as he expressed his frustration with British elected officials and Whitehall civil servants. They knew he would not give them a chance to interject their thoughts or even respond to his rhetorical flourishes. They just had to wait until he was finished "setting the stage" and until his mug was empty and he stopped to refill. Only then would he reveal what he wanted them to accomplish.

After preparing a new mug of tea, Winslow-Heath finally focused on why the Bankrofts were in his office. He said, "I know you have traveled as individuals in the past, but I want you to consider a new assignment where you would travel together. In fact, you would travel with your daughter as well. What do you think of that?"

Francis Bankroft was devastated by the thought of involving his little girl. The very thought of placing Elizabeth in harm's way broke through his normally formal responses to his commander. He said, "Sir, our daughter is only just starting her second term at the college. She is hardly ready for an assignment. Her training is nowhere near complete."

Winslow-Heath understood only too well a father's concern for his child. His voice was quiet and by no means martial in style. He said, "Francis, I can imagine no better tutors for a young intelligence officer than you two. I know your skills and I know Mary's skills. You complement each other very well. And, honestly, I can't wait until Elizabeth finishes school. I need a family to travel into Persia. I need three agents to go spy the land where our interests collide with the Russians and the Germans. Mary, you already reported that O'Connell and the Germans were headed to Persia. Francis, your sources have already identified Colonel Naglieff as moving his forces toward Western Afghanistan.

"I need an understanding of the state of play in the border region between Persia and Afghanistan and I need it quickly. If we know what we are facing, it will be easier for us to determine the next move. If James O'Connell was still in the game, he would be returning to Mesopotamia to determine the German efforts on the Ottoman-Persian borders. In fact, his mission in Mesopotamia was supposed to be the first step to determine the nature of these threats in and around Basra. Now…well, now, we don't know what has become of James but we must hope he is not an adversary. But as you have heard from me many times before, hope is not a plan. So, there it is. You must go. You are my best agents and as a family you could easily slip into these areas in ways that no singleton, man or woman, could."

Mary could see that refusal was not an option, so she decided to ask a more focused question. "Sir, when would we need to leave?"

This provoked an angry glance from Francis who had not yet given up his argument. Mary was certain there was nothing to be done. They were agents of the Crown and short of surrendering their commissions and returning to England to find new jobs, they were obliged to obey orders.

Winslow-Heath laughed through his enormous mustache. "At last, I have an ally in the Bankroft family. I believe we should give Elizabeth a few months of training. I have already instructed Guru, more properly Major, Naismith to take Elizabeth into a specialized training program for the next twelve weeks. Elizabeth will feel pressured, but I suspect she will also find one-on-one training to her liking."

J.R. Seeger

He paused for another sip of tea and said, "Oh, and we have already established an explanation for her departure. The school, and Elizabeth, will be told that she must leave term early to assist the Kew researchers in identifying that orchid she found last year. I have been told she is quite the botanist already. Perhaps she actually will help them for a bit when they arrive and then she will meet with you in Chitral. Guru Marian Sandusky will accompany Elizabeth and the Kew Researchers north from the school and then she will guide Elizabeth to Chitral. It should be spring by that point and the passes will be open. So, Mary, the short answer to your question is you will need to leave Rawalpindi in six weeks to arrive at Chitral in time to meet your daughter in early May."

Francis finally calmed down sufficiently to begin calculating what needed to be accomplished in those six weeks. He asked, "Sir, what identity will we use? My previous identities are well known in the north and especially to Naglieff. I suspect Mary's Russian identities will not work."

"Francis, I have been working on this with the staff. Given your language skills, we think a wealthy family of Jowzjani horse traders will work for the initial leg of the journey across Northern Afghanistan. You will be returning from a lucrative sale of horses for the Raj remount. We can provide you with a dozen trusted riders, ruffians all, led by one of your own men, Francis. They will serve as protection and also enhance your cover story. Honestly, after you get to Mashhad and head south into Persia, I will have to defer to you on whether you want to remain in the horse-trading business or build some other story. No matter how clever our boffins in the service are, I always assume the field officers know best."

Winslow-Heath smiled and concluded, "By the way, if you could recover the plans to the analytic engine and capture Mr. O'Connell, that would be most acceptable."

Mary said, "Sir, it will take until summer to get to Persia even if we travel at a fast pace. And, we still do not know where O'Connell is in Persia. How will we communicate with you? Do we have trusted couriers already in place to take the reports?"

"Mary, I think you already know the answer to this. It is something we have talked about for years but never actually tried. It turns out Naismith thinks Elizabeth is probably the best candidate we have ever had in this regard."

Francis and Mary looked at each other. They understood the mission had just become far more complicated. And, now they knew why Elizabeth was needed.

Starting on a New Path

01 March 1912 — Viceroy's College

ELIZABETH WAS BEWILDERED WHEN SHE WAS CALLED INTO THE OFFICES OF Master Guru Naismith in the third week of her second term. She knew of no student who visited the Guru's offices and ever returned to class. What precisely had she done to cause such anger or disappointment that she would have to leave the college?

She arrived wearing her new saffron robes after a morning session on agent debriefings. After all this work, Elizabeth was crushed by the thought that she had not made the grade, that she would be sent home, and today would be her last day wearing the saffron colours. As she waited in Naismith's outer office, Elizabeth went through every aspect of her training and her evaluations. She could think of nothing that hadn't passed muster.

When she was finally invited into the office, Naismith's first words shocked her even more. "Elizabeth, I have been watching your progress in the first term. I am very pleased."

Elizabeth bowed slightly and said, "Thank you, Master Guru."

"While you may have expected to attend the rest of your classes with your saffron classmates, I have to disappoint you. You will not be returning to classes."

Elizabeth felt her heart sink. It was as she had feared: she was being sent home. She used all of the skills she learned in her first term to avoid breaking into tears. She recited her internal mantra taught by Guru Marian and measured her breathing. She paused long enough to make sure her voice did not betray her disappointment. Then she said, "I am very sorry to hear this, Master Guru."

"Elizabeth, this is not a criticism of you at all. You must think you are being sent home. Not at all. You have been selected for an intensive training program. It will require you to receive training from Guru Marian, Guru Standish and myself every day for the next six weeks. There will be no breaks. There will be no rest. You will be covering material in days that your peers in both saffron and white class cover in weeks. And, just to add to the pressure, in a month, you will be taking the scientists from Kew on a field trip to the location where you found your orchid."

Elizabeth could feel the blood rush to her head. Intensive training? Personal training? She decided it made no sense to ask for an explanation at this point. As with the Reckoning, only acceptance of the plan would do for now. Eventually, she would begin to understand, assuming she survived. She said, "And when will I see my classmates? How will I train in the Circle of Decision?"

"Elizabeth, you are no longer going to have classmates. You are no longer going to wear saffron. As we speak, Guru Marian has already had staff move your clothes and books to separate quarters on the campus. Before you leave here to go to the new building, you will change out of your saffron. Your classmates will only know that you are gone."

Naismith handed her a cardboard box tied with a string knotted on the top. Elizabeth stared down at the box lying flat in her hands and against her chest. Naismith waved his hands like an orchestra director and the string appeared to untie itself. He raised his left hand and the top of the box lifted on its own and gently fell to the floor. Inside the box was a heavy cotton shalwar kamiz in a shade of indigo like the colour of the early night sky. Not quite black, not quite blue. Light seemed to sink and disappear into the fabric.

Naismith said, "It is a special uniform. It is, in fact, a uniform made for combat. It is worn by a group in our community known as the Ravens. Now, I want you to go into that room and change. Put the clothes you are wearing into the box, cover it and tie the string." Naismith smiled. As she headed into the side room, he added, "Oh, and Elizabeth, once you have returned your saffron to the box, feel free to tie the strings without touching them."

Elizabeth went into the side room where Naismith directed. She pulled out the new uniform. She stripped off her saffron shalwar kamiz and was about to try on the new indigo uniform when she realized that under the new shalwar was a one-piece undergarment with multiple pockets sewn in the front, the sides and even the legs. Puzzled by this, Elizabeth held up the undergarment to the light and noticed that unlike her current set, this was cut for her quickly maturing woman's body. She blushed as she wondered who had noticed that she no longer had a plank-flat body. She hoped it was Guru Marian, but she suspected all of the instructor cadre had noticed. When she tried on the new underwear, it fit perfectly in all the right places. She couldn't help herself. She tried a few yoga and martial arts exercises and realized that for the first time since she started wearing a school uniform, she felt completely free in her clothes. For Elizabeth, it was truly the first time since she had been a child in simple shalwar kamiz that she felt...liberated.

Next came the indigo trousers. Unlike her saffron trousers, they were less baggy in the legs and had belt loops rather than a drawstring. Inside the box was a leather belt, more like the belts she saw her father wear than anything she might have seen on a woman. She laced the belt through the loops on the trousers and tightened the cinch. The trousers now fit precisely on her waist with just enough looseness around the pelvis and thighs to let her continue to move through her exercise routine.

Finally, she pulled out the overshirt. Not exactly like a standard Indian kamiz which would reach to her knees. And, not exactly like an English blouse. Instead, the length seemed more like the shirts she used to wear tucked into her jodhpurs while riding. At mid-thigh, the shirt covered the top of her trousers and her belt. Also, instead of a garment she had to pull over her head, the shirt closed in the front with six fabric buttons in the same indigo shade.

Just before she put her arm in the left sleeve, she noticed tucked inside the shirt an indigo hood which would cover her hair but not her face. It was nothing like the hood on her wool jacket that protected her from the cold wind, rain and snow in England. Instead, it was almost as thin as the finest linen she had ever worn. Before putting the shirt on, Elizabeth held it up to the light of solar lamp. It was as if the light disappeared into the shirt. She found the entire outfit stunning, fascinating, and puzzling all at once. Precisely what did any of this have to do with espionage? In what sort of combat actions did intelligence officers perform? And who were the Ravens?

As she put the shirt on, she decided there were too many questions to sort out at present. She would have to wait until she could ask Guru Marian.

The last items out of the box were a pair of cloth boots with rubber soles. Also dyed indigo. Elizabeth tried them on and, again, they fit perfectly. Before she put her saffron robes into the cardboard box, Elizabeth did a quick pirouette, worked through two yoga positions and sat on the floor in the modified lotus position she had learned from Guru Marian. She was comfortable, so she took a moment to relax her breathing and recite the mantra that her gurus had taught her.

Guru Marian and Guru Naismith were watching from a hidden window that used a set of mirrors to observe Elizabeth's room. Marian turned to Naismith and said, "Master Guru, I know she is physically ready. Do you think she is mentally prepared?"

Naismith smiled and said, "Look into the room."

Marian looked into the room to see Elizabeth, eyes closed, in a full lotus position and levitating gently six inches above the oriental carpet. Marian gasped, "I haven't taught her that yet."

"I suspect she hasn't realized she is doing it. We will have time to teach her control, but we do not have much time. She has the mental gift. With this one, we do not have to forge a blade, we simply have to sharpen the blade. Let's see if she decides to try to tie the string without touching the string. I suspect she is far more advanced than either of us realized."

After finishing her meditation, Elizabeth neatly folded her saffron uniform into the box, put the top on the box and then puzzled over the string. She waved her hands imitating Guru Naismith's action. Nothing happened. She stared at the string as if it was a recalcitrant pet. Nothing happened. Finally, Elizabeth just sat down next to the box, closed her eyes, and measured her breathing that way that Guru Marian had taught her.

From the observation window, Naismith whispered to Marian, "Let's see what happens now."

The two ends of string came to life as they crawled up the side of the box. Just as they were about to merge, Elizabeth opened her eyes and the string stopped moving. She said to herself, "Well, isn't that odd."

Elizabeth found herself wondering if she had entered some sort of world imagined by Lewis Carroll. Had she passed through the looking glass when she entered the college? Now, so many things that she thought she knew "for a fact," were instead simply points of view in a much more complex reality. Elizabeth shook her head, stood up, tied the string in a bow and walked out the door and into Guru Naismith's office. She saw Marian and Naismith standing in front of the teak desk that served as Naismith's workspace at the school.

Naismith offered no sign that he and Marian had been observing their young charge. "Elizabeth, from now on, Guru Marian will be your guide. Guru Standish and my good self will join you for specific training, but Marian will be your teacher as well as your mentor. She will take you to another location in the college and from there you will be studying until the arrival of the Kew researchers. When they arrive, you will take them to the location in the mountains where you discovered the rare orchid. After that…well, after that, we shall see."

Elizabeth offered a bow with her hands at her side, keeping her eyes on the Master Guru in the manner taught at the school and reinforced in the Circle of Decision. You never took your eyes off anyone, friend or foe. "I will do my best, Master Guru."

"I have no doubt, Elizabeth. I do want to let you know that this training is something that we impart to students with special talents that need to be nurtured. We have not had such a student for some time." Naismith paused trying to decide what he would say next. Eventually, he said,

"Elizabeth, you are going to learn many techniques that are central to the world of espionage. These are techniques that have been used for centuries both in the West and here in the East when the world was filled with less technology and innovation. Central to these techniques are two fundamental principles: pay attention to the little details that people reveal about themselves; and pay attention to the world around you so that you can remain safe."

Elizabeth did not know what to say. These principles seemed obvious to her. She said, "Yes, Guru Naismith."

"Now Elizabeth, I know you think these are simple principles that everyone knows. In fact, the majority of people do not follow these principles. They engage others with preconceived notions of who they are or their place in society. They do not pay attention to the person in front of them, seeing that person only with regard to their place in society or their job. And, when they don't pay attention to the people around them, they stop paying attention to the world that is filled with opportunities and with threats. These are the basics."

Elizabeth nodded.

"Elizabeth, the training you are starting is designed to enhance your skills. And, you have exceptional skills, I might add. We are going to train you to use your mind in ways that most people would find impossible or, when they see the ways with their own eyes, they insist it is some magic trick. Indeed, we will teach you some magic tricks for your work, but the real magic will be based on skills that have been passed down from masters in the East. Centuries of knowledge on how to master the power of the mind. Skills used by warrior monks in Japan, in China, in Tibet and here in India. You have seen the book on your shelf titled *Athrashashtra*, no?"

Elizabeth nodded.

"This is a book designed to guide the princes of India. It is a book of how to govern. It is also a book that describes our trade and how we may be used. It is only one of the books of Asia that you will study now. You will study the translated works of the Chinese military philosopher Sun Tzu and scrolls from Tibetan Buddhist masters, texts from Japanese shadow warriors and even works by Persian Sufis. They all offer insights into the mind, Elizabeth." Naismith paused and then said, "You started on the path today when you moved the strings on the box without touching them. It is a simple trick, but that is how these skills start. Small acts. Simple acts. Eventually, practice opens the mind to other skills. Now go with Guru Marian. Please work as hard as you can."

Elizabeth did not know if she was expected to say anything, so she said nothing. She offered another bow.

As she did, she received a simple instruction from Marian. "Elizabeth, follow me."

Elizabeth had expected to return to the regular classrooms in the college that had been her home for the previous term. Instead, Marian moved one of the bookshelves. Behind the bookshelf was a door. She opened the door and led Elizabeth down two flights of stairs in the cadre building. As Marian and Elizabeth disappeared down the stairs, Naismith closed the door and moved the bookcase back into position. He returned to his desk and a cup of green tea. He was pleased to see Elizabeth willing to accept the first steps into the mysteries of the mountains. He remembered his own introduction. He had not been as accepting.

Dark Magic

12 September 1883 — Kathmandu

QUEEN'S COMMISSIONED OFFICER CAPTAIN BURGESS MAKEPEACE NAISMITH was seated in his tent on the outskirts of Kathmandu looking at a sketch map of the region north of the city. A newly minted Captain in the 5th Gurkha Rifles, Naismith's instructions were to leave the Rifles' headquarters in Abbottabad, travel to Kathmandu and engage the Gurkha recruitment team. The Rifles had just expanded to include a second battalion and headquarters wanted someone from the unit to take a hard look at the Gurkha recruitment process.

For all of the accolades received during the Second Afghan War, the 5th Gurkha Rifles were not the only, or even the most famous, inside the Gurkha Regiment. The commander, Lieutenant Colonel Fitzhugh, needed a man who could speak the local language and who knew enough about the Army to report on whether *his Rifles* were getting their fair share of good recruits. After a month in Kathmandu, Naismith was bored with his mission. He could see that all of the

Nepali recruits were worth the Queen's salt and any recruit who ended up in the 5th Rifles would be a good soldier. When he sent that dispatch back to Abbottabad, the return post instructed him to stay in place until the recruitment season was over. That would mean staying in Kathmandu until October. Naismith interpreted that to mean he could do some exploring on his own, so long as he returned before the winter snows closed the passes.

Seated next to Naismith was a retired Gurkha non-commissioned officer, in Indian Army parlance a halvidar. Halvidar Gurung had been essential in sorting out for Naismith what was and was not recruitment policy for Gurkhas. In the process, he displayed a degree of earnestness that Naismith recognized as a trait that helped explain why the Gurkhas were such successful soldiers. Every Gurkha was instructed from day one that success in every task, no matter how trivial, served to prove to all and sundry the honour of the Gurkhas. Slackers were simply returned to their villages in short order. Now, Naismith had given retired Halvidar Gurung a new tasking and Gurung was determined to exceed Naismith's expectations.

Gurung said "There is a simple ride north from town. It is the traders' route into Tibet. Of course, there is a mountain pass that we must not cross at this time of year, but we can enjoy a few days ride, we can do some hunting, and then return. You might even see a trader willing to sell his goods or, perhaps, one of the gurus of the mystic way."

"Mystic way?" Naismith grew up in a community of Hindu sadhus living on the gifts from the faithful and practicing a number of different yogic arts that seemed magical until you learned the trick. Naismith had gained the trust of several of these sadhus. They had taught him the way of an open-hand martial art and how to use a ribbon sword which looked like a simple rope belt. He also learned more than a few magic tricks from travelling Sufis. In fact, his preferred mode of reconnaissance in Afghanistan and on the Indian frontier was disguised as a Sufi traveler. Even after all of these years of study, he had not heard of this mystic way. He asked, "What mystic way?"

"Captain, you do not want to know more. These Tibetan mystics, they follow a dark path in Buddhism. It is said they can do powerful magic, they bring dead men to life, they kill men at a distance, and they can fly."

Naismith smiled and said, "I would very much like to fly. My feet get tired of walking."

"Do not joke, Captain. These monks can fly and they do so using cadaver parts and a mystic knife known as a *phurba*. It is a dark magic."

"Halvidar Gurung, between you and I, I doubt any man can threaten us."

"This is not something I wish to test, Captain."

As Halvidar Gurung promised, the ride out of Kathmandu was pleasant. They did find game to shoot and enjoyed nights where a campfire and the bright stars in the sky were their only light. It was not exactly as exciting as some of the reconnaissance work that Naismith did in Afghanistan or on the frontier, but it was very interesting as they approached each high plateau and looked out on grasslands to their front and the great mountains of the Gods, the Himalayan Giants to the east. Naismith enjoyed travelling with Gurung and listened carefully as the retired soldier related his experiences serving the Crown.

One morning as they were breaking camp, Naismith saw a figure in the distance, coming from Tibet and moving at an incredible pace. Naismith pulled out his binoculars and started to track the man as he approached. It seemed as if the man was running or leaping or, perhaps, both. The distances he covered in a single bound seemed impossible. Naismith called out to Halvidar Gurung, "Gurung Ji, what is this?"

"Sir, I mentioned these mystics from Tibet. This one is practicing what is called *lung gom pa*. The mystics use the technique to cover great distances between the various monasteries. This one must be a novice, a *naljorpa*, on a pilgrimage to the Tibetan Buddhist monastery near Kathmandu. Please do not engage him, sir. It is too dangerous."

Naismith watched as the man continued toward their camp. He seemed to be carrying a staff in one hand and a brass knife in another. His pace was as disciplined as any military march, but Naismith could see that he was covering over twenty feet with each step. The mystic wasn't running or jumping or bounding to cover these distances. He seemed to be walking but each step covered twenty feet. Naismith could not help himself. He placed himself in the mystic's path. Recognizing that Naismith fully intended to stop the mystic, Gurung ran to prevent the interruption. He arrived just as the mystic landed a few feet from Naismith. "Sir, stand clear. He is dangerous!" Just as Gurung said this, the mystic swept the staff in his right hand in front of him as if to clear the way. Though he did not touch Gurung, the old Gurkha dropped to the ground. Naismith had seen more than enough dead bodies in his years as a soldier. He recognized immediately that Gurung was dead. He turned to the mystic and pulled out his revolver. His only thought was vengeance.

The mystic was now close enough that Naismith could see him more clearly. Clad in brown woolen robes, the shaved-headed mystic looked to be in his mid-twenties. He was barefoot and carried no bag for food or water. Naismith also recognized the staff that the mystic was holding was clearly a long bone, the correct size and shape to be the leg bone of a man. Naismith's knowledge of human anatomy was limited, but it seemed certain this was the femur of a man or a beast.

Naismith cocked his service revolver fully intending to shoot this man down for the crime committed seconds ago.

The mystic smiled and raised his left hand, palm skyward. In his palm was a foot-long brass knife balancing on its tip. The knife started to spin and Naismith could see three ghoulish heads carved into the hilt. Naismith could hear nothing, but in his head, he felt a terrible pain. He fell to his knees as he dropped his revolver. A calm voice from inside his head said, "You will not die today, soldier. You will go with me. You will disappear now for a time. When you reappear, you will no longer dismiss the power of the mystic path. And, if you are lucky, you might even learn something."

Naismith struggled to speak. It was difficult, but he finally said, "You killed him!"

"Who, soldier?"

"Halvidar Gurung. I saw you kill him."

"Look again, soldier. What do you see?"

Naismith looked down. Gurung's body was nowhere to be seen. He looked up and Gurung was breaking camp as if nothing had happened. He didn't appear to be aware that Naismith was on his knees crying for help.

"Soldier, he cannot hear you because you are not speaking. Now, you will stand and follow me. You must keep up. You do not know how but you must." The mystic waved the bone in his right hand and Naismith rose as if in a trance. His revolver dragged behind him on its lanyard as he followed the priest. He could not understand how he was passing so quickly along the grasslands. It was almost as if he were flying. Much later, after lessons in a monastery near Kathmandu, he realized he was.

A Journey into Illusion

WHILE NAISMITH DRANK HIS TEA, PONDERING HIS OWN INTRODUCTION TO the mystic way, Marian and Elizabeth reached the bottom of the stairs and walked into a tunnel lighted by more of the solar lamps described as Naismith's invention. The glow of the lamps reflected off the polished stone walls and tiled floor. Marian turned to Elizabeth and said, "We have no time to spare, so run." Marian started a double-time pace that was just short of a sprint. Elizabeth matched her pace as they raced inside the tunnel. Elizabeth guessed it was a half hour before they stopped. She was breathing heavily though Marian seemed unaffected by the exertion.

Marian turned to Elizabeth and said, "I was practicing the act of not-running. It is called *lung gom pa* or control of the internal air. You were fighting the air as you ran. Movement for most people is a struggle that increases the faster they run or the higher they climb. We are going to teach you to

135

control the air around you so that you do not struggle. Soon it will be easy."

Elizabeth nodded as she caught her breath. She understood training and how a person improved as they trained. Certainly, this must be just another level of that training. Elizabeth did not want to appear foolish, so she said between deep breaths, "Yes...Guru...Marian."

They stood before a ten-foot-tall iron door covered with what Elizabeth now knew was Tibetan Buddhist iconography. Saints and demons looked down on Marian as she pulled the bolt open. Out of the corner of her vision, Elizabeth thought she saw the eyes of one of the iron images look down on her. "A trick of the light," she said to herself. At this point, Elizabeth was too tired to even worry if she was looking at real demons.

Marian opened the door and Elizabeth saw a scene of the foothills of the snow-capped Himalayas. She was standing on the path that she had taken on one of her field trips. When she followed the path from the college, it had taken her a half day to get to this spot. Through the tunnel, through the center of the mountain, it took 30 minutes. She looked back at the door to the tunnel. It was gone. All she faced was a sheer rock wall. The door was nowhere to be seen.

"Do not believe everything you see, Elizabeth. You are being trained to live in the shadow world of intelligence, where things are rarely what they appear to be. Turn back to the rock face. What do you see?"

Elizabeth turned back toward the place she was certain was the exit. She could not see any sign of a door, a hinge or even a crack in the rock wall. "I do not see anything but rock."

Marian passed a hand in front of Elizabeth's eyes and said again, "Now, what do you see?"

Elizabeth's jaw dropped as the rock wall appeared to dissolve before her eyes. The outside door was not iron. It was covered in a plaster that matched the rock around it, but now she could see the fine edge that made up the hinge where the door would open. "It's magic!"

"Elizabeth, this is not magic. It is simply illusion created by man. You were expecting a rock face so you saw a rock face. I just forced you to look away and suddenly you could see details that were there all along. We use illusion as a defense. In this trade, you are often alone with no hope of assistance. You will need to create illusions to stay alive. That is what I will teach you in the next six weeks."

"Illusion?"

"Here is another example, Elizabeth. Look down at your uniform. What do you see?"

Elizabeth was slightly frustrated with this child's game. She knew what she would see and prepared her response which she intended to begin with "my shoes, my trousers, my shirt…" But as she looked at her new uniform, she was surprised to see it had changed colour. Instead of indigo, it was now the colour of the rock face. A mix of grey, black, and brown with small green flecks just the colour of the lichen that was embedded into the rock face. Elizabeth said, "But, how?"

"How indeed, Elizabeth? You claim to be a naturalist. What has happened to your uniform?"

Elizabeth thought hard for a moment and then said, "The dye absorbs light differentially. Much like a raven's feathers. When you look at a raven one way, he seems black. From another direction, he seems blue. Sometimes grey. But this is far more dramatic. It is as if the uniform knew what colours surrounded it."

"Again, an illusion. We use weavers who are experts in their trade. They know how to build layers of cloth in our uniforms. These layers reflect different light in different environments. They also allow your uniform to be very flexible. I suspect you noticed that."

"Yes. So, the uniform is like a prism. It splits the light and appears to change colour when, in fact, it is not a single colour. Perhaps never a single colour. Our brains just think it is one colour."

"Elizabeth, that is your first lesson. Our job is to make others think one thing when we are doing another. Now, let's move quickly to your new quarters before the sun drops. This trail can be dangerous in the dark."

Airships to Afghanistan

Late March 1912 — Rawalpindi

FRANCIS AND MARY BANKROFT BEGAN THE DEPARTURE PROCESS. IT WAS NOT as if they could just disappear one night. Neighbors would talk, servants would talk. On the Raj Frontier, gossip was one of the mainstays of entertainment along with card games and illicit love affairs. The cantonment in Rawalpindi was a small bit of the Raj surrounded by a trading town with a mix of expatriates from Britain, China and Central Asia. Muslims, Sikhs, Hindus, and nomads who professed the Islamic faith but were truly animist passed along the Grand Trunk highway. In that mix were spies and informants, men and women willing to trade information for profit. If you wanted to disappear for a month, a season, or a year, you had to design a story that fit the natural flow of arrivals and departures and made sense to the entire community, both friend and foe.

For this reason, shortly after they received their tasking from Winslow-Heath, they told everyone they could, including their household staff, that they were receiving letters describing Mary's father as ill. After three weeks, the "news from England" said that her father was seriously ill and her mother needed their help. They would have to return to England. Of course, Mary's father and mother were in fine health. The last time they needed to disappear together, they had used the same story except it was Francis' parents who, in fact, had died in Calcutta years before. They received many condolences and promises to stay in touch through the mail, promises which would never be kept by either party. They paid their staff in advance for a year and instructed them to keep the house ready for them because they were certain they would return, but had no idea when. The household staff offered tears and promises to care for the house as their own. These were promises that both Francis and Mary were certain their staff would keep.

Their neighbours in the cantonment were very impressed when they saw the regimental commander's carriage arrive to take them to the airship port. Francis explained that Mary's family were well connected in Parliament and the commander had allowed them to travel by airship to the port of Karachi. After all, the airships traveled in all directions in support of the Raj, so why not carry a passenger with connections to Parliament? The regimental commander and his subordinate knew very well that they were not taking the Bankrofts to Karachi. This was not the first time they had disappeared.

The Bankrofts loaded their steamer trunks on the airship and took their positions in the passenger cabin, which had been cleared for them. After all, it would not do for some other military VIP to see where the couple would leave the airship. Certainly it would not be Karachi, Peshawar, or any of the standard military routes. The airship would be taking them deep into the foothills of the Himalayas. After that, the

Bankrofts would be on their own in the wild borderlands of Afghanistan.

Once the ship took off and the executive officer passed through the cabin to make sure everything was proper for these agents of the Empire, Francis turned to Mary and said, "I hope we made the right decision with Elizabeth. I think we should have taken this mission without her. Her training is not complete."

Mary placed her hands on her husband's cheeks and said, "My love, you have to trust Guru Naismith. If Elizabeth is not ready when we need her, then he won't send her. You need to know that both Naismith and Marian Sandusky have reported that Elizabeth is making progress at a speed that far exceeded our time in school."

"Dear, that would not be hard. I struggled in the college. I passed all the sections, eventually, but only through the help of Naismith and you."

"You were doing fine. You just had trouble concentrating in the final exercises. I blame myself for your lack of concentration. You were courting me, after all."

Francis blushed and said, "And I always wondered if you used the voice on me during those last weeks. You were always so good in the classes on mesmerism."

"And you were very good in classes on secret writing. No, I did not use mesmerism, I simply asked you to love me and you did! Now, Elizabeth is apparently well beyond simple mesmerism. They say she has moved to a level that we never achieved, a level of Tibetan mysteries that will help us along the way. They also said she has been trained in some sort of electronic wave communication. I know Mr. Marconi has sent messages to ships at sea, but I don't know if this will help us."

"So long as she is able to keep herself safe, I will be happy."

"Francis, you didn't ask her over Christmas, but I did. Her highest marks were in the Circle of Decision. She nearly accomplished guru status herself in the open-hand, dragon style of the martial arts before the term ended. I am sure her intensive training will make her more than capable."

Francis was already digging into his steamer trunk. He laid out three oil-cloth parcels and said, "I still prefer Mr. Colt's solutions. Especially now that the service has acquired his automatic pistol as well as his service revolvers." He unwrapped the parcels and displayed a dark blue automatic pistol: thin, easily concealed and deadly. Next to that were the two well-used Colt double-action service revolvers that Francis had carried for the past two years.

Mary remarked, "I hope you packed at least one of Mr. Colt's new pistols for me as well."

"Always dear. You know that I have wanted you to have a more robust cartridge for your weapon. The new Colt is the same size as your Browning but has a cartridge in caliber .380. I packed two for you. I also packed one for Elizabeth and a small revolver. I don't know if we will need them, but she will be prepared." Out of the steamer trunk came a leather rifle case. Inside was a German Mauser with a polished Mannlicher stock that ran to the end of the barrel. Francis had carried this rifle into Afghanistan many times. He handed Mary a smaller leather case and said, "I think you might find this interesting."

Mary opened the case to find a short-barreled weapon that looked like a shotgun, but with a much larger bore than anything she had seen. It was barely twice the length of the long-barreled, Colt revolvers that Francis carried. It looked more like the brass flare guns used in the British Navy to send signals between ships. The stock was beautifully carved and the barrel engraved with the broad arrow seal of the British Army and the phoenix which was the symbol of the Raj Military Intelligence Bureau. On examination, Mary realized that the bore was even larger than the guns her father had used duck hunting with Maharajas in the Punjab. "It is beautiful, but what is it?"

"It is a creation of the colonel's boffins, as he calls them. They said it fires a number of different cartridges. I only fired two when I picked it up. They were explosive charges and I was able to hit targets at a range just short of two hundred yards. They gave me a number of cartridges including explosives, smoke cartridges, a phosphorous cartridge that makes a large flash, and even two that are just shotgun pellets. I promised we would carry it with us and give it a test. They call it the hand cannon. By the way, they want it back. It is a prototype. One of only two in the entire Raj. If it is useful, they might issue it to the Gurkhas or the frontier scouts."

"You are certain it works?"

"It definitely works. I thought you might like it because of its size."

"You are so kind. I would prefer my Winchester carbine."

"And, indeed, your carbine is here as well!" He handed her another leather gun case.

"Enough of the guns. Any new toys?"

"Sadly, it appears that we have seen all the newest toys that come out of the colonel's quartermaster. We did get more of his potions. Oh, and one more thing for you from the same shop." He pulled out a thin wooden box and handed it to Mary.

She opened the box to find tucked inside the red satin interior a pair of tan leather gloves. She pulled out the gloves and noticed a heavy spring system placed on the underside of each glove. She pulled them on and carefully turned toward the window of the compartment. She flexed her left hand and the spring system pushed a thin wire club into her palm. She flexed her right hand and the glove delivered a needle-thin blade with a leather-wrapped handle. "I suspect these were both Badger's ideas?"

Francis knew that Professor Michael Budge-Lowe, the Bureau's experimental engineer, hated to be called Badger by anyone other than Mary. "Yes, dear. He made them just for you. Take care as you reload the spring. I tried a man's version and ended up sending the club across the room and out the window in Badger's laboratory. He wasn't pleased."

"I should think not." Mary carefully loaded the spring system and placed the gloves equally carefully back into the box. She knew Badger had a soft spot for his female agents and was always thinking of new defensive tools. At the end of the day, Mary preferred her mesmerism skills and her use of pressure points to disable the odd adversary. Still, one never knew.

They spent the next hour changing from the standard clothes worn by civil servants of the Raj into the travelling clothes they would wear for the first leg of their journey. Each had their one-piece inner garment with all their special tools, followed by their initial outer garments. Over that, Francis wore a leather jerkin vest which ran to mid-thigh and covered his Colt pistols in a pair of leather shoulder holsters. He added a leather bandolier with cartridges for the Mauser and a sheath for a Khyber knife. Finally, he donned a long Uzbek coat. In one of the pockets he placed his new Colt automatic in a thin leather holster. He put on his sheepskin cap and leather boots and looked at Mary. "All correct?"

"You wear the cap too far back on your head, but otherwise, all correct." Mary adjusted the cap. While Francis was putting on his clothes, Mary had donned her disguise. It was similar to the garb she used in Mesopotamia but topped with a heavy leather coat. Once fully attired, they sat side by side in the cabin watching snow-capped mountains approach. "This is the most beautiful view in the world," Mary said. "I wonder when the whole world will be travelling by airship."

"I think there will be a time in the future when that is the case, love," Francis mused. "For now, it remains the best possible way for the Empire to enforce the law in these remote mountains. For the present, only the British are using this design. We shall see. The designer is a German named Zeppelin. His own country has been slow to understand the value of these machines. I suspect the Germans will eventually understand. Then, they will give him a commission to make a fleet just like our own."

The hours passed gently as the airship engines ploughed the sky heading toward the remote Raj outpost of Chitral which had once been a kingdom in its own right. The princes of Chitral, sometimes willingly and sometimes unwillingly, acknowledged the Raj as their protector from Russian incursions as well as Afghan and Chinese bandits. The foothills of the Himalayas were still snow-covered and the roads to Chitral impassible. Those passes clogged with snow and ice seemed to drift by below the airship.

As the sun started to set in the west, the executive officer from the airship came down from the cockpit. Dressed in a navy-blue wool toggle coat, he looked like any other officer in the Royal Navy. When the armed airships were designed, the obvious service to take charge was the Navy. The airships were originally to be used as patrol craft for the coasts of the Empire. Now, they were essential to patrolling this remote area of the Indian Empire. The officer said, "Sir and Madam, we are approaching your drop-off location. Please follow me to the lower deck."

Francis and Mary shouldered the slings of their two gun cases and Francis picked up the two carpet bags that held the remaining items from the steamer trunks. The aircrew would return the steamer trunks to Regimental Headquarters for recovery when the Bankrofts returned.

They followed the executive officer through a polished oak door in the rear of the cabin leading to the more utilitarian engine deck. They continued on the circular metal staircase down to the combat deck where the airship's gunners manned water-cooled Maxim machine guns. The transition from the closed, formal cabin above through the noise of the steam-powered engines finally to the open combat deck was dramatic. The roar of the engines filled the lower deck. To survive the near-freezing cold of the open windows, the Maxim gunners were outfitted with specially designed, sheepskin-lined jackets and trousers. They wore leather helmets with integrated hearing protection and large, dark snow goggles. The goggles along with the bulbous, leather ear coverings gave each of the gunners the appearance of some sort of lizard man. As the Bankrofts walked down the stairs, passing from the hot engine room to the cold deck below, Mary could see the frost coming from the breath of the gunners.

The lieutenant shouted over the noise of the engine, "Major, we are approaching the drop off point. You will need to climb down the rope ladder because there is insufficient space to land our airship. Will Mrs. Bankroft be able to descend without assistance? We do have a rope chair that we can lower."

Mary turned to the executive officer and said, "Mrs. Bankroft has abseiled down a 100-foot Alpine cliff on a single rope, lieutenant. I believe I can handle a rope ladder."

Francis smiled and said, "Lieutenant, don't feel bad. She corrects me on a regular basis as well."

The lieutenant stood back as one of his crewmen opened the large, clam-shell cargo hatch in the rear of the cabin, revealing brilliant blue sky, snow-capped mountains and grey rocky terrain. Until they looked down, the image was one of a perfect painted canvas of the Himalayas. There was no sense of distance or height. When they did look over the edge, they saw a small outcrop on the edge of a cliff. On the outcrop were four horses and an armed man dressed in the same garb as the Bankrofts. Next to the man was a small box with red smoke swirling out and straight up into the sky toward the airship.

A bell rang and an electric light near the hatch turned from red to iridescent green. The airship came to a complete stop. The lieutenant turned to one of the crew and ordered, "Deploy the ladder for the officers and deploy the cargo." At his instruction, a leather-clad crewman leaned out over the opening to ensure the deployed line would not become wrapped around any of the steam-driven propellers or torn from the airship by some rock outcrop. Satisfied that the area was clear, he walked back into the cabin and checked the attachment point for both the rope ladder and a separate hawser that would be used to lower the carpet bags. Satisfied that both were well attached to the floor of the cabin, he tossed the rope ladder off the edge. Next, with the help of another crewman, he tied the two carpet bags and the gun cases to the hawser and lowered them to the ground. He laid on the floor of the cabin and watched as the man below untied the bags. Once clear, he stood and pulled the hawser back into the airship. He saluted the lieutenant.

The lieutenant then turned to the Bankrofts and said, "We recommend you sit on the deck, engage a lower rung with your feet and then push away from the deck. There will be a slight swaying motion initially and then your descent will be relatively stable as if you were climbing down a regular ladder.

Francis nodded to the lieutenant. "Ladies first," was all Francis said to Mary.

Mary nodded to the lieutenant. Instead of following his instructions and sitting on the deck, she took a short hop, grabbed the outside of the ladder with her riding boots and gloved hands and slid down the thirty feet to the ground in a few seconds. Francis turned to the lieutenant, shook his head and said, "My wife always has been a show-off. Please thank the captain for the ride. We shall see you in Rawalpindi."

He hopped off the deck and, using the same technique, disappeared over the side. He was on the ground in seconds as well. On landing, he waved to the crewman looking out over the hatch. Once Francis Bankroft was clear, the crewman pulled up the ladder. The airship's propellers started to turn and the black smoke from the steam engine poured out of the stacks on the underside of the airship. In a few seconds, the airship nose turned up, the ship turned south and headed to the next mission.

"Welcome, Baba Jan! Welcome. It has been too long since we worked together!" A bear of a man, clad in a sheepskin coat, karakul sheepskin hat and knee high riding boots walked forward and hugged Francis. "We have work to do so there is no time for tea, but tonight we will have a feast and enjoy our time together."

Francis turned to Mary and said, "Mary, I am pleased to introduce you to Abdul Rashid Jowzjani, expert horse thief and the best shot in Northern Afghanistan. My very best colleague in the North. Abdul, please welcome my wife, Mary. She is one of us."

Jowzjani bowed and said in exceptionally formal, British-accented English, "Madam, it is my pleasure. I heard of your successes well before I started working with Francis. I hope you will tell me tales of adventure tonight. After that, we will be with others who are not to be trusted. We will have to assume our roles as returning horse salesmen or, as Francis so accurately stated, horse thieves. I know Francis speaks Dari and Russian. You?"

Mary responded in unaccented Uzbek, "The pleasure is all mine!"

Jowzjani smiled, revealing white teeth below his enormous black mustache. "We shall be good friends, I know this for sure." He turned and mounted his white stallion as easily as if he was taking a seat in a dining room chair. Francis tied their carpet bags to the pack horse, and then both he and Mary mounted their stallions. They settled into the Central Asian saddles made from wooden frames covered by beautifully woven carpet squares. Their brass stirrups were carved and their bridles decorated with carpet remnants of red and black. They moved off in a single file along a path that was barely wide enough for a man but somehow the horses found their way as they headed west into Afghanistan.

As the sun began to set behind the Hindu Kush mountains, revealing the glacier peaks of the Pamirs to the east, Abdul Rashid led them down a narrow valley to a small encampment that he established hours before meeting them at the airship. He had set up two canvas tents facing east. A small fire pit still glowed from earlier in the day. They dismounted, took the saddles and pack saddles off their horses, lightly combed the horses dry and hobbled them on a small grassy field behind the tents. Abdul Rashid took one of the leather water jugs from the pile near the pack saddles and filled a series of small, rubber nesting buckets to water the horses. Each animal was allowed to drink exactly the same amount before its meal.

As he cared for the horses, he said to Mary, "You know we have to be sure they stay staked out tonight. These stallions will fight all night if we let them get too close to each other." Mary nodded. She hadn't ridden stallions before. Even the Army mounts were geldings or mares. She noticed as they were riding on the trail that her stallion tried repeatedly to bite the rump of the horse in front of her, while defending himself against the attempts at biting by Francis' horse behind her.

Francis reset the fire from branches of the dwarf trees that surrounded the campsite. Mary took their canvas bags into one of the tents, set up their sleeping bags so that their heads would be away from the tent entrance, and placed their rifles within easy reach in case they were disturbed that night. She also placed next to each bag another new device from the office of the quartermaster. Based on the recent invention by David Misell, they were called battery torches. They looked much like the lanterns used by miners, but instead of the small oil lamp, the base of the torch had a Columbia dry-cell battery which provided a charge to a vacuum tube set inside a mirror so that the lantern sent out a directed beam of light.

Previous light bulbs had been too fragile to take to the field and, without an electric power source, of no great use. Apparently, the quartermaster laboratory had experimented with different materials for the filament, as it was known. They found tungsten was less fragile and provided a brighter light. Mary had tested the lights in Rawalpindi. Even more than the new weapons, she thought these electric torches were the most important tool the quartermaster could have provided. As she had several times in the last decade, she marveled at the changes in their life in this new century.

Once they were settled, Abdul Rashid served them an Afghan stew made of apricots and lamb. He baked simple flat bread on a flat piece of iron placed right on the fire. After dinner, they sat by the fire, drank tea and watched as the night sky turned from mauve to purple to jet black. First the planets started to appear and then a few stars and eventually the entire Milky Way spread across the sky. By the time the stars were fully out, Mary had returned to the tent leaving the two men to share stories of past adventures and plans for future successes.

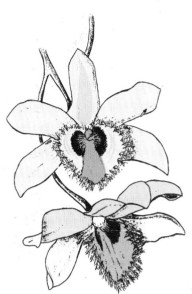

Cabins on a Mountain Trail

Late March 1912 — The Viceroy's College, Nathiagali cabin

ELIZABETH'S PROGRESS DURING HER ONE-ON-ONE SESSIONS WITH MARIAN was as Naismith had expected. Within a few weeks, she became an expert climber and, with the assistance of Guru Standish, she quickly gained skills in pistol, rifle, crossbow and knife. Between these lessons, Marian began to teach Elizabeth the ancient Tibetan ways of mesmerism. She also taught Elizabeth a class in camouflage, though to Elizabeth, it almost seemed as if she was being taught some magic on how to be invisible. She struggled to cope with these new ideas of how she could bend nature to her advantage. It was a difficult task to change her expectations of natural philosophy, where laws were immutable and humans had no effect on these laws.

Marian responded with the same argument every time. "Elizabeth, there is no such thing as magic. There is simply advanced science. Especially advanced science of the mind. The mystics who lived in these mountains did not have the engineering marvels of our culture, but they did have something else. They had time. With few distractions, they used their time to develop their minds in ways that we have not. We have taught you the power of meditation. It clears the mind. Ordinary people — who live their daily lives, working, raising families, and enjoying what seems to them a normal life — have minds cluttered with people, places, and things. The gurus in these mountains focused on what they would call enlightenment. They focused on emptying that clutter. I am not going to teach you enlightenment. That is up to you. What I am teaching you is how to empty the clutter. Once it is gone, I expect you will be able to expand the power of your mind."

Elizabeth listened and learned. But what she knew of natural philosophy and science made one thing more obvious to her with each passing day: Marian was teaching magic.

Their quarters for this part of Elizabeth's training were a pair of rustic cabins on a remote mountain trail. Each cabin had a bedroom, little more than a monk's garret, a training room which in Elizabeth's cabin doubled as her study, and a kitchen that served as a dining room. The cabins were heated by wood stoves which doubled as cooking stoves. One of Elizabeth's duties each day was to bring wood from the woodpile into both cabins and maintain the fires that kept them warm. The basic food supply was delivered once a week by two soldiers from Ft. Burnes. These supplies were stacked along the far wall of the kitchen and in cabinets around the stove. Elizabeth watched as each day the supplies dwindled until the next resupply from Ft. Burnes. It was, in that sense, an uncomplicated life. In another sense, Elizabeth's life was complicated beyond her previous understanding. Each day was filled with a mix of skills training and reading.

At the college, Sundays had been set aside for contemplation and personal time. In Elizabeth's new world, it meant another day of training with slightly more time between lessons to think about her future assignment as an agent for the Empire. On this Sunday, Marian and Elizabeth were sitting in the study as Marian continued the class on mesmerism. She explained how it could be used during intelligence collection, especially while debriefing individuals who might not be entirely truthful. "Elizabeth, the reason we teach you mesmerism is to control how you are perceived by the outside world. It is a world filled with allies, neutrals and adversaries. Unfortunately, at first you may not know who is friend and who is foe. So, you need to control how you want to be perceived. You must be certain that you have some degree of control over individuals you meet. It is about controlling your own mind, but also about controlling the minds of those around you. We do that through many techniques." Marian paused to watch the aura around her acolyte. A green-blue hue around Elizabeth's head and shoulders argued Elizabeth was ready to receive the next lesson.

"First, we create an impression in the target's mind as to what or who you are. We do that through the clothes we wear and how we walk, how we talk, and how we act. Think of that as camouflage the same way animals camouflage themselves in the wild. If and when needed, we use mesmerism to enhance that view. *IF* you do this correctly, you will disappear in the target's mind. Of course, you don't disappear, but the man, though it won't always be a man who is your adversary, will believe you have disappeared. After that, it is just a matter of controlling his mind through your voice and your actions."

Elizabeth resisted at first. "Marian, I have been raised in natural philosophy, in what is becoming known as the scientific method. As natural philosophers we don't perceive the world. We observe the world. It is one of the reasons why I found the orchid."

"Indeed, Elizabeth. It is one of the reasons why you have a great future as an intelligence officer. You observe the world in detail. Many do not look as carefully. Most don't have the mental strength you own. Most people walk through the world focusing only those things they care about. They see the world through a lens of self-delusion. They don't look left, they don't look right, and they definitely do not look up. They don't observe, they only perceive. They would say they see the world as it is. In fact, they see their own creation of the world. That self-creation is a very small part of the real world because it fails to see the links among all living things and even between living things and inanimate objects."

Marian realized that Elizabeth's aura was transitioning from blue-green to green-yellow. She was still resisting the concept.

Marian continued, "First and foremost, I am teaching you to guide their thoughts so that the world they see is not as it is, but as you want them to *believe* it is. Once you have that control, you will be a better and safer agent of the Empire. You won't lose your ability to observe the world. Instead, you will have the ability to control the way others see the world. Further, when you are debriefing a contact, you will have a better understanding of what that contact is offering. Is it truth, half-truth, or falsehood? You will know even before the contact decides to lie to you. And, with the mesmerism skills you are learning, you can force the contact to tell you why he is lying."

Marian paused and decided to fold one lesson on another. "Now, I want you to concentrate, close your eyes, and then tell me everything you have seen in the classroom, down to the smallest detail."

Elizabeth had faced this same challenge every day for the past two weeks. Sometimes it was when they were out riding or walking, sometimes at the evening meal, sometimes outside in the pitch dark with only the light from the stars. It was an exercise designed to enhance Elizabeth's observation skills and her memory. Elizabeth assumed this time it would be easy. After all, Marian was asking her to describe where she lived and the room where she spent hours every day.

She closed her eyes and said, "The room has a table and two chairs against the wall. It has an oil lamp and two windows with drapes. In the ceiling of is one of Guru Naismith's solar lights. The wooden floor is covered with an Afghan carpet in reds, blues and golds. The design is what you have taught me is the design of the Yomut Turkistani tribe. On the table are two of my notebooks, a pencil, a pen and an inkwell. In the corner of the room is my locker. The doors are closed. Next to the locker are my crossbow and my rifle as well as my field pack. The pack is closed. The space where we are standing is approximately ten feet by ten feet. We are standing two feet apart. Do you want to know what is inside the locker and the pack?"

"No, just continue with what you could see."

Elizabeth paused. She thought she had described everything in the room. Then she said, "There are new things in the room!"

Marian smiled. She said in a quiet voice, "Continue."

"On the floor next to my pack is a leather-bound book. It has engraving on the cover and on the spine. The title is in some script that I don't know. I do not know what it says."

"Good. What else?"

"At the end of the carpet is a small knife about the size of the palm of my hand. It is made of brass. It has a triangular blade and it has….it has a demon's head on each of the three sides of the knife. It is a spirit knife like my father keeps in his study. He says it brings us good luck."

"Perhaps an exaggeration, Elizabeth. What it may do is ward off negative energy. That energy might be called evil spirit or misfortune. You have to make your own luck. Anything else?"

Elizabeth concentrated. "There is a small canvas bag leaning up against the door of my locker. I had not noticed it before."

As Elizabeth concentrated with her eyes closed, Marian noticed that her pupil was beginning to levitate off the floor. This was not the first time she had seen Elizabeth do this over the past month. Just a few inches, but still something she had not seen in a student before and something that took Marian years of practice to accomplish. Naismith had said that the only student he had who could levitate without years of practice was James O'Connell. Given the recent news Naismith provided that O'Connell was missing and possibly had defected to the Germans, Marian was not certain that any of this offered good fortune for Elizabeth or the school.

"Elizabeth, I want you to open your eyes slowly. Don't move. Just look at me when you open your eyes."

Elizabeth did as she was told. In Marian's palm was the spirit knife balanced on its point and spinning clockwise, apparently of its own accord. As the knife turned, the carved faces of the three spirits seemed to be alive and looking at Elizabeth. As she stared at the knife, she realized she was floating about a foot off the ground. Her concentration broke and she dropped sufficiently hard that she nearly fell to her knees. "What in the world happened?"

"My dear, you are learning to fly. So far, you are only beginning to fight gravity, but if you practice, you will first be able to leap great distances."

"How? How can this be? And how did you make the spirit knife spin?"

"As I said, we know from the mystics there are energy links among all things, living and inanimate. Some individuals, through powers of concentration, tap into that energy. Clearly, you came to the school with some inherent power. I cannot give you a scientific explanation at this point because we have not been able to design an experiment that measures this energy or how it can be manipulated. Members of the college have been experimenting for years. So far, we haven't been able to design instruments to capture the information. I know we will eventually succeed, but for now, I only know our minds can use that power to defeat gravity."

"You can do this?"

Marian smiled, "You saw me do this on your first day at the College. It is most helpful when climbing stairs or, for that matter, climbing mountains."

"But Guru Marian, gravity! I know that we are bound by gravity."

"Elizabeth, we are only bound by these laws of gravity because your mind tells you we are bound by gravity. The mind is powerful. If it says you cannot do something, then you cannot. However, if you free your mind and expand your skills, your mind will allow you to free yourself from limitations that you have set for yourself."

Elizabeth shook her head. It seemed so…impossible. She said, "Guru Marian, I am confused. What does your mind have to do with the physical world?"

"Confusion is the only possible emotion if you allow yourself to live in a world constructed by limitations. Let me show you an example."

Marian turned the palm of her hand and the spirit knife left her palm, flew across the room and settled gently next to Elizabeth's notebooks. There was a noise in the kitchen. A drawer opened. Suddenly a spoon flew out of the kitchen and landed in the palm of Marian's right hand. Marian held the handle of the spoon between her thumb and forefinger and extended her arm toward Elizabeth. Showing no sign of effort, Marian concentrated on the spoon and it began to bend until the spoon curled around her forefinger. While it was moving, the spoon acted alive, almost like a snake with the bowl of the spoon as its head and the end of the spoon held by Marian its tail. When she was finished, Marian slid the curled spoon off her fingers. She stroked the spoon once with her left hand and it returned to its original shape. Elizabeth watched the demonstration with her mouth wide open.

"Is this real or is it some mesmerism skill you are using on me?"

"Elizabeth, the answer is yes to both parts of your question. Please don't dismiss the possibility that there might be a scientific explanation that you don't yet understand. There are many things that you can do, many more things that you will observe, and even more things that you can make someone else see, smell, feel or think."

"But…"

"Elizabeth, just accept what you saw as real for the moment. Explanations will follow. We need to continue the lesson."

"How do I get better at this? What do I need to do?"

"Elizabeth, Guru Naismith is a scientist, an inventor, and a medical doctor. He spent years studying the teachings of Hindu Sadhus and Tibetan Buddhists and many more years studying the importance of espionage in ancient India. It is written in the *Athrashastra* sitting on your bookshelf. It is also written in the Tibetan text known as *Hevajra Tantra*. We may have time to study them together, but if not, you should study them on your own. When he first taught me these skills, he said that it was not magic. Instead, it was using more of your mind to engage the powers that link all things. The human brain is a magnificent machine." Marian paused, turned her palm and the spoon shot across the room, back into the kitchen and Elizabeth heard the drawer close.

"Nearly all people use so little of the true capability of their minds. We are teaching you to use more of your brain. The problem you face is that you can't do anything to improve on this ability. If you focus on doing, you will fail. You have to empty your mind and focus on not doing. That is why we teach you in first term to meditate. Meditation is all about emptying and opening the mind. Let your mind wander free. Let it fly on its own. Then you will be able to free yourself from what you think are boundaries in this world. It is the portion of your mind that is trained in hard science that is holding you back. The more you think, the less you will succeed. We do not want you to stop thinking like a natural philosopher. We simply want you to be able to switch from one part of your mind to another. When you switch, you will remove as many boundaries of your mind as possible."

Marian paused and said, "You are familiar with Isaac Newton, correct?"

"Of course. He was one of the early natural philosophers who began the study of gravity."

"Indeed. He was also something of a mystic and an alchemist. He was convinced that there was a means of transforming one material into another. Often it is simplified as turning iron into gold, which you know is impossible. But, with what we know today about chemistry, we know that chemical reactions do change materials. In Newton's day, what we know today would have been considered alchemy or, possibly, black magic. So, boundaries are often limitations that prevent you from seeing and doing things that you might otherwise accomplish. I am working at teaching you to avoid creating artificial boundaries. You will soon graduate from the college. The Crown needs your skills."

Marian could see she had completely confused her young charge. Her aura was now a golden yellow. It did not mean she was hostile to the idea, merely confounded by the improbability of the discussion. It was hard enough for Marian to understand how she herself did this after years of concentration. She had been exposed to Naismith's training when she was in her twenties. Marian could imagine how hard it would be for a girl still in her teens. She decided to change pace while working the same subject. "Elizabeth, it is time for us to practice additional self-defense skills. Ready?"

Elizabeth smiled. She was always ready for this mix of fighting skills they were teaching her. She expected Marian to pull out the drawing of the human body that identified the pressure points. She was learning which points were used to numb, which to disable and, if needed, which to strike in order to kill. Instead, she noticed Marian picking up the canvas bag that was leaning against Elizabeth's locker.

Elizabeth bowed to her guru and said, "I am ready."

Marian pulled out a three-foot-long bamboo pole with one end wrapped in a thin band of canvas, providing an excellent grip. It reminded Elizabeth of the wooden poles called lathis used by the garrison police to control crowds. Marian grabbed the wrapped end and started to swing the pole back and forth as she came closer and closer to Elizabeth. Suddenly she spun in a circle and swung the pole from right to left at Elizabeth's feet. Before Elizabeth could think, she had jumped just high enough to avoid being struck by the pole.

Marian nodded. "Excellent. Again."

This time she swung the pole from left to right approximately a foot higher. Again, Elizabeth's leap was just high enough to avoid the strike. Marian dropped the striking end of the pole to the ground, tapped it twice and then swung the pole at Elizabeth's waist, far higher than Elizabeth could jump. This time Elizabeth flew straight up and almost hit the ceiling of the training room as the pole passed below her. Elizabeth landed crouched on her feet with one hand on the floor.

"You see! You can fly when you need to, but not when you want to."

Elizabeth was out of breath. Before she could recover, Marian swung the pole directly at Elizabeth's head. Elizabeth didn't know what to do when the pole came straight down.

She cringed at the thought of the bamboo pole striking her in the head or the shoulders. She formed a cross with her hands above her head with her palms facing the pole in an attempt to deflect the blow. Instead, the pole stopped an inch from her hands and flew straight back almost pushing Marian over with the force of the move. Marian smiled and said, "And that, Elizabeth, is a skill that you have that no one can teach. You have found the ability to move objects with your mind. Guru Naismith sensed you had the ability."

"But I didn't do anything."

"Exactly. Again, this was about not thinking, not doing. Please observe." Marian dropped the pole on the floor. She looked at the pole and then looked to the far wall. The pole stood up on one end and appeared to jump on its own into the canvas bag. Then, the bag moved across the room to the wall next to her locker. As Elizabeth watched, the top of the bag closed on its own and the bag and its contents seemed to pass through the wall of the training room and disappear.

"Where did it go?"

"Elizabeth, where did what go? Did you ever see the pole? Was it all an illusion? Or did you make it disappear?"

Elizabeth shook her head. She was tired from the events of the day, and this little bit of exercise had been surprisingly difficult. She only managed a croak as she said, "What is happening, Guru Marian?"

Marian smiled and said, "That is enough work and enough questions for today. Now, we must return to the world as others see it. You need to prepare for the arrival of the botanists who are coming from the Royal Botanical Gardens at Kew. They will arrive in one week and we must accomplish much before they arrive. You will guide them to where you found your orchid. We will walk on the trail and they will follow us on horseback. They will not be able to walk as easily as we will because they will not be used to the altitude. Remember your first day at college? Now, please return to your desk and continue your writing on your natural history observations. You will need to provide those observations to the men from Kew. Meanwhile, I will make us dinner and we can eat while we watch the sunset."

Elizabeth walked to the desk at the end of the training room, sat down, and opened her notebooks. Once she heard Marian beginning to cook at the stove, she walked quietly toward the corner of the room where the canvas bag had been. She stopped to look for some secret door that she missed before. No door, no window, no compartment. She wondered where the bag had gone. She walked to the door of the training room and peeked into the kitchen. There, leaning against the wall, was the canvas bag with the handle of the bamboo pole sticking out. As Elizabeth returned to her desk, Marian smiled and continued to make dinner. She wondered how long it would be before Naismith came to the cabin and began intensive training of his new student.

01 April 1912 — The Viceroy's College

Naismith sat in his office reading Marian Sandusky's reports on Elizabeth Bankroft. He was pleased and not terribly surprised at her progress. From his first encounter with the young girl, he sensed a level of mental energy that he rarely saw in others. The girl developed quickly but he wondered if she was developing quickly enough. Winslow-Heath's instructions were clear. She had to be ready in the next few weeks. There was so much to teach her and so little time. The mystic arts required a very specific training regimen.

First, revelation. The student had to be introduced to the arts, and the introduction had to proceed in a way that would be acceptable to the student. In the case of Elizabeth, Marian and Naismith had agreed to explain the arts as extensions of the natural world.

Next would come practice. Starting with small elements of the mystic arts such as telekinesis, telepathy, and *lung gom pa,* Marian would teach Elizabeth how to move in the shadow world.

Once Elizabeth had mastered at least some of these skills, Naismith would take over. His role would be to teach her how to use her powers to engage a shadow world that could not be explained by the scientific method. And, certainly as important, to teach her to keep clear of the part of the shadow world where demons and evil spirits lived. Would there be time to teach her how to avoid evil? Naismith was not certain. As he drank his green tea, Naismith stared at his spirit knife. On its own, the knife jumped up on its point and began to slowly spin.

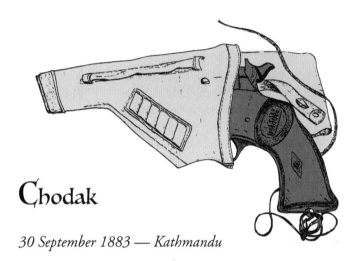

Chodak

30 September 1883 — Kathmandu

THE GURKHA SEARCH PARTY FOUND NAISMITH AT THE HEAD OF THE PASS
leading into Tibet. He was wrapped in the tan wool robes of
a Tibetan monk and walking toward Kathmandu. He had a
small leather pack on his back. In the best of times, Naismith
was a small, lean man. When the Gurkhas found him, he
looked as if he had not eaten or slept in days. They took him
back to Kathmandu on horseback wrapped in a good English
woolen blanket taken from the Gurkha barracks.

Halvidar Gurung rode beside him. "Sir, we never gave up.
I knew you had been captured by that Tibetan devil. We are
so very happy you are alive."

Naismith turned to Gurung and said, "You warned me
and I did not listen. I apologize for being such a fool."

"Sir, we all are children until we see evil in the world. I
have seen things in Afghanistan that I could not imagine,
and wish I could forget. I know you thought I was simply a
child afraid of the dark."

"Gurung, I have seen the darkness now. There are good reasons to be afraid."

"Indeed, sir. But now, you are safe. You are in Gurkha hands and that means we will take care of you. No devil can hurt you now."

Naismith nodded. But, from his days in captivity, he now knew that the Gurkhas could not protect him if the spirit of the *naljorpa* wished him more harm. This Tibetan priest was unlike the Sufis and the sadhus that he had known. This priest's heart held a truly evil spirit. Naismith realized he was lucky to be alive and lucky to have kept his sanity.

In combat in the past, Naismith had spent little time worrying about the souls of the men he killed. In intelligence operations, the goal was to obtain the information and remain invisible: to make no contact with the enemy. The only times in his career when he had to fight were those times when it was kill or be killed. One on one. Naismith had no regrets in killing the Tibetan priest. After all, the priest had intended to kill him. The problem this time was Naismith wasn't certain that he had truly dispatched the priest to his appropriate Tibetan hell.

Early in his captivity and while still in the mesmeric trance, the priest bragged that Naismith's death would release great power that the priest would capture and use. Killing a soldier from the most powerful country on Earth was the priest's goal when he came down from the mountains. He had expected to capture and kill a Gurkha. But, finding and capturing an English officer was much better.

The priest had assumed that his mesmerism techniques would keep Naismith under his spell. That was true for the first week, but eventually, the *naljorpa* got lazy and ignored his captive. He was busy preparing the location for a human sacrifice and the necessary potions that would end the life of his captive without harming the body or damaging the blood. After all, it would be after the sacrifice that the soldier's blood would be most powerful. The poisoner needed to have precisely the right measurements to ensure a quick death where none of the bodily fluids were expelled.

Naismith came out of the spell the way one emerges from a deep sleep not knowing which is true: dream or wakening. He found himself in a shallow cave, no more than ten feet square and six feet high. He was naked and, as he revived, he realized he was very cold and very hungry. How many days had he been there? He had no idea. He touched his jaw and felt the beginnings of a beard, not just a stubble, a beard. No more than ten days? Next he ran his hands down his body to see if there were any obvious injuries. There were none.

Around his neck was a thin rope of woven cotton. In dream-like memories, he recalled being bound by chains. As he came to his senses, Naismith realized that this was simply an illusion created by the *naljorpa*. He untied the cotton rope. It was ten feet long. He followed the length of the rope until he found the large metal hook in the wall where the rope was secured. He looked over to the other wall and saw another metal hook. The original purpose of these hooks was lost in the mists of time, but Naismith could imagine sinister uses. Next to the first hook was a brass water dish. Naismith smelled the water. It appeared fresh and without any odor of the drugs used by Sufis and Sadhus to create hallucinations. He took a sip. Nothing odd on his tongue or in his stomach as the water coursed down his throat. Naismith decided it was safe to quench his thirst.

The water revived both his mind and his body, and Naismith began to plan his escape. First, he knew he would never outrun the *naljorpa* since he observed the priest's ability to run faster than any horse. That meant, regardless of the risk, he would have to fight the priest before he made his escape. The front of the cave was covered by an animal skin. Daylight cascaded through the gaps on both sides of the skin. Naismith guessed it was mid-day. He had no idea when the priest would return, but at least for the time being, he had enough light to explore the cave. The rope and the water dish seemed the only items, so these would have to be the weapons he could use. On one end of the rope, he tied a slip knot on a loop. He passed a loop of the rope through the hook on the wall and then tied a bowline knot on the running line. He placed the loop from the bowline around his wrist. Nothing short of dislocation of his wrist and arm would now prevent him from maintaining a good purchase on the rope. He intended to use the slip knot to secure the priest and the brass dish for his weapon.

Naismith took the empty brass water dish and the rope from the back of the cave and walked to a spot near the entrance. He waited there, leaning against the cave wall with the patience taught to him years ago by a Sadhu from his homeland in Assam. Naismith decided the way to stay alert and pass the time was to do complex mathematics in his head. As a child, he had proven himself to be adept at basic mathematics and he enjoyed simple math puzzles. At the beginning of his Army career, Naismith was sent to the school for the Bengal Sappers and Miners. As he waited, he calculated in his head the requirements for building a bridge across a river. It kept him awake and he was ready when the *naljorpa* returned.

Naismith knew that when his captor pulled back the animal skin and entered the cave, there would be a moment before his eyes could adjust to the difference between broad daylight and the gloom of the cave. In that instant, Naismith struck. He hit the priest as hard as he could on the head. The brass water dish cracked from the impact. Immediately following the strike, Naismith threw the looped slipknot over the priests head, around his neck, and pulled the rope taut. The priest smiled and then extended his right hand, palm outward, toward Naismith. Naismith was pushed against the far wall with a force that nearly knocked him senseless. As he flew across the cave, Naismith summoned all of his strength to pull on his end of the rope. When the priest turned to confront Naismith, he had stepped over the cotton rope. Naismith's yank on the line pulled the rope between the priest's legs and forced the *naljorpa's* head down to his knees. Naismith realized that this was his one and only chance. He ran to the back of the cave and pulled with everything he had. As the line tightened around his neck, the priest tumbled to the floor and somersaulted onto his back. Naismith continued to pull on the rope as fast as he could. The priest was dragged along the dust of the cave floor and then up the wall until he was off his feet hanging by the rope a few feet below the hook. Naismith kept applying pressure and the knot around the priest grew tighter and tighter. It was not an easy killing, but it was effective. In less than a minute, the priest stopped struggling. To be certain that he had done the job, Naismith continued to hold the rope taut for another few minutes before he walked over to the other hook embedded in the opposite cave wall. He took the rope off his wrist and tied a second knot, this time a tautline hitch that allowed him to keep the line as tight as possible. It was only when that was completed that Naismith took the time to breathe.

As Naismith headed out of the cave, the *naljorpa* came back to life for a moment. No longer struggling, he opened his eyes and looked straight at Naismith. He said, "I am a corpse. If not flesh and blood, my spirit remains between this earth and the shadowland. I promise my spirit will hunt you and your offspring down." Once the priest completed his statement, his head drooped again and his eyes closed. Naismith was chilled to the bone as he walked naked into the sunlight.

As he walked out, he realized he was no more than a hundred yards from where he had been captured. Next to the cave entrance was a small lean-to made of branches and leaves. Under the lean-to were a number of bowls next to a series of closed bottles. Naismith recognized a leather bag with his clothes and another bag with a single set of Buddhist priestly robes. In the bag with his clothes, he found his Webley revolver still in its holster. He pulled out the revolver, untied the lanyard from the pistol grip and walked back into the cave. Only the songbirds and carrion birds nearby heard the six shots fired inside the cave.

1883–1890 — Nepal

It was a year after the confrontation in the cave that Naismith returned to Nepal and to a Buddhist monastery nestled into a southern cliff face on the road to Tibet. That trip was based on both his successes and failures in his regiment. When he returned to the Gurkhas, his soldiers had realized that Naismith was on what they called "the mystic path" to enlightenment. They were pleased, but also scared. Naismith's orders were now considered commands that must be obeyed for fear of not only their honour but their spiritual lives. It made Naismith a less-effective commander as word of his mystic skills was passed from Gurkha to Gurkha.

While the regimental commander had no real idea why this young officer was now considered by his Gurkha troops to be more god than man, he knew that it would not do for a junior officer to have this sort of power over the troops. He reported to Bengal that Naismith could not continue in his role as a reconnaissance troop commander in the 5th Gurkhas. In a moment of clarity that Naismith found rare in the Indian Army, the Military Intelligence Bureau in Calcutta recommended Naismith's attachment to the intelligence section supporting the entire Gurkha Regiment. Once there, the commander of the section dispatched Naismith to Nepal to gain additional insight into Tibetan mystics.

"These longi-wearing, barefooted sadhus threaten the regiment," the commander said. "They undermine morale, and heaven only knows who might use them to subvert the regiment at a time of greatest need. Naismith, you have seen their power. You are, after all, part local yourself, so you need to be our eyes and ears against these fakirs and mystics. Go back to Nepal, find monks who are friendly to the Raj and sort this all out. I don't care how long it takes, make it so!"

Naismith took the commander at his word and returned to Kathmandu and approached the monasteries near the capitol of Nepal. He entered a monastery in the foothills of the Himalayas at the base of the mountain the Nepalis called *Gaurishankar*. He came as a seeker of insight, or *trapa* as the monks called him. The monks knew who he was well before he was announced at the temple gate. The master of the temple approached him and thanked him for ending the threat of *naljorpa* Chodak. Chodak was exiled from the temple when it became clear that he was committed to what the temple master called serving the wrathful diety called *Mahakala*. The master said that Chodak intended to usurp the powers in Lhasa and overthrow the living saint, the Dalai Lama.

Chodak's stated goal was to establish a mystic kingdom with himself as supreme leader, and to use his powers to drive foreigners out of India. To succeed, Chodak needed to expand his mystic power through any means necessary, the master explained. That was why he intended to kill Naismith. The temple master said that Naismith's ability to kill Chodak demonstrated that Naismith had great power himself, and that he would use it for good. The master and the entire temple welcomed him and offered to help enhance his nascent powers.

Three years later, Naismith departed the monastery as a

master of some of the mystic arts the priests taught. He returned to the Gurkhas with full intention of serving the Queen as a scout for the Gurkhas. Instead, the Military Intelligence Bureau found him a series of new assignments until, finally, he was made the head of a new training program for Raj Intelligence, The Viceroy's College. Once the college was established and the first class graduated in 1890, Naismith offered military intelligence headquarters the chance to create a new, special force made up of graduates: men and women who could fight an invisible war against the enemies of the Raj. He called them the Ravens.

The Ravens were born of necessity. There were times when operations short of war had to be conducted on the edges of the Empire, in the lands of allies, neutrals, and sometimes even adversaries. These teams were used instead of more conventional units from the Gurkha Regiment because the missions were designed to be completely deniable. In the twenty years of their existence, they had conducted multiple hostage rescue missions inside the tribal areas near the Afghan border and, in one case, a sabotage mission against a pirate warlord operating along the coast of Oman. Instead of pure intelligence missions, Raven teams conducted operations that might involve elements of reconnaissance, intelligence and combat. Based on the recent Boer War, the Indian Army leadership called these missions "commando" missions.

Interlude with the Botanists

10–11 April 1912 — the foothills of the Pamirs

ELIZABETH LED THE KEW BOTANISTS ALONG A TRAIL STILL COVERED IN SNOW. She and Marian had traded their shalwar kamiz for clothes more fitting for English travelers. On their feet they wore knee-high winter boots that allowed them to walk the trails without difficulty. The three visitors on horseback were completely awed by the views of the mountain peaks and the pine forest, and barely paid attention to the trail. Elizabeth was equally enthralled by the beauty and, she had to admit, a day of freedom from her intense training. But, she knew it was important for Marian and her to keep focused on the mission. It would not do to lose a civilian over some mountain cliff. Still, the dry air at this altitude matched with the bright white snow and deep green trees intoxicated the mind. It was wonderful.

After nearly two months of travelling by train, carriage and horseback, the Kew researchers arrived at the main gates of The Viceroy's College. Members of the military staff guided the researchers to visitors' lodging on the edge of the property and reported their arrival to Naismith. He met them that evening at their lodge dressed in his uniform as a major of the Gurkha Rifles. He hosted them for dinner in his private quarters. It simply wouldn't do to reveal to the scientists the true nature of the place. They had no reason to know about the existence of The Viceroy's College or the students training to be intelligence officers for the Raj.

Over dinner, Naismith provided a fictitious explanation for a garrison in the mountains. It was simply one of many outposts on the frontier. Well before they left England, the Kew scientists were aware of the importance of the Raj and knew that security was maintained by remote military garrisons on the edge of Empire. Naismith used his mesmerism skills over dinner to embed in their minds the story that he and Marian had devised to explain Elizabeth's discovery. He made sure they believed Elizabeth to be the daughter of one of the senior officers in this remote garrison, and that Marian was her highly skilled tutor. He explained that they found the orchid during Elizabeth's training and, when the discovery was reported to him, he sent the information to Calcutta and Kew. It was not completely true, but it was true enough, particularly when Naismith deeply embedded the story in their minds. It was what they would believe and what they would report when they returned to England.

The next morning, Marian and Elizabeth waited at the rear gate to the college with horses for the Kew researchers and their equipment. The researchers were reluctant to ride while their guides, female guides no less, walked. Elizabeth was about to say something when Marian looked at the most senior botanist and said, "We shall take turns. You can walk for the first stretch and we will walk for the next. There are only five horses. Three to ride and two to carry your equipment and tents. This is not England, gentlemen, and we are not English maidens. We are used to these mountains and you are not."

With that Marian and Elizabeth slid into the saddles of the first two horses and started down the trail. The eldest of the three botanists climbed onto the third horse and followed. The two remaining botanists took the leads of the pack horses and followed. In less than an hour, the two were falling far behind the riders. At that point, Marian and Elizabeth rode back and changed places with the two exhausted botanists. They led the pack horses forward and walked the rest of the way.

The botanists were thrilled with the mountain glade where Elizabeth originally found the orchid. Sunshine through the gaps in the trees had melted the snow, and in one of those gaps was Elizabeth's discovery. Not only was the orchid previously unidentified, it was also surrounded by other plants that had been previously identified by Himalayan explorers, but neither photographed nor collected. Marian and Elizabeth watched as the three men scampered like children between the glade and their horses, acquiring measuring tools, photographic equipment, and collection boxes from their pack horses. Riding on top of the pack horses were two glass boxes, which Elizabeth suspected to be small versions of glass Wardian Cases designed to take live samples back to England. In no time at all, the cases were off the saddles and pressed into service to take plant and soil samples. Elizabeth was slightly jealous as the scientists thanked her for guiding them to what they seemed to regard as their own discovery.

Marian watched carefully to make sure her student did not say or do something to reveal the real training that took place at the college. After several condescending remarks by one of the scientists, Marian could imagine Elizabeth accidentally using her new-found skills to send a rock or a handful of snow flying toward the least polite of the Kew biologists. She had already warned Elizabeth of their cover story, but Marian could see Elizabeth's aura change from blue to yellow to red as she was pushed aside by the visitors. Marian knew it was dangerous to push a student with Elizabeth's skills and there was no doubt that the visitors were nearing her limit of courtesy. Just before Elizabeth was about to launch invective if not projectiles at the botanists, Marian asked if the three intended to spend the night so they could continue their study.

When they said they did intend to stay, she looked at Elizabeth and said, "It's time for us to go. The Kew botanists will probably stay here until their provisions run out and we have other things to accomplish."

Elizabeth nodded. She was definitely relieved to be rid of the men who saw her as little more than a local guide. As she looked at Marian, she said, "I really wouldn't have hurt them…much."

Marian smiled and said, "And that was why it is time for us to leave before you hurt them at all!"

Elizabeth blushed. It was clear that Marian had known all along that she was becoming jealous and angry with the visitors. As she calmed down, she said, "Will they find their way back to the college without any difficulty?"

"I believe so," Marian said. "But just in case, I have already asked Guru Naismith to dispatch a squad from Ft. Burnes tomorrow. We have too much to accomplish to serve as their guides or their nurse maids. I suspect this is not the first time these men have been plant hunting. I looked at their tents and provisions. They will be fine for two days. By that time, the college guards will pack them up and lead them back down the trail. Now, Elizabeth, it is really time to go."

Marian turned and started to run down the trail. The trail was a mix of switchbacks separated by one hundred yards of open terrain. On the climb up, they had focused on keeping the visitors and their horses safe, so Elizabeth had not spent time looking back along the mountain face or the switchback trail which looked like multiple "z" letters carved into the hillside. After weeks of one-on-one training, she knew that Marian never wasted a moment. If this run was designed to increase her fitness, then so be it. Elizabeth took off after her mentor. After two turns on the trail, they were out of sight of the botanists. Marian changed her pace. Instead of running, she seemed to be leaping along the trail, covering ten to fifteen feet in a single bound. Marian turned to Elizabeth. She smiled and challenged Elizabeth. "Keep up if you can!"

Elizabeth started running faster, but soon realized she would never catch up. She stopped for a moment. If this was some new technique, then certainly Marian expected her to be able to master it. She remembered Marian's guidance to stop thinking and just act. She turned, sprinted for a few strides and then leapt. What she hadn't expected was she landed over twenty-five feet down the path and nearly on top of Marian.

"What did I just do?"

"You just started practicing something that Buddhist monks have been doing for years here in the Himalayas. I told you about *lung gom pa*. Controlling air. You have started using your levitation skills to travel on these mountain pathways. Now that you know you can do this, let's begin again. Only this time, focus your attention on landing, because we are going to…" Instead of finishing the sentence, Marian jumped from one level of the trail, down a thirty-foot embankment to the next level of the switchback and then again and then again. Before Elizabeth could imagine, Marian was nearly fifty yards below her.

Elizabeth was uncertain that she could do the same thing without a broken bone. "How?"

"Just leap and please focus on your landing this time."

Elizabeth made a tentative hop and found herself only about halfway down the first face. She slid the rest of the way using her mountain boots and the rough wool of the seat of her trousers. It was not graceful nor was it comfortable. Elizabeth was blushing as she recovered her balance and called to her guru.

Marian shook her head and said, "Trust yourself and your skills. Just leap." With that bit of advice, Marian disappeared down the next embankment. Now, Elizabeth had to cover three switchbacks if she intended to keep up with her guru.

This time Elizabeth walked to the edge of the trail, looked down where Marian was standing and gave a forceful leap. She covered the distance and landed with a thump next to Marian.

"It does take practice," was all Marian said as she started to hop from ledge to ledge heading toward their cabins in the forest. Elizabeth decided to follow as best she could. Sometimes the leap was successful, sometimes she ended up sliding down the ledge again. They covered a distance in fifteen minutes that should have taken an hour.

They were on a flat stretch of ground and using the *lung gom pa* technique to cover ten yards at a time when Elizabeth collapsed. Her feet came out from under her and she did a successful shoulder roll to end up seated on the side of the trail. She had a blinding headache and couldn't catch her breath. Marian was immediately at her side. She was worried that she had pushed her student too fast. "What happened?"

"I don't know. I suddenly had a picture cross my mind and

I lost my concentration." Marian knew that for this bounding technique, Elizabeth had to concentrate. Her charge was, after all, still a young woman who could be distracted by almost anything in the natural world. She said, "Tell me what crossed your mind. Was it something about the botanists?"

"No, it was...it is hard to explain." Elizabeth closed her eyes as she tried to recapture the image. She suddenly turned white and a tear rolled down her cheek. She said, "I must be going mad!"

"Elizabeth, are you injured? Where does it hurt?"

"Guru Marian, it doesn't hurt anywhere. It hurts everywhere. I have an image of my mother and my father. They are bound hand and foot. My father is gagged so he cannot speak. They are in a dungeon. They are afraid. What sort of dream is this? I am wide awake. I am someone who is not taken with silly whims. I am not someone who sees visions."

Any teacher from England might have dismissed this as just the musings of a young girl who has been away from home for months. Marian knew at once this was not what was happening. She said, "Elizabeth, focus on the image. Where are your parents? Are they alone? Can you see what they saw when they were captured?"

"They are not alone. There is another man nearby. He is also bound and gagged. Somehow, I know him. No, my parents know him. His name is Abdul Rashid. He is very angry with himself. I can see..."

Marian knew what Elizabeth was going to say next. She was revealing a new skill in the mystic way. It was not something that she taught or, for that matter, Marian even practiced. Still, she knew precisely what was happening. "You can see your parents as if you were above them..." Marian reached out and held Elizabeth in her arms, rocking her ever so gently.

"Yes. I see them as if I was above them. Mother and Father are on a single rope bed. A charpoi. Abdul Rashid is on the floor. The room is dark but there is a light coming through the small window in the door. Just enough light to see. I can feel my father's anger. He has tried to pull apart his bindings. Instead, he has just torn his wrists. Mother is concentrating on some type of chant. She is trying to…"

Marian said, "She is not trying, she is succeeding in communicating with you, dear. Now, you must try something very difficult. You must imagine yourself floating away from your parents. You must leave them behind, rise above them, passing through the walls of their room. Floating until you get outside. You must look and listen and find out where they are. They can't tell you. Only you can find out."

Elizabeth was crying now, but she followed Marian's instructions. She imagined floating above her parents, passing through the ceiling, through another room, then outside on a parapet of a fortress. She was floating next to a pair of guards. They were speaking in Afghan Persian. Their accents were hard to understand. She had not practiced her Persian in months and Afghan Persian was a very different dialect. She sobbed, "I can't understand them."

Marian decided to use the mesmerism voice on Elizabeth. Her calm and soothing voice surrounded Elizabeth. "Of course, you can, dear. It is easy. Just listen. You will understand them. You will understand them."

Elizabeth repeated in a dreamy voice, "I will understand…" She paused and said, "They are Afghan guards. They are talking about their lives and their family. They are talking small talk about life in…" another pause, "Mazar-e-Sharif. They do not understand why the king needs a fort this big in the north. It is a fort of war and they don't see the point."

Marian nodded and said, "Did they say Qalai-e-Jangi, Elizabeth?"

Another dreamy response, "Yes, Qalai-e-Jangi. It means fort of war."

Marian used a tone which would bring Elizabeth back to the present and back to the trail near their cabin. "Elizabeth, we must leave your parents now. We must get back to the college and we must plan how to rescue them. We must hurry." Elizabeth turned to Marian and said, "Yes, we must hurry." Marian said, "Now Elizabeth, we are about to make a journey. We are about to travel in a manner you have not imagined. You must not show fear for if we are to accomplish this together you have to trust me. Are you ready?"

Elizabeth had no idea what Marian was talking about but she said, "Of course, Guru Marian. I trust you." With that, Marian took Elizabeth's hands in hers. She looked directly into Elizabeth's eyes and the two women disappeared.

When they reappeared seconds later, they were standing in Guru Naismith's office at the college. Naismith looked up from the paperwork on his large teak desk. Sitting next to him was the spirit knife standing on its point and spinning so fast that it was impossible to see each of the Tibetan spirit faces on the hilt.

He nodded to Marian and said, "There is trouble."

"Master, there is trouble indeed."

"Then we must get to work." Naismith led Marian and Elizabeth into a room behind his office. The walls were lined with shelves filled with books, an assortment of weapons both old and new, and a number of copper and steel devices that Elizabeth could not identify. In the center of the room was a large globe on an oak frame. Any other time, she would have been like a child in a toy store reaching for items to handle. Today, she realized that she was no longer a child.

Naismith said, "Elizabeth, you need to share with me what you have seen. To do so, you have to let me come into your mind. Will you do that?"

As with her comment only minutes ago on the mountainside, Elizabeth said, "Yes, master guru. I will do that."

Naismith sat Elizabeth on a hard bench near the library table. He pulled up a second bench across from her and sat down. He motioned for Marian to join him on the second bench. Once he was facing Elizabeth, he gently put his left hand on Elizabeth's right temple. He said, "Elizabeth, you need to concentrate now. We are going to rescue your parents, but you need to be part of that rescue. Open your mind and let me see."

Ready or not, Elizabeth had just become an agent of the Empire and a student of the mystic arts.

Captives!

11 April 1912 — Mazar-e-Sharif

Francis Bankroft sat in the cell in the basement of the Afghan Army headquarters in Qalai-e-Jangi. He was furious with Abdul Rashid and, moreover, with himself for allowing himself and Mary to be captured so easily. He should have expected some degree of treachery from the tribal outriders who were supposed to provide them with safe passage from Chitral into Afghanistan. The only thing that he could see as positive at this point was that at least Elizabeth wasn't with them when they were captured.

Francis reviewed how they got into this predicament. Surely there was something that he could have done to prevent their capture. He thought back on the last ten days to explore what, if anything, he could have done to avoid their current predicament.

After they spent the pleasant night on the Afghan — Indian border, they rode for two days on the trail with Abdul Rashid. They arrived in a small side valley of the River Pech in the Konar. Not far from Chitral and a reasonable place to wait for their escort. It also seemed as good a place as any to wait until either Elizabeth arrived or a messenger arrived saying she wasn't going to join them. Abdul Rashid had a cabin in the valley, not much more than a stone shed for shepherds with a small corral for the horses. As they approached the cabin, Mary said to him, "This is like some small valley in the Alps. I know we will have to move on as soon as Elizabeth arrives, but it will be a wonderful place to wait for her."

Abdul Rashid's English was as good as any man's in the region and he noted the tone as well as the subject of Mary's comment. He said, "I have tried to make you as comfortable as possible Mrs. Bankroft. We can expect the riders to arrive tonight and, if everything goes as you have planned, then we can expect your daughter by next month. Meanwhile, the horses will have a good rest with excellent grazing, and you will enjoy more of Abdul Rashid's cooking!" His smile was broad and sincere.

After placing the horses in the corral, they carried their bags into the small stone cabin. Abdul Rashid led the way, followed by Mary and then Francis. They were surprised to find it occupied. Before their eyes had adjusted to the darkness, a man used a match to light an oil lantern at the far end of the cabin. He used the same match to light a thin cigar made of very strong Turkish tobacco.

"Welcome, travelers. I hope you have had a pleasant journey!"

Francis recognized the voice long before his eyes adjusted to the light. He uttered the name as if it was a curse. "Naglieff!"

The man near the lamp stood up and from the darkness the new arrivals could see four rifles pointed at their chests. The trap was complete. Naglieff was tall, a good two inches taller than Francis, though bone thin. His high cheekbones and, as near as Mary could make out, ice blue eyes argued that he was a European Russian rather than a member of the

Don Cossacks that surrounded them. He spoke nearly perfect English, arguing for an early childhood nanny from Britain. "Francis and Mary, I would prefer if you called me Sasha. Of course, if you insist on being formal then you may call me Baron Colonel Alexander Naglieff of the Russian Imperial Guards currently assigned to the Tsar's Cossack Regiment in the city of Merv. I would like to make this as reasonable as possible, so if you would please drop your cases and remove your weapons." Naglieff smiled. Mary thought it was not the smile of a man who was enjoying his success. Instead, it was the smile of a man who might have just won a chess game with an old friend.

Naglieff continued, "I know it will be an inconvenience, but I will also need you to accept my men binding your hands. Francis, they were exceptionally impressed with how you dispatched the three Pathans we sent to kill you. They would prefer to shoot you now, but I would prefer to hold you hostage, ideally to exchange you for some future Russian intelligence officer captured in some Indian city by your service."

Francis could see Abdul Rashid taking a series of deep breaths which would precede some sort of Uzbek berserker attack on their captors. Francis was certain that Abdul Rashid's actions would result in all of their deaths, whether Naglieff wished that or not. Francis rarely used the mesmerism voice on any of his men, but there was no time to spare. In a calm, sugary voice, he said, "Abdul Rashid, my friend. We are going to follow Sasha's instructions."

The Uzbek's shoulders fell. His breathing slowed and he said in a dreamy voice, "Yes, Baba Jan. I will obey."

The Russian shook his head in bewilderment. Finally, he said, "That is a powerful trick, my friend. You will need to show me how it works. Sadly, it means that for the time being, we are also going to have to gag you so that you can't use the same skills on my men. If you can transform an

Uzbek berserker into a compliant prisoner, I can imagine it would take very little for you to transform my Cossacks into my assassins."

Mary finally decided to speak. She used just enough of the mesmerism voice in her perfect St. Petersburg accented Russian to insert a level of doubt into Naglieff's mind. It would be of no use now, but it might be useful later. "Sasha, we are willing to accept you have played the game well and we have lost. Please do us no harm. An honourable man has no interest in killing hostages."

Naglieff looked at Mary with a cocked head. He couldn't decide what to do with this beautiful woman who spoke beautiful Russian. All he could think to say was, "Mrs. Bankroft, I presume?"

Mary continued to use the voice as she replied "Mary Louise Bankroft, daughter of Sir Maxwell Frobisher-Smith, member of Parliament and Colonel of the Regiment for His Majesty's Scot's Guards. Like my husband, I am also a major in Indian Army Intelligence. I hope you will call me Mary."

"My pleasure, madame. I will do my best to reduce your hardship, but please do nothing while we are on the trail. While I am in command of the Cossacks, I will honestly say I am not always in control." Naglieff suddenly wondered why he had added this last part of the sentence. It was as if he wanted, no, he needed to let Mary know his concerns.

"Sasha, thank you for the warning." Mary switched to English and said, "Abdul Rashid and Francis, I know you do not speak Russian. The Colonel has asked for us to indulge him and avoid any altercations while we are on the trail. He wants to be sure we arrive at our destination, wherever that may be, safe and sound."

Francis understood the opening gambit created by his wife. She knew full well that he was also fluent in Russian, albeit barracks Russian. He had heard her use the voice on Naglieff and it appeared to work. Given the odds against them at present and the odds while on the trail, Francis was more than willing to accept the terms and play for time. He swallowed his pride, calmed himself and said, "Colonel, you have my word that we will not do anything to impede our journey. I suspect these men are only one part of your patrol and there are more men waiting. We accept your conditions."

"Francis, that is wise. Indeed there are a total of twenty-four Cossacks in my squadron. The rest are waiting outside. We have another few hours of daylight and I intend to use them to get clear of this location. While we were able to bribe your Uzbek's riders, I suspect there are more than a few bandits in this area who would try to take us all hostage. It would be unwise of them, but more than one of my men and perhaps one or more of us would die. I have no interest in dying today." He waved his hands toward the door. "Please go back to your horses while we arrange for the rest of the patrol to join us. Oh, apologies for being insistent, but please remember to take out your weapons now so that we can be certain that nothing untoward happens in the next few days."

Francis reached under his coat as carefully as he could so that none of the Cossacks were challenged. He pulled the two Colts out of their holsters, placing his thumb and forefingers on the two grips. He placed the guns gently on the floor of the cabin. He reached into his pocket and reluctantly retrieved the new Colt automatic. He placed it next to the two revolvers. Finally, Francis pulled his Khyber knife from his belt and placed them on the floor. He said, "My saddle bag has my Mauser rifle. Colonel, if anyone is going to acquire these weapons, I would hope you will get the Mauser and my Colts." He then spoke to Abdul Rashid who was still in the waking dream. "Abdul Rashid, please put all of your weapons on the floor." The Uzbek complied.

Naglieff bowed in thanks. He turned to Mary and said, "I do not intend to search you madame unless I have to, so please surrender your weapons as well."

Mary smiled and said, "If you insist." She pulled her new Colt automatic from its concealed holster and put it on the ground. Next she pulled out her dagger and her sharpened throwing stars from their respective carrying cases attached to her leather belt. Francis noted that somehow Mary believed she could successfully conceal her small Browning pistol and some of the various potions and tools that were in her undergarment. He hadn't noticed where she had the second holster when they changed clothes. If she wasn't going to be searched, perhaps she felt they were things she could keep without risk.

The Russian said, "I thank you for your cooperation. Francis, I promise I will keep the Mauser as a memento. However, I suspect I will have to surrender your pistols to my senior sergeants. Spoils of war and all that."

"Understood. At least someone will continue to enjoy the hunting rifle."

"Indeed. Now, we need to go back to the corral and leave this place. Once you are mounted, I will have to bind you and, Francis, I intend to gag you, but that inconvenience will be temporary, I promise."

It was Francis' turn to bow. Once he did so, he did a formal about-turn and walked out the door. As soon as he returned to the sunlight, he faced the remaining mounted Cossacks, swords out and ready to deliver any order given by their Russian commander.

Francis was certain that Mary already had a plan. In his experience, she always had a plan. He realized he would have to wait to hear it because he certainly had no plan for escaping from a patrol of armed Cossacks. As they headed west, Francis Bankroft was pleased to see that neither Naglieff nor his Cossack minions were in the least concerned about Mary. While he and Abdul Rashid were bound and gagged, the Russian limited the restraints for Mary to a single rope loop around her waist. The longer they failed to understand that Mary was at least as dangerous as he was, the better the chances for their future escape.

After another day's ride, they were transferred to a covered, wooden freight wagon that bumped along for two more days. At the end of each day, they were allowed to leave the wagon to relieve themselves, share a meal with Naglieff and his men, and then return to the wagon. Naglieff spent the evenings talking to his prisoners about his times in the Imperial Guards, including combat experiences with the Cossacks as they extended the Tsar's reign past Merv and into the emirates of Bukhara and Samarkand. By the second day, Mary had convinced Abdul Rashid to wait for a moment of treachery that would mean their freedom. Each night, their Uzbek colleague sat scowling at Naglieff but he made no effort to fight his captors.

At the beginning of the final days of the ride, Naglieff said to his prisoners, "I'm sorry to do this to you, but we are going to have to put the canvas over the wagon so that you are not visible as we head into the city. It would not do for you to be seen by villagers and tradesmen. I have no doubt that Francis still has allies here in Mazar-e-Sharif and I do not want to have to fight my way to my headquarters."

Francis had not been gagged as Naglieff said this. He said, "Colonel, I have to commend you. If you have established a true headquarters here in Mazar-e-Sharif, then it is clear I have failed in my previous mission."

Mary understood Francis' ploy and addressed her husband though she was talking to Naglieff, "Northern Afghanistan was a long stretch for you, Francis. You should not be surprised that Sasha had more resources than you. He had the Cossacks and he had the Tsar's gold."

The Russian was taken with this praise, delivered with just a hint of "the voice," so he said, "You had a good run, my friend. We almost didn't make it. But, when General Stanekzai from the Afghan Imperial Guards joined us, it took very little gold to turn the garrison into our headquarters."

Francis bowed his head. "Colonel, you have performed magic here in the north."

Naglieff almost purred at the compliment. "Thank you, Major Bankroft. It has been a pleasure to play the great game against you." At that point, Naglieff put the gag on Bankroft's mouth as he led his three prisoners to the wagon. Abdul Rashid was already gagged so all he could do was growl.

Now, after three days in an underground cell in Qalai-e-Jangi, Francis was tired of waiting for an opening. He had tried to free himself and all he had done was wear his wrists raw. He thought about strangling any jailer who came to feed them, but they only came in groups of ten: three to provide food and seven armed with pistols aimed at the prisoners' chests.

Francis might be impatient, but he was not suicidal. Abdul Rashid was like a caged tiger, barely able to sit still even though he was bound hand and foot, but he also realized that it would be a wasted effort. He might kill one or two, but not enough to recover the honour he'd lost when he led his friends into a trap. Only Mary, who was unbound, remained calm as she focused her attention elsewhere.

Late on the third day after the guards had come and gone with their meal and emptied their toilet bucket, Mary looked at Francis. Her voice entered his consciousness though she spoke no words. "I have summoned help."

Francis' telepathic skills were never as strong as his wife's and he was out of practice. Telepathy, like a foreign language, could only be maintained through use. He managed to say to her, "Help? Who?"

"Both Naismith and Elizabeth."

Francis' raised eyebrows and increased breathing behind the gag emphasized his displeasure. "Elizabeth?"

"Dear, she was here. She saw us. She knows where we are. Naismith has already said to me that they are coming. We need to be patient."

This time, it was Francis who could only growl.

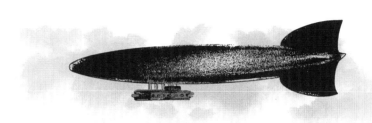

Enter the Ravens

13 April 1912 — The Viceroy's College

As Elizabeth walked down the corridor of the mountain headquarters with Guru Marian, she had not expected to see her Gurus from the school: Guru Lawrence, who served as the senior instructor for mathematics; Guru Standish, who taught chemistry; and Guru Maloney, the martial arts instructor. Each of them had two followers. The six individuals, three men and three women, were not students and they walked in a manner that Elizabeth had seen in Rawalpindi when watching the soldiers of the Corps of Guides prepare for operations. Confident, energetic, and absolutely silent. Now that she was in formation with these individuals, Elizabeth felt completely out of place. These were men and women who had proven themselves in operations in the far-flung reaches of the Empire. Even their uniforms, which were designed exactly like Elizabeth's, showed field time while hers looked fresh, almost starched. She worried that she was unprepared for the adult world she was entering.

Naismith stood as his team entered. It had been some time since he had used the map room carved inside the mountain. Generally, he trained officers to serve the Military Intelligence Bureau of the Indian Army and he seldom saw them after they left on their individual missions. Rarely, he had assembled a team to conduct a specialized raid where the government in Calcutta or the mandarins of Whitehall wanted success but discretion. It had been nearly three years since he had assembled a Raven Team. This would be the first time a Raven Team had a dozen men and women, and it was the first time in ten years that Naismith was the team leader. It was also the first time that all of the most arcane of the Tibetan skills would be used. It was a gamble, but the lives of two former students depended on its success.

Naismith prepared the room beforehand so that there would be no distractions and no delays. Opposite the door was a large campaign desk that had dozens of file folders of reports. In front of the desk, bathed in bright light from his solar lamps, were three large map tables. On the first table, he had placed an Indian Geographic Survey map of the border between the Indian Northwest Frontier and the kingdom of Afghanistan. The second table had two less-detailed maps. The first was another geographic survey map of Northern Afghanistan and the Russian-controlled emirates to the north. The Amu Darya, the river that served as the border with the periphery of the Russian Empire, running east to the Himalayas, ran through the center of the map. This map covered the cities of Badakhshan, Konduz and Mazar-e-Sharif. Below that map was a more detailed, hand-drawn map of the city of Mazar-e-Sharif. On the third table was a large and very detailed sketch map of the fortress on the outskirts of Mazar-e-Sharif. Qalai-e-Jangi, the House of War. This was the objective for his team.

Naismith looked at the eleven men and women in front of him. In the past, he might have used fewer of these combat experts, but the urgency of the mission meant that some of the standards of clandestine warfare would have to be compromised to guarantee success. Naismith and his team were all wearing what they called the ghost uniforms. A hooded cotton blouse that ended at the hip over a pair of heavier cotton trousers and then laced-up boots with rubber soles. The colour of the uniform was difficult to describe. When in the shadows of the room, it would be called black or midnight blue. When nearer the map tables, the light from the incandescent bulbs turned the uniforms a flat grey or lighter blue. It was a uniform for night operations.

Naismith began with no prologue. "The mission we are tasked with is a hostage rescue of two of our colleagues. Majors Francis and Mary Bankroft, and their principle agent, Abdul Rashid have been kidnapped by a Russian officer and his Cossack squadron. They are being held in underground cells in the Afghan Army fortress called Qalai-e-Jangi in Mazar-e-Sharif. I will not spend any time on background information. I assume you have already read your files."

When he saw each of the Ravens nod, he continued, "The meeting here is to outline the plan and begin a discussion on how to best execute that plan. Time is of the essence because we do not know for certain how long our colleagues will be held in the cells and, if they are moved, where they will be going." Naismith paused to review the auras of each of the fighters. All but one were a blue-green which suggested they were completely ready for the briefing. Only Elizabeth Bankroft's aura was a pale greenish yellow which argued for her confusion. Naismith had expected this and was not worried.

Naismith continued, "Some of you may know each other, but I would like to be certain of this. Our lives will depend on each other. Captain Lawrence, you first."

"Major, my team has Lieutenant Beverly and Lieutenant Alexander. They are back from assignments in Mesopotamia."

Maloney was next. His Scot accent came through in the

room just as it did in the Circle of Decision. "Major, my team has Lieutenant Christopher and Lieutenant Eugenia. Christopher was working on the border when we contacted him. Eugenia has just returned from Tashkent."

Standish closed the session. He said, "Major, my team has Lieutenant Jonathan and Lieutenant Martha. Jonathan was most recently working in Bhutan and Martha was in Tibet."

Naismith nodded and said, "My own team will be Captain Marian and Cadet Elizabeth. Cadet Elizabeth is the daughter of Francis and Mary Bankroft." Naismith noted slight colour changes in the auras of two of the lieutenants, but nothing of concern, yet. He waved the team toward the first two maps and started the briefing.

"We are going to travel to Northern Afghanistan in the newest airship, *HMFS Talon,* which is the fastest and longest-range flying ship yet deployed here in India. We will depart tonight from the college embarkation point and fly into Afghanistan." He pointed to a red pencil line that ran from their current location west over the tribal areas and toward a blue circle located west and north of the Hindu Kush mountains. He looked up at the team and said, "It will take us eight hours to make this leg of the trip. We will be landing near dawn tomorrow in a remote location north and west of the city of Konduz."

Naismith looked at one of the members of the team and said, "Christopher has already arranged for a reception committee that will secure the site in advance of our arrival. We will spend the day in hiding." Another look at the team to check their auras. While there was certainly some concern over the route, they were still confident of success. Naismith continued, "Once it is dark, we will make the run directly to Qalai-e-Jangi."

Naismith moved from the first map to the second. He had choreographed the move so that the team would have to follow him. He could watch their body language as well as their auras to see how well they were accepting the mission. He was pleased to see that they continued to be committed to the mission without reservations.

"We will approach the fort from the north, avoiding the city," he said. The airship will switch to battery power to run the propellers. The approach should be nearly silent and the *Talon* is painted slate grey so it should be invisible. We will drop down on this parapet," he pointed to the hand-drawn map on the third table. "At that point, we split into three teams. Lawrence, your team will remain on the parapet. You will secure the space and protect *Talon.*"

Lawrence nodded.

Elizabeth was used to military protocol, but this was the first time she had seen this level of informality. Clearly, she was watching an entirely different world, the world of what her father had called "the special services." These men and women may not have worked together, but they trusted each other implicitly. It was something that Elizabeth had heard her father describe on the frontier, but this was the first time she saw it with her own eyes. She was pleased to be part of the team even if she would have admitted being concerned about her own abilities and her own courage.

Naismith continued, "Maloney, your team will be responsible for securing the descent and the parade ground between the parapet stairs and this area." He pointed to the area on the hand-drawn map. Maloney nodded his agreement. Naismith looked at Standish and said, "You will lead us into the garrison headquarters and toward the cells. Once there, I will take my team and we will recover the hostages and return. At each step in our return, we will recover the teams, protect the hostages and then board the *Talon.* We intend to be back inside India and landing in Chitral garrison before dawn on 16 April. Now, what are your questions?"

The first came from Lawrence. He said, "Major, is the *Talon* commander aware of our mission and is he comfortable with loitering above the Afghan fort for the amount of time it is going to take to complete the mission? I have found airship commanders to be uncomfortable with our style of operation. They are more used to working with the Army."

Naismith nodded and said, "I expressed the same concern to Winslow-Heath. The colonel said he was in direct contact with the Royal Navy on this. The *Talon* commander is on rotation from the torpedo-boat squadron operating out of Bombay. He will have an experienced airship crew, but he has been selected because he has done similar operations with his torpedo boats up and down the Arabian coast. He has delivered and recovered Gurkhas from punitive raids against tribals nominally operating under the protection of the Ottoman Empire. Of course, this is the first time he has worked with Ravens, but the colonel assures me that he will be a steady hand." Lawrence nodded and Naismith noted that his aura turned a blue-green that suggested he was comfortable with the answer. Naismith said, "Any other questions?"

Elizabeth watched as the female officer identified as Beverly spoke up, "Sir, I wish no disrespect, but what purpose does Cadet Elizabeth serve in this operation? I understand that she is the daughter of our hostages and the fact that she has our uniform argues that she has been trained. Still, this is a complex operation. Why is she here?"

As Beverly completed her question, Elizabeth noted that all eyes turned to her. She could feel the blush rising from her neck. She focused her breathing and fought the internal battle to say something or, perhaps, to run from the room. Beverly looked to be in her early 30s. She had a tanned face and, Elizabeth noticed, calloused hands that hinted at years of hard work and martial arts training. Elizabeth decided to stay in place and hoped for an answer from Naismith.

Naismith started by recognizing Beverly's concern. "Lieutenant, I am fully aware of the challenges in this operation and, honestly, I have thought about your concerns as well." He looked over to Elizabeth. Her aura had gone from light green to orange. He could see she was trying to control her fight-or-flight response. Naismith realized that he needed to explain this quickly before Elizabeth did something that would turn the team against her.

"For all of you here, first I want you to know that the hand-drawn map of the fort is the result of the cadet's reporting. In fact, our understanding of the situation is entirely based on her reporting."

Again, a pause to watch the team. The colours across the room shimmered and ranged across the spectrum from blue through green to yellow.

"Cadet Elizabeth has a strong...no, to be clear, a brilliant telepathic capability. She has been in direct communications with her mother, who is one of the prisoners in Qalai. As most of you know, I have a strong telepathic ability myself, so I reached out to Francis and Elizabeth Bankroft. They acknowledged that they had been in contact with Elizabeth and passed her details of their situation."

A pause to watch the auras move closer toward green, and some to the blue-green of acceptance.

Naismith had expected these questions and he structured his response so that the final comment, if delivered properly would convince the team of Elizabeth's utility. He said, "Cadet Bankroft has another skill which we have been improving over the past week. Martha, you may understand it better than the rest of the team. We call it remote viewing, but the Tibetans call it..."

Before Naismith could complete the sentence, Martha issued an awed whisper, "the illusory body."

"Exactly. She has travelled to the fort and passed through the various hallways from the cells to the parapet. She knows this fort better than anyone in this room. More important to our operation, she can maintain contact with our hostages so we will know if they are moved and if there is a greater or lesser threat as we approach our target."

Beverly nodded. She hoped she spoke for the team when she said, "Elizabeth, welcome to our team."

Alexander immediately asked, "Elizabeth, what do you know of the threat on site?"

Naismith turned to her and said, "It is time you said something, Cadet."

Marian nodded and Elizabeth swallowed hard and started her report, "While the Afghans are holding my parents, correction, the hostages, they do not have a clear understanding of why they are doing so. The hostages were captured by Russians, but are held in the fortress by Afghans. The Afghan guards I have observed think their leader, General Mahmoud Stanekzai, does not trust the Russians so he does not allow them to live inside the fort. He likes their gold and he hates his king, so he works with the Russians. That does not mean he is their ally. The Russians are forced to live on a compound outside the fort. I saw only a few guards on the parapets and at the gate early this morning. The Afghans stay in their barracks on the south side of the fortress. There was no one in the garrison headquarters and only one guarding the cells. They believe the fortress is impossible to attack. I felt their confidence. I cannot say how the Russians think. They live too far away for me to see."

Alexander said, "Well done. It is clear you will be a good guide."

Elizabeth nodded. Naismith noted that while there were still some auras that were yellow green instead of blue green, Elizabeth's comments had convinced completely Beverley, Martha and Alexander. They would serve as the catalyst for the change over the next few hours. He said, "I want each team leader to design your plan and return here in two hours. We need to leave on the airship at 8 pm tonight. Dismissed."

Beverley walked over to Elizabeth. She said, "I hope you don't hold it against me for asking hard questions. It is our lives we are playing with on this operation. And, you are... well, you are very young."

Elizabeth nodded. She honestly didn't know what to say to this intelligence officer who was obviously also an experienced fighter. She smiled and said what she accepted as the obvious, "I fully understand. I am not an experienced officer by any stretch."

Beverly touched her on the arm and said, "If you will accept my help, I will help you get your kit straight before we leave. On my first assault, I needed that help."

Marian entered the conversation and said, "Beverly, that would be a very great help. I have to work with the major and I worried about Elizabeth."

They loaded the *Talon* at dusk on 13 April. It was already dark and the twelve officers dressed in black disappeared into the cabin with no sound and little sign that they were joining the airship. As she walked to the embarkation deck, Elizabeth noticed the dramatic difference between *Talon* and her previous experiences with airships. The *Talon* was longer, nearly half again as long as *HMFS Resolve*. It seemed to be narrower as well, almost as if the designers had worked off a torpedo drawing and then expanded it into an airship. Unlike *Resolve*, *Talon* had three pairs of propellers, but each pair were smaller than the previous airship. Finally, there was something about the colour of the skin of the airship. Unlike the silvery shimmer of the other airships, this one seemed to be a flat grey with large streaks of even darker grey running diagonally along the exterior skin of the aircraft.

As soon as they boarded, Elizabeth noticed the spartan surroundings. The passenger deck had simple, painted plank floors. The seating on the passenger deck was simple wooden benches that ran along the length of the cabin. Once the team was onboard, the airship nosed up with little fanfare and moved off to the west at full speed. The roar of the engines caused a vibration through the plank floors in the passenger cabin. The various teams sat together in the order that they would depart the ship, with Lawrence and his team in the rear of the cabin near the stairs to the lower deck, and Naismith, Marian and Elizabeth in the front of the cabin.

Elizabeth was still not comfortable with the mix of weapons and equipment that filled the black leather jerkin she wore over the black uniform. After the initial briefing, Beverly took Elizabeth to the quartermaster and walked her through the chore of drawing weapons, equipment and the leather jerkin which carried them all. She helped Elizabeth choose items and load the various pockets in the jerkin. She said, "Elizabeth, from the description of your mission tonight, I recommend you carry a small set of weapons. Your job is not to fight, your job will be to lead. So, I think you should not draw a rifle. Rather, a pistol and a knife. What do you think?"

It was the first time an adult had asked her opinion on anything of this importance. Previously, she had been a student. Now she was a junior member of a team. She said, "I am comfortable with pistols and throwing knives. Unless you think otherwise, I would prefer to have my hands free."

"Very good. Here are your pistol choices: a revolver or an automatic. Personally, I prefer a revolver. It is heavier and has a slower rate of fire, but it will not jam the way the modern automatics seem to at the worst possible time." Elizabeth picked up a Colt revolver and holstered it inside the jerkin. Beverly said, "Take these throwing knives. They are beautifully balanced and work just as well for close-in combat. Also, you need one of these." She handed Elizabeth a leather bracelet holding a watch with an illuminated dial. "Members of Raven Teams wear them so that we are all operating on the same time, down to the second. The illuminated paint is…"

Elizabeth could not help herself, she said, "It is radium paint. The element discovered at the turn of the century by Marie and Pierre Curie."

"Exactly, Elizabeth. Later, we will set all our watches based on a time synchronization the airship commander will issue. Is there anything else?"

Elizabeth smiled and said, "No. I think a pistol and the knives will be more than enough for my part of the mission." Elizabeth paused and asked, "Lieutenant, may I ask how many times you have been a Raven?"

Beverly said with a straight face, "Enough times to know it is never easy when the Ravens are called to do the mission."

Elizabeth had begun to observe auras over the past month and in this case she noticed the lieutenant's aura turning toward yellow. She decided further questions would not be proper. She bowed her head slightly and, with that, Beverly reached into several trays and started to load Elizabeth's jerkin with ammunition and several chemicals in glass vials. Elizabeth knew from her training the vials would shatter on contact with a floor or a wall and immediately create a smoke screen allowing her to disappear, literally in a "puff of smoke." As they walked out of the quartermaster's office, Elizabeth noticed that Beverly had taken two revolvers, a Khyber knife, and a crossbow. If a fight was necessary, Beverly would be ready.

Now, inside the airship, bathed in red light from electric lamps in the passenger bay, they traveled west along the foothills of the Himalayas. Elizabeth once again checked her equipment to be sure that she would not lose any of the items when she left the airship. She observed her new colleagues checking each other after first checking their own equipment. After she completed her own check, she turned to Marian and said, "Would you like me to check your equipment?"

Marian smiled and said, "Absolutely. We must be thorough. I don't know how many times you have used a rope ladder, but it is easy to get turned upside down if you are not careful. It simply won't do to lose your weapons before you even arrive on the ground. That is why my crossbow has both a leather shoulder strap and a cotton lanyard so I can wear it on my back until I drop off the ladder. Now, please check my jerkin, most especially in the back."

Marian looked up at Naismith who smiled as he watched Elizabeth work carefully along Marian's equipment. He noted that her eyes followed her hands as she moved along Marian's jerkin in a systematic top-to-bottom routine. Elizabeth was already demonstrating that his decision to include her on the mission was correct.

Early morning 14 April 1912 — Mazar-e-Sharif

The door opened and candles from the hallways cast long shadows into the cell. The three prisoners looked out of the gloom to see Naglieff and two of his Cossacks. For the first time since their capture, both Francis and Mary could feel Naglieff was no longer their confident captor. Mary had a better grasp of the emanations that Guru Naismith called the human aura. The halo around the Russian was a bright yellow-orange. Naglieff was afraid of something. Mary passed the telepathic message to her husband. "He is afraid. Also, he is not afraid of an imminent rescue. Something else has happened." Francis nodded acknowledgement.

"I am afraid there is an unpleasant situation outside that is not in my control," the Russian said. "Given how honourable you have been throughout this situation, I wanted to both warn you and ask your indulgence. It is not something that I expected, nor will I complain if you are reluctant to help me." After this puzzling interlude, he walked over to Francis

Bankroft and released his bonds and removed the cloth over his mouth. "If you can control your Uzbek colleague long enough for him to avoid trying to kill me, I will release him as well."

Francis nodded and, using the mesmerism voice, said to his Uzbek colleague, "Abdul Rashid, we need to trust the Colonel long enough to hear him out." Abdul Rashid nodded though his eyes showed his compliance would last only so long. Eventually, the berserker would come out. Francis stood up as he rubbed his wrists where the bonds had bitten into his skin. He said, "Please free Abdul Rashid. He is willing to avoid a confrontation," Francis paused and looked into Naglieff's face before completing the sentence, "…for now."

Mary stood up, faced the Russian and said in her most powerful mesmerism voice, "Sasha, please tell us what is troubling you."

Naglieff responded in far more detail than he expected to offer, but it seemed to him that it was absolutely the right thing to do in response to Mary Bankroft's request. "As I said when we first met, the Afghans came over to our side as part of a deal to support General Stanekzai against Kabul. He was well paid, but still demonstrated no real commitment to our side. Tonight, my sources reported to me that Stanekzai intends to betray us. He intends to kill us all and blame your deaths on Russia."

Francis understood Mary was the best interrogator for this exchange so he waited for her to ask, "What possible purpose does that serve Stanekzai?"

Naglieff said, "My source says that a German contingent has arrived in Mazar-e-Sharif. They want to create a rift between our two countries; a rift far greater than the great-state competition that we share. The Germans believe the murder of a British couple in Northern Afghanistan, a couple on a mission to determine Russian actions here, would cause both Calcutta and London to take a more aggressive tone with the Tsar. Meanwhile, the Afghans will kill my Cossacks and yours truly to ensure there are no witnesses to their perfidy. The Germans believe that will leave an opening for the Kaiser. It is mad, of course, but that is what my source reported. I have real confidence in the accuracy of his reporting. Further, the Germans have outspent me, and Stanekzai has returned his loyalty to the Afghan king. My entire plan is in shambles." Naglieff lowered his gaze in frustration.

Francis used his limited telepathic skills to ask Mary, "Do you believe him?"

She responded in kind, "I believe he believes this story completely. What is the real truth? We can only guess."

Francis decided to enter the conversation. "Colonel, if we accept your tale, what can possibly be done?"

Naglieff said, "I believe we need to escape and ride north to the border. If we can cross the Amu Darya before the Afghans realize we know their plan, I think we will survive. We need to leave now, before dawn. If you give me your word, I am prepared to return your weapons and your horses. I have my men ready outside the fort if we have to fight our way to escape."

Francis offered his hand and said, "Colonel, if you are faithful to your word, we will be as well."

Naglieff took Francis' hand and shook it. Mary noticed the Russian's aura turned from fearful orange to a pale green. Relief, if not precisely acceptance. She looked at Francis and nodded. Then she said, "If you will allow me to lead, I think we will be able to leave the fort without any difficulty."

Naglieff looked puzzled and turned to Francis. He said, "What is Mrs. Bankroft saying?"

"I think you will be surprised," Francis answered. "She should be in the lead if we are to get out without a fight. Trust me."

Naglieff said, "If so, this will help our escape to be sure. Mrs. Bankroft, please lead the way. I follow and then your husband, your Uzbek colleague, and finally my Cossacks." He turned to allow Mary to pass.

As Mary passed the Cossacks, she said in perfect Russian with a strong use of the mesmerism voice, "Gentlemen, please let me pass. I will keep us safe." The Cossacks parted and allowed her to pass. She walked unerringly along the corridor to the stairs. Over the previous days, Mary had used her skills in remote viewing to map the way out of the prison and, eventually, out of the fort.

At the top of the stairs, she met the single Afghan guard, a large Pashtun wearing a black turban and a long wool coat much like their own, with crossed bandoliers, a rifle and a three-foot-long Khyber knife. He offered a dangerous challenge to any who might try to pass. That said, it was early morning and he was half asleep. He looked completely puzzled as he saw the bedraggled woman dressed in clothes like his own coming up the stairs. Before he could either raise his rifle or the alarm, Mary raised her hand, palm down and stared directly into his brown eyes. To the guard, her blue eyes seemed to drill directly into his mind. A voice heard only inside his head said in perfect Pashtu, "You have been ordered to let us pass. When we are gone, you will continue to guard the corridor. Let no others pass. You must obey."

The guard bowed and said, "Chashem."

In the darkness on the stairway, Naglieff said to Bankroft, "What did she do? Will he let us pass?"

Bankroft responded, "We can only walk past him to see. Follow Mary. I will stay behind to be sure he stays compliant."

"Compliant?"

"He will either remain compliant or he will be dead."

"Do you need a weapon?"

"Not at this precise moment. Now move quickly and quietly. The spell is strong, but it can be disrupted by loud noises."

Naglieff nodded, made a hand sign to his two Cossack

guards to be silent, and climbed the stairs. The team passed by the guard and entered the parade ground of the fort. Last through the outside door, Francis closed the door quietly. He was convinced the guard was still under the spell and had not needed to ensure his silence. Francis recognized long ago that his wife remained his superior in the art of mesmerism.

Walking slowly and with a purpose, they moved silently across the parade ground. Pale moonlight shed shadows across the compound as they moved from light to darkness. Naglieff led them to a small gate on the north wall, guarded by two Afghans. Francis realized that Mary might not be able to capture the minds to two men at once, so he moved up to the front beside his wife.

As they approached, the guards puzzled over the group. They had not been told of the foreigners using their gate and certainly not at this time — well before dawn. Still, they recognized the Russian Colonel as a frequent visitor to General Stanekzai's headquarters. What they did not understand was the faces or the garb of the first two in the group. As Francis and Mary approached, they came to attention and raised their weapons to ensure the visitors halted before they were allowed to leave. Their actions were too late as they allowed the visitors to come within arms-length of their position.

In the shadows of the pale moon and the mauve sky known as false dawn, Naglieff did not see Francis or Mary strike the guards. But they must have, because both Afghans dropped like marionettes whose strings were cut. Before the men fell to the ground, Francis and Mary caught them and leaned them against the gate, using their rifles to hold them upright. As Naglieff followed the Bankrofts through the portal out of the fort, he stared into the open eyes of two dead men. At that point, he understood that he had been lucky to stay alive when he first decided to capture these two English spies.

Waiting outside were the remaining Cossacks on horseback and six additional horses. On the saddles of three of those horses were long Cossack coats and what appeared to be the weapons confiscated when they were first captured. In a moment, Francis, Mary and Abdul Rashid recovered their handguns, donned their Cossack disguise and mounted their Afghan stallions. Naglieff turned to his men and said in Russian, "It is time to go."

Leading the column of riders, Naglieff rode north from the walled fort and toward the river that separated Afghanistan from the Russian surrogate, the emirate of Bukhara. They moved not at a gallop but at a trot as might be expected by authorized visitors. That said, every member of the column and, most especially, the two English riders and their Uzbek colleague, were prepared for an ambush at any moment and from any direction.

As they rode side-by-side, Abdul Rashid whispered to Francis Bankroft, "Baba Jan, do you trust the Russian?"

Bankroft whispered back, "Brother, I will trust him until the moment I do not. I believe he is afraid for his life and would prefer we not die on this ride to the Amu Darya. After that, I do not know if he will try to take us prisoner. Of course, the advantage we have this time is we know the strength of our adversary."

"Twenty five against two are not odds I favor."

Mary's voice entered the conversation, "Twenty five against three are reasonable odds if we are the three."

Abdul Rashid's white teeth gleamed. As they passed outside the small village near the fort, Naglieff said in Russian, "Ride as our lives depend on it!" The riders thundered into a gallop in the early morning light.

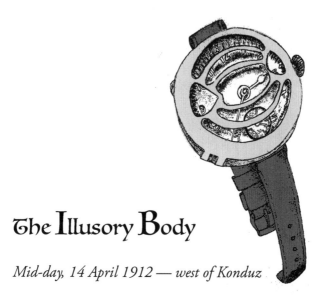

𝕲he Illusory Body

Mid-day, 14 April 1912 — west of Konduz

ELIZABETH BANKROFT WAS DOZING UNDER THE AWNING STRETCHED OVER the sides of *HMFS Talon* in the mid-day sun. The crew of the *Talon* had landed and secured the airship just before dawn, and quickly covered it with a net. From a distance, the torpedo-shaped ship would appear to be just another hill of sand among hills of sand and rock northwest of the Afghan city of Konduz. With the craft secured and protected, the crew allowed the twelve passengers to leave the crew compartment and join them on the ground. The *Talon* could easily have made the trip to Mazar-e-Sharif and back in one twenty-four hour period, but success in the operation meant that they needed to arrive on target at night. So, for the next twelve hours, the crew would spend their time on basic maintenance while the small *Talon* guard force of twenty men deployed in a defense perimeter around the airship. This allowed the Ravens time to review their plan and, by mid-day, to get some sleep. Naismith told each team member, "We will be up all night tonight and into tomorrow. You need to get sleep. If you have trouble sleeping, let me know. I can help you relax."

Elizabeth had no trouble relaxing. She had been on full alert for days with little sleep as she worried about her parents, drew detailed maps of the fortress, and focused on being "one of the adults" on the team. It was this last effort that tired her the most. She wanted to be sure she did not disappoint Guru Naismith or Guru Marian.

"Elizabeth."

She had slept for several hours. Suddenly, she jerked awake. Was someone calling her?

"Elizabeth".

She realized the voice was in her head. It was her mother's voice. It took serious concentration to maintain some level of communication through telepathy. Elizabeth strained as she responded, "Mother?"

"Elizabeth, we have escaped the fortress. We are now on the run heading toward the Amu Darya. We are riding with the Cossacks and being pursued by Afghans and, we think, Germans. Where are you?"

Listening wasn't hard because her mother's telepathic skills were very powerful. It was sending telepathic messages that was hard. She sat quietly in a full lotus position that Marian taught her. She centered her body and her mind, her *chi*. She half closed her eyes and focused her breathing, placing her tongue on the roof of her mouth. Breath in through the nose, exhale through the mouth. While she did not see him, Naismith approached. He saw Elizabeth begin to levitate and float nearly a foot off the ground. He knew not to disturb her.

"Mother, the airship has landed and we are waiting for dark. We are west of Konduz. I don't know the precise location. Where are you?"

"We are moving north on an old smuggler's trail. Come see. I know you can do it. We need you to know where we are so you can help."

Elizabeth had little experience in what Naismith had called remote viewing, but it helped that her mother was in telepathic communication. It was almost as if she drew a map and then drew a line between their two locations. Elizabeth felt her body lighten and suddenly she felt her *chi* in spirit form depart her physical body. She seemed to fly in a straight line to see her mother, her father, and other men riding along a trail that was not too far away from the airship. Once she had their location, she turned back to the airship and her waiting body. As she did, she saw another troop of cavalry, some miles behind her parents, riding at full gallop. In between the two sets of riders, she seemed to see another ghostly form searching the ground. In an instant, the wraith saw her and approached her in a flash.

The wraith looked at her. He seemed a skull and bones wrapped in robes. He was a slight figure with an angry, bone-white face. He spoke to Elizabeth in a voice she knew all too well. "You will be too late to save them, Elizabeth. You are too late." With that, the spectre turned back to the hunt, laughing as he flew.

With a gasp, Elizabeth returned to her body and collapsed.

Naismith called out to Marian, "Bring a wet compress, a cup of tea and the spirit knife. We have to see what Elizabeth just saw."

It took nearly ten minutes for Elizabeth to revive and open her mind to Naismith. He used the spirit knife to focus her concentration and to finally see with his mind what Elizabeth had seen. Naismith placed the compress on Elizabeth's throat, on her *vishudda chakra,* one of the five body centers or *chakras* known to Buddhist mystics. The rest of the team assembled to watch as Naismith held his left hand, palm up, so that the spirit knife could spin in front of Elizabeth's eyes while he cradled her head in his right hand. The two of them were sitting side by side, both with half-closed eyes. Finally, Naismith nodded. The spirit knife stopped spinning and fell into his palm, and he eased Elizabeth down onto her back.

Naismith turned to the team and said, "Elizabeth has just seen her parents. They have escaped from Qalai-e-Jangi and they are less than a half hour away by airship. They are being pursued by Afghans and some German intelligence officers. The Germans have a powerful figure with them. He has the ability to project his astral self in ways that are most dangerous. I have felt this presence before. We need to intercept the Bankrofts before they are recaptured. Please load up. We leave immediately."

Naismith turned to Beverly and Marian and said, "Help Elizabeth onto the airship. She has had a shock and needs to recover before she can move on her own."

Naismith turned and walked toward the airship captain, who was sitting in a folding chair reading a navigation chart and checking his planning for the evening attack. "Captain, I fear we have had a change in plans," the Guru said. "We just received word that our hostages have escaped and are on horseback heading toward the Amu Darya. We need to intercept them immediately so that they are not recaptured."

When he received his initial briefing on this mission, Lieutenant Commander Hightower of the Royal Navy was told that he was to accept the instructions of Major Naismith without question. He was selected both for his audacity and his flexibility. When Naismith explained what had happened, he realized he would need both traits to accomplish the mission. He stood up, shook Naismith's hand and said, "We shall do our part."

He made an about-face and shouted to his crew. "Action

stations. We leave immediately!" The crew of the *Talon* proved their skills as members of an elite community. They had the netting off the ship and the steam plant running in minutes, and they were aloft as soon as the pickets were recovered from the defensive perimeter.

As the nose of the airship tilted skyward, Naismith turned to his team, now inside a well-lighted crew compartment. He said, "I will be back shortly. I have to tell the skipper of this craft our heading and his job once we get there. Once he has his directions, I will come back and we will build our plan. One thing at a time, colleagues. One thing at a time."

Afghan cavalry was some of the best in the world. Both Russian and British intelligence officers had reported that Afghan cavalry was made up of riders in some cases literally born on a horse. They could fight from horseback with rifle or sword and they demonstrated no fear. The Afghan pursuit of the Russian Cossacks proved these reports to be true.

General Stanekzai had gone to visit the prisoners, just after dawn and discovered his prey was on the run. He had intended to inform them that he was now in charge, and that the Russian was no longer their captor. He might even have told them that he was planning to sell them to the Germans, though the real plan was to kill them all and create havoc between the two regional superpowers. The German officer, Colonel August Liemann, had offered that idea as a possibility and Stanekzai immediately saw the benefits to himself. He could build a new and deeper relationship with the king just long enough to decide if he was going to remain loyal or take the throne for himself. Now, with the Russians and the British captives running for their lives, all Stanekzai wanted was to catch his prey and kill them all.

Liemann and two of his men were riding with Stanekzai.

The Afghan general had to admit that the Germans were good horsemen. He had no idea what the German's meant when they said they were hussars but he assumed it meant cavalrymen. The only delay had been the Irishman and his son. They were reasonable riders, but could not keep up with hours at a full gallop. Stanekzai still didn't understand why Liemann kept them in the pursuit. At least until Liemann asked for a halt.

"Tired, German?"

The German spoke to Stanekzai in formal Persian. He said, "General, I suspect by now you know that Germans do not tire easily. I wanted to let you know what we just found out from the boy."

"That he is tired?" Stanekzai smiled a humourless smile. At last the German was going to send these two back to the Qalai.

"Sir, I know you have wondered why we kept the Irishman and his son with us. Both are what you might call…" Liemann struggled for the proper term in Persian. Finally, he decided, "They are mystics. Seers. The Irishman has proven himself invaluable to our efforts both here and in Mesopotamia. His son is an even more powerful mystic. He has seen the Russians and reported that we may be able to overtake the Russian and his captives before they reach the Amu Darya, but there is a complication."

"Colonel Liemann, what do you mean a complication?"

"There is a rescue force on the way to meet with the Russian."

"From?"

"The east. They are coming by airship."

Stanekzai looked at the colonel with disappointment. If he had changed his mind about the pursuit, he should just say so. "Colonel, I don't believe in flying carpets. I have heard you have both a horseless carriage that travels faster than my best steed and a winged machine that carries two men. I doubt that any airship the British might have would carry enough fighters to defeat my Afghan cavalry."

"General Stanekzai, I realize it is hard to imagine an airship that can carry troops, but our reporting from the Pashtun lands inside India has described combat airships that carry soldiers. The boy says it is on its way, carrying soldiers."

"Seers and mystics," Stanekzai snarled. "They are often confused and their visions usually are based on a demand for money. If you do not want to continue the pursuit, I recommend you, your men, and your mystics go back to Mazar-e-Sharif."

Stanekzai turned his horse toward the north and shouted to his men, "*Buru, bekhair!*" Leaving behind a cloud of dust, Stanekzai and his cavalry departed at a full gallop.

Liemann rode back to James O'Connell. He smiled as he said, "The general says he doesn't believe in visions or mystics."

James O'Connell shook his head and said, "You know he is heading toward disaster."

Michael O'Connell looked completely exhausted. He responded in anger, "I followed the Russians and their captives, I tracked their route, and I saw the impending rescue plan. I know this as much as I know anything. And now the Afghan has decided he doesn't believe me?"

Liemann said, "Even if you are wrong, it is clear that this general is not willing to take instructions from a German. There are more Afghan generals out here. We just have to build a story that shows Stanekzai to be a traitor to the king and decide who we will be our new recruit for the North. Do you think that can be accomplished?"

James O'Connell said, "Colonel, there is no doubt. I have been reviewing the possibilities already. There is an Afghan colonel at Qalai-e-Jangi who is a perfect choice."

Liemann turned his horse back toward Mazar-e-Sharif and said, "Then let us make haste to the fort. You can work your magic there."

O'Connell pulled his horse even with the German and said, "Colonel, you know very well what I do is not magic. It is simply mesmerism and an understanding of the human mind."

As the colonel started off at a trot, he said, "O'Connell, I don't care what you call it so long as it works. I've seen your work in Mesopotamia. One moment the tribal leaders were ready to sell us as slaves to the Persians and the next minute you had them agreeing to support our work with the Ottoman governor. That to me was magic. If you are successful this time, I promise we will help you and your son get back to your native Ireland. And, when you are there, we will work together to free your country from the British overseers. That is my promise."

O'Connell laughed. He turned back to Michael and said, "Son, your efforts are not in vain. The Germans understand our power. So, there are no battles for you today, but success in the future."

Michael O'Connell nodded. He had tried to keep up a grim determination as they headed toward the fight with the Russians, but now he was glad to be returning to Mazar-e-Sharif at a trot rather than into battle at the full gallop the Afghans used. He was a reasonable horseman, but hours in the saddle at a gallop had been exhausting, especially while projecting his astral self to follow the trail left by the Russians. Now, he could take his time to observe the Germans, appreciate the Afghan landscape and watch his father build a relationship with the colonel through a mix of reality and mesmerism.

As his father said at the beginning of the trip, he was learning more about espionage and intelligence work than any of the gurus offered at that school in the mountains. And, he now understood his own skills.

Sadly, he also understood that his greatest adversary in the future would be his former classmate, Elizabeth Bankroft.

Stanekzai and his troops caught up with their prey at sunset and just before both columns started downslope toward the river known as the Amu Darya. He had no intention of letting the Russians and their English prisoners cross the river, where they would be in Russian territory and free. He turned to his men as he drew his sword and said in Afghan Persian "*Hamla!*" His men were a mix of Pashtuns and Uzbeks. Even if they didn't hear the command, they all knew what that meant — attack! They drew their swords, drove their heels into their Uzbek stallions and charged.

Naglieff looked back at the enemy and looked forward toward the river. He knew his horses and his men well. They would not make it to the river in time. He pulled up and dismounted. His Cossacks dismounted and formed a half circle facing the charging Afghans. They had their rifles at the ready. Francis Bankroft dismounted and walked over to his Russian captor. He said, "If we are going to live through this, I will need more than my pistols. I need a rifle as will my wife and Jowzjani. It is time you decided if we can be allies."

Naglieff spoke to his men in Russian. "Wait until they are in range. We have the advantage because they are staring into the setting sun, but we will have to take them in the first volley!" He then spoke to Bankroft in English with a grim smile on his face. "I don't think it will make much difference, but you are certainly welcome to help. Your rifles are strapped to my senior sergeant's horse. Help yourselves and, I am afraid to say, prepare to die."

Bankroft nodded and walked over to the horse Naglieff identified. He pulled the two rifles and the special weapon made for Mary. He checked they were loaded and walked over to his wife and Jowzjani.

He said to Mary Bankroft, "It doesn't look very good, my dear. I hope you are a good shot."

Mary nodded as she checked the weapon he gave her. "It is always darkest…"

"Before the dawn. I know the saying, dear, but right now we are a platoon against a company of Afghans. I suspect it may get very dark."

"Pashtuns. I hate Pashtuns," Jowzjani said as he shouldered his rifle. "I will kill many of them today."

Naglieff stood in the center of his men. He had two heavy-caliber revolvers in his hands ready to fire. For some odd reason, at that moment Francis Bankroft focused on Naglieff's revolvers. Bankroft's training and experience said that instead of Colts, the Russian was using a pair of Smith and Wesson .44 caliber pistols which were long-barreled handguns designed for cavalry officers and sold in small lots to the Tsar. Clearly, Naglieff was a favourite of the court if he was carrying two of these pistols. It seemed unlikely that this favoritism would mean much against over fifty mounted Afghans.

Naglieff faced the charging Afghans with full awareness that no matter how lucky he was, this was likely to be his last day on earth. His men were disciplined and knew that they should not open fire until they heard their commander's orders. They would kill a row of Afghans in the first volley, after that it would be chaos. He had twelve rounds to fire and then it would be bayonet versus Afghan curved sword known as a tulwar. In his case, a Russian cavalry sword of Damascus steel versus tulwar. It was a moment of great tension as they stood watching the charging Afghans approach. Naglieff smiled. If this was his last day on earth, it would be a glorious day.

The noise from the first volley was deafening and the first row of Afghans fell off their horses. Naglieff had not yet given the order to fire and he looked around to see which of his men had broken discipline. Their lives hung on a thread, but he might shoot the coward in his force before he shot anyone else. Then he noticed, none of his men had fired. The second volley was even louder and now he could hear the distinct noise of a pair of Maxim guns sending a hundred bullets a minute into the Afghan ranks. A brass casing hit Naglieff on the shoulder. He looked up and to his right to see the silent form of an airship spitting fire into the Afghan cavalry. Naglieff was no expert in modern airships, but he realized at once that the ship must have approached using some sort of silent propulsion. It had established itself so that the full firepower from one side of the airship was turned on the Afghans.

Naglieff decided that it was time to engage. He raised both long barreled pistols and aimed at the remaining lead Afghans. He fired both. Less than a second later, his Cossacks opened fire as well. Stanekzai and twenty more Afghan riders fell from their horses. The Maxim guns from the airship continued to fire as the charging Afghans began to disperse in every direction to avoid the deadly rain of bullets.

An explosion like a small mortar round covered the struggling Afghan riders in smoke and flame. Mary Bankroft looked at the barrel of her still smoking launcher. She said to her husband, "I quite like this new invention."

Francis smiled as he aimed his Mauser and fired another round into the crowd. Jowzjani was working the bolt on his rifle as he said, "I must have one like Mrs. Bankroft's, Baba Jan. Please."

Well before Mary could load another round, the fight ended. The few remaining Afghan riders from the rear of their company had no intention of dying. Once they saw their commander fall, they knew there was no longer any obligation to continue the fight. There was no honour in fighting to the death and no dishonour in retreat once the commander was dead. They pulled their stallions to a halt, turned quickly and headed away from the river. The airship nose spun in the same direction and with a thunderous noise as the steam engines poured on power to the propellers, it pursued the last of the company.

Naglieff spoke to his men in Russian and Bankroft realized that the Cossacks were now aiming their rifles at Jowzjani, Mary and himself. Naglieff smiled and said, "A strange fortune of war, my friend. The Afghans are retreating, your airship is in pursuit and we are only a mile from the river. By the time your airship commander realizes his mistake, we will be across the border and, once again, I will have three captives that I can trade for some future colleague captured in India or even in England."

Mary Bankroft smiled and spoke in perfect Russian using her best mesmerism voice, "My dear Colonel. Have you not noticed who is at your side?"

Naglieff looked to his left and his right. He was surrounded by two figures clad all in what looked like grey cloaks. Both had knives drawn inches from his neck. Naglieff turned to look at his men. He found each of them collapsed on the ground. Ten of these grey wraiths were standing next to the men and removing their weapons. He heard a voice, this time in his head rather than in his ears, that said in a most gentle voice, "Colonel, I think the game is over and you have lost. We have no reason to harm you or your men. We are here simply to rescue our colleagues. Please sit down and keep your hands away from your weapons." Naglieff complied, not because it was an order but, for some reason, he seemed to want to comply. It was confusing, but restful at the same time.

Francis Bankroft turned to the hooded figure and said, "Guru Ji, I haven't seen you in years and I am most pleased to see you now."

Guru Naismith pulled back his hood, revealing a shaved head and his grey beard. "Francis, you were always a troublesome student," he said. "The least you can do is to help the Ravens secure these Cossacks so that we can make good our escape before they awaken."

Francis nodded and turned to his Uzbek colleague, "We need to make haste."

Jowzjani smiled and said, "I have heard of your magics, Baba Jan. But this was something that I did not expect to see."

He walked over to the closest Cossack who appeared to be in a most restful sleep. Next to him was another of the cloaked figures tying the ankles of the Cossacks on a long loop. Just enough to slow them down but not enough to prevent them from escaping the eventual wrath of the Afghans. Jowzjani was dumbfounded when he looked more closely and found the wraith to be a woman slightly younger than his wife. He could only laugh. "They sent English women to defeat Cossacks. What a tale!"

The subject of his humour stood and gently waved her hand across Jowzjani's eyes. "You did not see a woman and you will not tell."

Jowzjani responded in a slightly dazed voice, "I did not see, I must not tell."

Marian switched to her command voice and said, "Please help me secure these men. We must leave soon." Jowzjani obeyed without comment.

Francis turned to the still-dazed Naglieff and said, "My friend, I know most of this evening will seem like a dream, but I need you to remember that we remain adversaries. When next we meet, I will do my best to kill you just as I expect you will do the same to me. The Germans are just a distraction. You will remember one thing: The real game is not between our two empires. It is between you and I. For now, we will simply leave you here and disappear."

The Cossacks were secured and the Bankrofts' weapons and equipment were returned to their rightful owners.

Jowzjani's rifle and Khyber knife were tucked back into his belt. The Cossacks' horses were picketed near their masters.

As Naismith had said, they had no intention of harming the Russians at this point. Instead, Naismith reached into his cloak and pulled out an odd-shaped, brass-barreled pistol. It was a flare gun used to recall the airship. He fired a red signal flare, then broke open the breach, loaded, and fired a blue flare. The two flares arced across the sky and within minutes the airship was above them. The crew dropped three rope ladders. The Ravens climbed the ladders, followed by Jowzjani and the Bankrofts. As soon as the entire British complement were secured, the sound of the pistons of two small steam engines and the smell of exhaust filled the air as the *Talon* turned to the east at all ahead full. They would be in India in six hours, and inside the Chitral garrison by morning. The smell of the exhaust was sufficient for the Cossacks and their leader to awake and see the airship disappearing over the horizon.

The Nature of the Grade

AFTER THE TEAM SECURED THEIR ARMAMENTS IN THE WEAPONS LOCKER IN the upper deck, they gathered for tea and stories. As the senior officer in charge, Naismith controlled the flow of information. First, he allowed the Bankrofts to tell their tale from start to finish. Naismith encouraged Jowzjani to add his thoughts. In part, this was designed to reinforce to their Afghan agent that he was part of the team. Naismith also knew that Jowzjani would have observed cultural nuances that the Bankrofts might have missed. This was indeed the case when Jowzjani offered a comment, "The Pashtuns that guarded us are all rebels. They were more than just minions of the Russians. They were actually working with the Germans."

"Germans?" Naismith was most interested in Jowzjani's insight. This meant that the Afghans were well aware of the German team and, apparently, fully accepting this new ally.

Francis added, "Guru Ji, it would appear that we are involved in a three-sided game now. Naglieff told me that the reason we had to flee was the Germans intended to kill us all in an effort to increase tensions between St. Petersburg and London. He said that his sources were reporting Germans working in the court in Kabul creating more trouble with the Afghan King."

Jowzjani said, "It is as I said. The Pashtuns in the Qalai were talking about how they were going to switch from hostility to loyalty to their king. Stanekzai would become general of all the Afghan armies. These Pashtuns have no honour."

Naismith nodded to Jowzjani. He winced at the thought of one Afghan ethnic group debasing the honour of another. The history of Afghanistan demonstrated that any ethnic group, any tribe or clan, would switch sides for survival or profit. He turned to Elizabeth who had been sitting quietly in the background still wearing her hood and cloak. "Elizabeth, why don't you tell your parents the rest of the story."

Elizabeth blushed as she dropped her hood and watched as her father's mouth dropped open. Obviously, he had not known her role in the events. She also noticed her mother showed no sign of surprise. Had she known all along? As directed, Elizabeth began, "As you know, I visited the fortress earlier and we had a plan to free you using the airship and the team. It would have been far less deadly for the Afghans and would have avoided revealing any of our capabilities to the Russians. But, once I knew you were headed for the river, we had to change our plan." Elizabeth paused and looked over at her colleagues and her mentors. She was expecting them to take on the story. Instead, they just nodded. Inside her head, Elizabeth heard Beverly's voice say, "It is your story. You should tell it. We are ready, but we want you to tell the story."

Elizabeth took a deep breath and said, "I worked with the airship's navigator to identify an intercept course. It was based on calculations of your speed of travel and the speed of the airship. The Captain decided to make the final approach using the battery-operated engines so we might surprise your pursuers. Unfortunately, during my last check of your travels, I was observed by a master from the other side. I do not know who it was."

Naismith turned to the Bankrofts and interjected, "I believe Elizabeth knows who might have been projecting his mental force, but is choosing not to say. That is for another time. Elizabeth, please continue."

Elizabeth was taken aback by Naismith's comment, but she decided to continue with her report. "Once we knew where the interception would take place, the airship dropped us off within walking distance of your final stop. We arrived before you and used our cloaks and our...our..."

Marian decided to help her young student, "Our mental abilities..."

Elizabeth continued, "to wait unseen. Guru Naismith influenced the Russian's mind to ensure he stopped precisely inside our ambush circle. The rest of the story you know well. The airship dispersed the Afghans and we used our..."

Marian again, "Understanding of the human body..."

"To disable but not harm the Cossacks when the Russian confronted you. It was a silent coup."

Mary Bankroft said, "Bravo to the Ravens. It was unfortunate that the Afghans decided to pursue to the point of facing the airship. Still, I applaud you all in disabling the Cossacks without a single casualty on either side. You are all a credit to our alma mater!"

From the back of the room, the fighter known as Alexander asked, "Guru Ji, were there Germans with the Afghans?"

"Initially they were part of the pursuit," Naismith said. "I suspect the Germans were warned of our approach by the remote seer that Elizabeth faced during her last projection. I think he saw us or, at least, he sensed the airship and knew the Afghans had no chance against the Maxim guns."

Naismith paused to look around the room. He continued,

"Alexander, since you have asked and I can sense you all want to know my opinion, I will tell you. As you know from your classes, we are taught to distinguish between what we know and what we think. This is only what I think, but I think one of our former colleagues, James O'Connell, has changed sides. He brought his son over to the German side as well. Michael O'Connell has great powers and I think he was the remote seer that is working with the Germans. I do not know why the O'Connells made their decision. I will not presume to guess. But, I felt their presence as we approached the ambush site. I believe they warned the Germans. They turned back to Mazar-e-Sharif before they were caught in the gunsights of the airship. I fear the young O'Connell has taken on the powers of an ancient, hostile Tibetan spirit known as Chodak. If so, we have much to consider."

The revelation that two of their own might be working for another side silenced the group. Elizabeth was dumbstruck by the thought that her former friend, Michael, was that white-faced ghoul who warned her. No further questions were asked and the intelligence agents withdrew to their own seats and their own thoughts.

Elizabeth walked over to her parents and gave each a hug. She was close to tears as she said, "I was so worried about you."

"And we are so proud of you," Mary Bankroft said to her daughter.

Francis said, "And I am so sorry that you had to risk your life for us."

The corners of Elizabeth's mouth turned upward in what she hoped was a mature smile.

"It is our trade, Father," she said. "You know it is the nature of our trade."

Additional Reading

A School for the Great Game is a work of fiction, but there are many non-fiction works that will provide the reader with additional background on the history of the Great Game and some of the historic figures mentioned in the book.

For those interested in the overall competition between Great Britain, Russia and Germany in South and Central Asia, I heartily recommend all of the works of Peter Hopkirk, most especially his first work *The Great Game*. The German incursion in the Middle East and Central Asia are described in detail by Sean McMeekin in *The Berlin-Baghdad Express: The Ottoman Empire and Germany's Bid for World Power* and Jules Stewart's *The Kaiser's Mission to Kabul*. Jules Stewart has written many books on British India. He works *Spying for the Raj: The Pundits and the Mapping of the Himalaya* and *Savage Border: the story of the North-West Frontier* are also excellent start points.

Readers interested in the transformation of the Royal Navy during the first decade of the 20th Century should read Robert Massie's *Dreadnought: Britain, Germany and the Coming of the Great War*. The analytic engine described in the book was never adopted by the Royal Navy, but there was a prototype prepared for the Navy and other military uses. That prototype is on display at the Science Museum, London. Also on display in the Science Museum are a small steam engine by William Henson and a display of the early British airships based on the designs of Ferdinand von Zeppelin.

Indian and Tibetan mysticism plays a significant role in my book. My two references were *Magic and Mystery in Tibet* by Alexandra David-Neel and Kautila's *The Arthashashtra*.

The structure of the intelligence service of British India is of great interest to me. Two books I recommend are William Beaver's *Under every leaf* and BG Bah Parritt's history of the British Military Intelligence titled *The Intelligencers*. Captain William Henry Shakespear was a real character working in Kuwait during this time period and the most recent biography of this intrepid intelligence officer written by Alan Dillon is definitely worth the candle.

Finally, the intrepid female adventurers that capture Elizabeth Bankroft's attention were all real people. Gertrude Bell was an amazing scholar and explorer who became a key figure in British military and intelligence operations during WWI and in the post war era. One of the best single volume biographies of Bell is Georgina Howell's *Gertrude Bell: Queen of the Desert, Shaper of Nations*. The story of the Agnes and Margaret Smith and their travels in the Middle East in the late 19th century remains a barely known tale of courage and scholarship. The best description of their travels is in *The Sisters of Sinai: How two lady adventurers discovered the Holy Gospels* by Janet Soskice.

These recommendations are only a start of the literary adventures available for the reader of the *Steampunk Raj* series. Good Hunting!

Recommendations for Book Clubs and Teachers

A School for the Great Game is designed to be a fun adventure novel. It can open a window into the British Empire and Great Power conflicts in the early years of the twentieth century. It describes a world filled with hope for scientific progress while also a world where mysticism was still accepted in polite society. While a work of fiction, the book raises questions that readers might well ask of themselves and fellow readers. Here are a few of those questions.

What pressures did Elizabeth Bankroft feel as a young woman growing up in Edwardian England? Victorian era models of "polite society" and the role of men and women were changing, but how much did that mean for a teenager living in India? Does Elizabeth face challenges in India that she does not face in England?

The British Empire just prior to World War I extended across the entire globe. What challenges did members of the British officers in India face at the time? How did they see their Indian subjects? How different was the British Indian government from the Russian expansion in Central Asia?

What role did Afghanistan play in "the Great Game"? Why was it important? What did the Great Power competition mean to the Afghans? To the Pashtun tribes in India? To the ethnic groups under Russian sovereignty?

How is natural philosophy compared in the novel to mysticism? How does Elizabeth Bankroft handle her own exposure to both? What if you were exposed to something you couldn't explain? How would you handle events you saw with your own eyes that did not match your own understanding of the natural world?

Also by J.R. Seeger

The MIKE4 Series

"Straight from CIA's war zone files, MIKE4 crackles
with authenticity, like a satcom phone in the field."
JASON MATTHEWS, author of The Red Sparrow trilogy

MIKE4
FRIEND OR FOE
THE EXECUTIONER'S BLADE
O'CONNELL'S TREASURE
A GRAVEYARD FOR SPIES

"If you like good tales of the shadowy, often hard-edged
world of counter-terrorism, read MIKE4!"
GENERAL STANLEY McCHRYSTAL, author of
My Share of the Task: A Memoir and *Team of Teams:
New Rules of Engagement for a Complex World*

J.R. SEEGER is a western New York native who served as a
U.S. Army paratrooper and as a CIA case officer for a total of
27 years of federal service. In October 2001, Mr. Seeger led
a CIA paramilitary team into Afghanistan. He splits his time
between western New York and Central New Mexico.

The Adventure Continues in

Like the Sound of Distant Thunder

Available in 2021

Bombay — August 1913

ELIZABETH LEFT THE TAJ HOTEL JUST AS THE SUN WAS STARTING TO SET INTO the Arabian Sea. She picked up a carriage near the Gateway of India and told the driver to take her to All Saints Cathedral at what was known to all the drivers as "zero point", the historic center of the English colony city in Bombay. The turbaned Sikh driver looked back at the young lady who seemed barely old enough to be allowed out of the house. She was properly dressed in a shalwar kamiz and dupatta, but in his family, the idea of a woman traveling alone in a port city like Bombay seemed foolhardy. Still, she was going to a church on a late Saturday afternoon, so she must be an honorable woman after all and there could be no harm in taking her to the cathedral.

Elizabeth Bankroft was not going to church. She was a British Intelligence officer meeting one of her local reporting agents, an exiled Russian Jew, code named Z1, who operated a gemstone trading business in the Bombay bazaar.

On Elizabeth's last trip to Bombay, just before monsoon in June, Z1 reported that he had seen a number of German engineers visiting Bombay on British-flagged steamships from White Star Lines and Cunard. The engineers would board a liner in South Africa, disembark in Bombay for one or two days, and return to the ship in time for its departure for Hong Kong or Singapore.

This seemed out of the ordinary to Z1, who expected passengers and merchant mariners to spend their time and money at the gin shops in Lal Bazaar near the harbor. When these more typical visitors finally ran out of money, they would come to his shop to sell valuable stones and gold from the colonial mines in Africa and Australia. Instead of frequenting these sailors' haunts, the Germans visited the Taj Hotel, the Victoria rail station, and the Navy lines and Royal Navy docks.

Elizabeth liked Z1 for his sense of humor, for his commitment to his family and for his commitment to his adopted country. They met in quiet parks in late afternoon after he closed the shop for the day. He always brought a tiffin of wonderful food made by his wife and, over tea and pastries, Elizabeth would use the conversations to improve her Russian language skills. He was like an adopted uncle who quoted Russian poetry and liked to play chess. It became clear over time that he liked Elizabeth because he could reveal his darkest concerns about his family's future.

Since the end of her training at The Viceroy's College, Elizabeth had served for more than a year in Bombay as an agent handler and direct observer of the city. She stayed in the Taj Hotel, Bombay's premier location, and ranged about the city as herself or using multiple disguises. As a junior officer, Elizabeth had already established a reputation for accurate and timely reporting. Most of those reports were from Z1. In the past month, Elizabeth realized that she had an obligation to this man who was central to her success. It became her personal goal to help him obtain British citizenship or, at the very least, British Indian travel documents. The carriage dropped Elizabeth off at the crushed-stone sidewalk leading to the large Anglican Church. As she turned the corner of the church toward their meeting place, Elizabeth heard a voice, more of a whimper, cry out, "No. No more."

She could see Z1 on the ground being kicked by a man wearing the uniform of a British sailor. Next to him, looking on as if giving directions to the sailor, was a man dressed in formal European clothes. Elizabeth shouted, "Stop that immediately!"

The sailor and the European looked up, surprised. While a woman might not stop their attack, she would certainly be able to call for the local police patrol and she would be a reliable witness against them. They looked at each other and ran in opposite directions leaving Z1 a crumpled mass on the ground.

Later, Elizabeth admitted to her mother she had a hazy recollection of what happened next. She was furious. Who would attack a man as gentle as Z1? A white hot anger boiled up and overtook her normal, quiet persona. The sailor was 50 yards away, and running. Before she had even considered what she should do, Elizabeth used the Tibetan skill of *lung gom pa,* controlling the air around her and allowing her to cover great distances in bounding leaps. In the mountains, this meant Elizabeth could span a distance of one hundred yards in a few seconds. At sea level, she was able to reach the sailor in a single leap. One second he seemed well on his way to escape and the next, he was confronted by a young women standing in front of him. In the receding light, the sailor was surprised, but not worried. After all, she was just a woman, and a slight woman at that.

He drew his long, sharp sailor's knife and said, "Girley, let me pass. This is not your trouble."

Baghdad, August 1913

For the first time, Michael O'Connell sat alone in the office of the senior intelligence officer for the Kaiser. The German mission in Baghdad was in one of many 19th century brownstone houses in the foreign quarter where the Ottoman government tolerated diplomats, scientists, business and, of course, spies.

Michael scanned the room as he waited for the German officer to invite him to sit down. The room, designed to mitigate the summer heat, had a fifteen-foot-high ceiling. To Michael's right, large casement windows were open to catch any breeze. The windows were bordered by embroidered drapes that would be used as needed to keep out the heat and the dust. Behind the officer's desk was a life-sized portrait of the Kaiser in military uniform. On either side of that were prints of scenes from German military successes during the Napoleonic Wars and the more recent Franco-Prussian War. To his left hung a six-foot by eight-foot map of the Ottoman Empire, flanked by two cavalry sabres.

Standing to the right of the desk was a German civilian, dressed in what could only be described as high-status Arab clothes. His garb included a white silk thobe and headdress matched with a khaki-colored, three-buttoned suit coat. Michael had heard of this man before. He was Wilhelm Wassmuss, Arab expert and agent provocateur for the German military based in Bushehr, Persia.

In contrast to Wassmuss, Colonel Manfred von Trier was everything Michael imagined a German officer would be. He was in full uniform of a German Hussar, with his sword, scabbard, holstered pistol and leather belt hanging behind him on a carefully polished coat tree. Michael judged the colonel to be slightly older than his father, perhaps 60 years old. At one point, he had certainly been an athlete, but Michael could see that von Trier was beginning to pick up weight.

Not portly, at least not yet. His hair was cut so short that Michael could see his pink scalp. Matching his German military presence, von Trier had a scar that ran from his jaw to his left ear, just missing his left eye. Based on the depth and width of the scar, Michael could see the wound was not from some frivolous duel in Prussia but from one of the past century's battlefields. As he concentrated, Michael used his growing synaethesia skills to identify the Colonel's aura. A halo of purple around the colonel meant this was a man of immense confidence in his own views. He was definitely not one who would tolerate informality. Michael prepared himself for interrogation.

The colonel spoke in formal English with a slight German accent, "Herr O'Connell, please have a seat."

Michael was relieved. He had been prepared to stand for the entire audience with von Trier and this small invitation suggested that the colonel might not dismiss his skills out of hand. It was interesting that the colonel intended to proceed in English. It argued that he had some advanced education in Britain. It also meant Wassmuss was fluent in English as well as Arabic and Persian. Once Michael sat down, he prepared both brain and body so that if he was given a chance to speak, he would use a light touch of mesmerism to gain some advantage. He bowed slightly and simply replied, "Thank you, sir."

In his best parade ground voice, the colonel shouted to his aide de camp, "Coffee for three if you please."

Behind him, Michael heard a voice respond, "Absolutely, Excellency."

The coffee was served by a Baghdadi in a resplendent white, servant's uniform. The three men spent a moment preparing the Turkish brew to their liking. Michael simply stirred the coffee with the provided spoon. Wassmuss swirled his cup after putting a sugar cube in his mouth. The colonel added two spoonfuls of brown sugar and stirred. The clinking of the spoons on the edges of the tall, cut-glass cups was the only sound in the room except for a ponderous ticking of a large clock on the colonel's desk. Michael thought about how von Trier had stage-managed this entire interview so that he maintained both a sense of control and superiority.

"So, young O'Connell, I have read your file. You have been very successful in your work for us," the colonel said. "I have a mission that I wish you to handle."

The Adventure Continues in

Like the Sound of Distant Thunder

Available in 2021

Made in the USA
Las Vegas, NV
18 November 2020